Everyone wanted to crucify a golden boy

Jesus Christ was a golden boy, a big-mouth like me, crunched under the stampeding feet of mediocrity. I was usually prepared for a shot in the balls, but today my defenses were down. I hadn't had much sleep, I was called a pig for breakfast, and I was worried about going blind.

"Got classes today, Ken?" asked Barb congenially, standing up and gathering her books.

"I'm not going to my classes because I've got an appointment at the eye doctor's. I think I'm going blind."

"Me, too," said Barb. "It's from masturbating."

"If that wives' tale is true, I'm a goner."

"You'll have to kick the habit."

"I've tried that before," I said. "I only lasted a few days. Then I locked myself in my closet with a library of pornographic novels and went on a bout of self-abuse that lasted three weeks. That was the beginning of my interest in literature."

TUDOR PUBLISHING COMPANY
NEW YORK AND LOS ANGELES

Tudor Publishing Company

This is a work of fiction. The characters, names, incidents, places, and dialogue are products of the author's imagination, and are not to be construed as real.

ISBN: 0-944276-42-3

Reprinted by arrangement with The Permanent Press

Printed in the United States of America

First Tudor printing — March, 1989

GOLDENROD
PETER
GAULT

Dedicated to Heather
who provided the torture
that was necessary to make
this book a reality

Acknowledgments

First and foremost, I'd like to thank Cinda, for her camaraderie and muscle power. I'd like to thank Joe, for his passion and energy and visual genius; Gary, for his patient hospitality and the use of his desk; Alonzo, for his shining enthusiasm and for using his credit card to get me drunk when things were at their bleakest; Margaret, for bringing me into the world and making me believe that anything is possible (anything *isn't* possible, but I'm glad she made me believe the opposite). I'd also like to thank the New York contingent: especially Dick, especially Kathy, especially Marty and Judy.

Introduction

Walking home one day last summer on 65th Street and Broadway I noticed a young man (earring in ear, crissclashing potpourri of pop art, jock and punk rock garb) selling books. Now this street is always crammed to bursting with peddlers hawking their wares: jewelry, sunglasses, old books, cutlery, watches, sneakers, African masks and mini-sculptures; one can purchase near anything. But a writer selling his own book!? This was a first! And so, drawn half by curiosity and half by empathy, I bought his book. So began my friendship with Peter Gault.

And now, hardly one year later, his publisher has asked me to write an introduction to Peter's novel: *Goldenrod.*

With pleasure.

Coming to the end of the eighties Peter Gault strikes me as something of an abberation, an anomaly, someone skewed way off the standard deviation of the bell-shaped probability curve. So many young people today seem to be afflicted by a contemporary malaise which attacks to the core and leaves its victims so exhausted and racked with pain that they only have strength enough left to become one thing: whether planning careers or planning marriages, whether entering the law or entering the bedroom, making debate or making babies, in one way or another: They're All Accountants! Not so Peter Gault. By word and deed, and writing a novel is a great deal of each, Peter Gault most assuredly comes from another age. Admittedly a simpler and less confused age, but for those very reasons, an age more vital, elemental, bountiful and bounteous. In a word: Abundant.

And his novel, *Goldenrod,* like Peter himself, is so filled with this abundance, this fecundity of youth (or what heretofore I have always associated with youth) that it veritably sweeps the reader along on an orgiastic joyride through this Gaultian timewarp. A time when Accountants knew their place and dared not trespass where not wanted (or needed). Yes: Miracle of miracles, *Goldenrod* carried me all the way back to my own youth whence my ego was rocklike certain, the point of it all clear, the good guys 'good,' the bad guys 'bad,' and the comic/tragic hunt for you know what: Everything. Where indeed people, especially young people, still believed that everything was possible. In short and in sum, where the letter 's,' whether it be placed before the words sex, self, or significance (as in human significance) was always written with a capital 'S.' And that is precisely what is special about Peter Gault's novel. It makes its readers young again. And if already young, younger still. It allows them to frolic gay and carefree. To partake in a journey where no reductionism debases and makes mockery of our human size, and no accountants and accountants' practices are permitted to muddy the waters and foul the holy land. Where Ken Harrison, Goldenrod himself, is not merely given youth's innate privilege and right to dream, but is a dream himself.

Now other intelligences might speak of literature and art, and the many ways to write a novel, post-modern and classical, stylistic and au naturel, but for me Peter Gault's way is as good and honest as any. For if you read his story, your hearts (as well as your lower parts) like mine, will swell with an appreciation of what it is to be young and whole and innocent and full-blooded. And if *Goldenrod* can do that for you, as it did for me, Peter Gault will have given you what he has to give. Not merely his art and his craft but all his love. HIS LOVE OF LIFE! And perhaps that is a first step, the shot in the arm our accountants' age needs, and what I sensed immediately and all at once when reading that young man's book which I purchased on that fortuitous day a summer ago on 65th Street and Broadway.

Richard Kalich, February 1988

1. Think Golden

I never tire of looking at myself. I can stare for hours, without a minute of boredom. I take off my clothes and stand naked in front of one of those full-length mirrors and simply contemplate my body. It's a narcissistic ritual—I don't deny that—but it is more than mere narcissism. It's like a religious ceremony. It expands my consciousness. It's a form of transcendentalism. If my confidence is low, and there in fact have been brief moments in my life when my confidence was low, I just have to look in the mirror, and I experience an overwhelming flood of inspiration. I feel I can do anything, comprehend anything, create anything.

I start by contemplating my feet and work up. Generally, I'm not enthusiastic about feet; there's nothing particularly profound about feet, but, as far as feet go, I have rather interesting ones. They're interesting because they resemble my hands and my genital area. My feet, hands, and sex organs have a similar look about them, a look which is distinct from the rest of my anatomy.

"I include my tongue as a sex organ," I say to myself earnestly, tickling the air with licks.

It's these three sets of dangling artifacts—feet, hands, and sex organs—that give me away, that expose the truth of my personality, that belie my reputation as a superficial, happy-go-lucky, all-star jock hockey player. The rest of my body is stereotypically, or perhaps I should say classically, male. A visible web of muscle is stretched upon a sturdy frame. I'm not tall, about average height for a hockey player, but I have a lean, hard, powerful build. I'm a sexual being. My body was created for sexual acrobatics. But my body is misleading because of the jealous myth propagated by anemic academics and sickly intellectuals that anyone who looks athletic is stupid. A deep understanding of life doesn't cause physical degeneration. I'm living proof.

"Feet, hands, and sex organs express the enigma of Ken Harrison," I say to myself, tickling the air with my tongue again.

I shall refrain from giving minute descriptions of my physiology, not because it's irrelevant or extraneous to the story—it's very relevant indeed—but because minute descriptions of any kind are often tedious. It's the story that's important. I want nothing to cloud the story. Before I delve into those three years of my life, those three years of bizarre change and discord, I should transgress briefly with one more description. I must give you a picture of my face.

For the sake of objectivity, I throw aside all modesty. I have a handsome face. My square brick jaw, delicate features, and curious expressions are somehow contradictory, masculine and feminine, emotional and intelligent, vulnerable and confident. It's a face that's difficult to understand, always in some stage of metamorphosis, yet never unpleasant to look at.

"My face is like a breath of fresh air," I announce magically, studying my reflection in the mirror.

Mirrors have had a special place in my life. They remind me of when I was a hockey player because in the team dressing room, spanning the full length of the wall from the floor to the ceiling, was a huge mirror. It was the last year of my hockey career. The mirror reflected a room cluttered with sports gear and gawky male adolescents in the final stages of puberty. The room was small, but the mirror produced an illusion of expansiveness. It made life seem larger, like art. Red was everywhere. Red was the color of the team sweaters. Since it was nearly time to go on the ice, most people had their sweaters on. Mine was still on the hanger. I secretly competed to be the last person dressed. I sat directly in the center of the mirror, still naked, quietly taping my hockey stock. The door opened wide enough for Mr. Winfield's unusually large head to fit through. "Humpty-Dumpty," I muttered under my breath. Mr. Winfield's enormous forehead was swarming with veins, like purple maggots feeding on his brain.

"When the buzzer goes, everyone better be dressed and ready to go on the ice. If you're not ready, you'll . . . there'll be trouble," said Winfield, unable to think of an appropriate threat. The door slammed shut. Coach Winfield didn't have to work at being obnoxious; he was that way by nature. This time his obnoxiousness was directed specifically at me, part of our private vendetta. What Winfield was bashing brains out to get, I got by smiling. I made life look enjoyable and free. This was what Winfield hated. He insisted that life wasn't that way, that life was bleak and serious and that only through suffering and drudgery could one obtain the things that are worthwhile in life. Winfield was obnoxiously Presbyterian. Meanwhile, I hadn't bothered to arrive at the game until the third period—due to some sexual escapade—and still managed to score three goals. Tonight I would be there for the whole game.

Winfield didn't know that I had a special technique for getting dressed extra fast. My garter belt, hockey socks, and knee pads were attached together. I slipped them on in one motion. When Vein Brain returned, I was dressed and lacing up my skates. I ignored Winfield. I didn't want to encourage him by acknowledging his existence.

"Shut up," shouted Winfield, even though no one was talking. Winfield looked like Punch Imlach with rabies. He began to pace, which made him feel important and tough. He suddenly started adjusting his tie so frantically it looked like he was beating himself off. I expected his nose to ejaculate sperm.

"We have to move together, work together, reciprocate as a team," said Winfield, ignorant of the sexual connotations of his words and actions. "I don't want to see any friction on the bench. No friction! Friction is wasted energy and we have to save our energy for the real thing. Do you know what causes friction? When the puck is in our end zone, and one of our men is out of the play, dancing around the center ice line like a faggot, teasing the opposition's goalie." Winfield was referring, not so subtly, to me. I'm the cock teaser at the red line. Dancing at the red line was my trade mark, and I scored a lot of goals from that position. Winfield had nerve calling into question—even covertly—my sexual integrity, while he was masturbating with his tie and foaming over Bruno. Bruno was a defenseman and Winfield's favorite player.

I felt that a hockey team was like a homosexual club. A bunch of men got together three or four times a week, took off their clothes, played games, and had showers with each other. Everyone had a favorite, a buddy, a lover. There were breakups and hurt feelings and jealousies. It was a physical environment.

"I want you to grab that puck," continued Winfield, "and hold on to it. Start moving it around slowly, but keep possession. Don't rush it. Look for the hole. When the time is right, split the defense and go for it."

Winfield was still fondling his tie. The veins on his forehead were starting to bulge. He carried on in a frenzied voice, "We can't stop, not now that we're on top of things. We've worked up to this moment. All the planning and practicing and friction leads to where we are now. Win the next two games, two measly games, and we got the big gold cup. I've coached the Dixie Queens for thirteen years, thirteen years of my life, and all to win that golden cup. I've never been closer than I am tonight. We have to hold hack a little longer on the shooting and start skating, start moving our asses. I can feel it inside me. I can feel it coming. Let's give it all we got."

Winfield rallied a crowd better than Adolf Hitler. It was like a strip show. The energy level was high, people either standing or sitting erect in their seats. Bruno, the coach's pet, was making foul grunting noises. His hand was pumping up and down on the shaft of his hockey stick. I was struck by a hideous image of Winfield doing rhythmic pelvis thrusts in a G-string. I shuddered and chased the image out of my head.

"I can feel it coming too, Coach," whispered Bruno pervertedly, emphasizing the word "Coach." Winfield loved being called Coach—it's such a sentimental epithet. Even his wife and kids called him Coach.

"I want you to prove that the Dixie Queens are the best Junior B team in the league," said Winfield. "I've got one question to ask you. Who's going to win?"

"WE ARE," exploded the whole team passionately, Bruno's voice ringing the loudest.

"THEY ARE," exploded Phuc Wildfong and myself in the silence that followed. Phuc and I feigned bewilderment. It was our joke. It was a way of giving Winfield's inspiring harangue an anticlimactic effect. We did it all the time.

Phuc Wildfong was nothing like the name implies. He was not the least bit aggressive. On or off the ice, he was a gentle, unassuming person. I was the one that instigated this rebellious streak in him. Although Phuc was Oriental and had an Oriental name, there was not a hint of foreign accent in his conversation.

I believed that Phuc had some kind of complex because of his name. It's difficult to trust someone with a name like Phuc Wildfong. He bore the brunt of a lot of ridicule. Roll call at school must have been terrible. With a name like that he was centered out all the time, and kids are so cruel. At a young age, "Phuc" was simplified to "Fuck," of course, which is a degrading thing to be called. Winfield would say at practice, "Get the fuck over here," and everyone would grab Phuc and act out a gang bang on him. It was meant in fun, but I could tell Phuc didn't enjoy it. I was self-righteous about pronouncing his name correctly.

I pretended to be fixing a strap until the players stampeded out, and I was alone in the room. The mirror was mine. I didn't like to hide myself in a helmet, so I carried it under my arm. Feet, hands, and sex organs were disguised. I was invulnerable. The red team sweater gave a flattering hue to my complexion and the big black C stood boldly on my heart. I was the captain. At the beginning of the season, I was the coach's pet, not Bruno. The loss of love between Winfield and me had nothing to do with my performance on the ice—I was leading the league in scoring—but with the fact that Winfield didn't understand my sense of humor. He thought I was being flippant, but it was really just my way of dealing with pressure.

I dismissed myself from the mirror. Confidence flowed through my veins like an hallucinogenic drug. The loud speaker was listing the members of the home team, the Dixie Queens. Bruno was organizing the warm-up with the enthusiasm of a lunatic. His mouth worked harder than any other part of his body, shouting at almost everyone in the rink, including his old Italian mother who was dressed in black and sat behind the penalty box. Bruno was assistant captain, and this gave his tongue license. He always climaxed prematurely, during the warm-up, and seemed to fall asleep by the time the game started. Bruno was trying to kill our goalie by blasting slap shots around his ears from five feet away.

"Number fourteen, Ken Harrison," said the loud speaker, catching my attention. I was standing by the bench, avoiding Bruno's warm-up, pretending that my straps needed more adjustment.

There was a modest uproar at the mention of my name. My cheering section consisted of a multitudinous array of family and a couple of friends. My father was the loudest. He was there with his common-law wife and her four daughters. My mother was the most zealous. She was there with my seven sisters. My girlfriend was the most mysterious. She was sitting beside my friend Phil. It was a predominantly female congregation of fifteen.

I inherited my mother's good looks and strong mindedness. She was a determined lady. My older sisters harbored a little resentment toward my mother, blaming her for the divorce. My mother wanted a boy, and when mother wanted something, there was no earthly means of discouraging her. She would wait for my father to get home from work, pounce on him the second he got in the door, and drag him into the bedroom. Fifteen years of pouncing, getting pregnant, bearing female children.

"Number twenty-one, Phuc Wildfong," said the loud speaker rudely, followed by a ripple of laughter. The only names that caught my attention were Phuc's and my own.

Father started doing disappearing acts. He was scared to come home at night. He had married the prettiest virgin in his high school class, and she had become transformed into an erotic monster, an insatiable sexual vampire in a perpetual state of arousal. I was the long-awaited boy. My birth was to be his salvation, like the second coming of Christ. He was mistaken. The pouncing didn't stop. It got worse. But I don't blame the divorce on my mother, she was only being herself.

Phuc and I were in the starting line-up. The referee blew the whistle and put his arm up, indicating that he was ready to drop the puck and start the game. I played the paragon of positions, center, and Phuc was my right wing. The center is a freedom lover, roaming the whole surface of the ice, expressing his creativity and leadership through the act of scoring. Defensemen are not as charismatic. They're the conservative sector of the team, concerned with preventing goals and protecting the status quo. The goaltender is the dullard. He stands there like a tree.

I let everyone wait as I circled around, strapping on my helmet and rearranging my balls. I would never win a face-off. I actually helped the opposing center draw the puck back and had my wings rush the defense. The opposition, the St. Charles Darlings, were in baby blue. Phuc moved at full speed from the moment the puck was dropped, indiscriminately pouncing on every Darling he could get a hold of with an inexhaustible passion that only my mother could equal. What Phuc lacked in size he compensated for in mobility. He was a bundle of energy. Despite his efforts, the Darlings kept control and shot the puck into our end zone. It was followed by a quiet invasion, like parachutists descending into enemy territory. Everyone floated into their positions, subdued and evenly spaced—everyone but Phuc. Phuc was a bullet, ricocheting off the ice, off boards, off players.

I acted as the foil. While Phuc was going hysterical in our corner, I relaxed at center ice. I hadn't budged since the puck was dropped, worrying their defense and cock-teasing their goalie. Phuc had one thing on his mind, "get the puck to Ken," and he didn't need to look to know where I was standing. He was conscious of my presence.

"Faggot," shouted Winfield from the bench, the veins in his forehead ready to pop.

I used the blade of my stick to nudge the defenseman where I imagined the crack of his ass was and stood back. He swung his stick at me, but missed. "Just looking for the hole," I whispered to him, and started my dance. The dance involved bouncing on my skates, an action akin to the pawing of a bull as it prepares to charge. I had a knack for bursting out of a static position, for springing forward and shifting speed with a swiftness that would catch my opposition off guard. The dance inspired my cheering section and intimidated the Darlings' defense, but it was a false alarm. Phuc was boxed in. He held the puck against the boards for a whistle.

Phuc's leg bounced nervously as he sat beside me on the bench. Hockey affected him like an amphetamine. Once it was in his system he couldn't stop moving. His performance on the ice was an expression of his personality, of not only an attitude toward life, but of a bloodline. Generations of Wildfongs were expressing themselves through Phuc's movements. I consider hockey to be an art form, a mode of self-expression. We were a team of dancers and choreographers. Someone like Bruno, barrelling up and down the wing with blinders on, devoid of imagination, had the technical skill, but lacked the artistic flair. He didn't have the delicate vitality of a creator. He was made for slavery.

"Goal scored by number fifteen, Steve Lawson," echoed the voice of the loud speaker, like a mechanical god. Lawson, captain of the St. Charles Darlings, had instigated and capitalized on a textbook passing play. The Darlings led one to nothing.

Near the end of the first period, I was overcome by a familiar surge of magnificence. I felt my mind and body suddenly grow in stature, like Pinnochio's nose, until my head was looming in the rafters and the ice surface had shrunk to a frozen puddle. Later in life I would exclaim to myself, "Ken, your emotions can jump from paranoia to delusions of grandeur in a matter of minutes." I perceived myself as the center of the universe, everything revolving around me. I had the power to manipulate the forces of fate. All the world was a stage, and the players were puppets of my whim.

I wanted the puck. It responded immediately, landing on my stick, and I carried it behind my net. My players set up along my boards and prepared for my rush down ice. Phuc, sensing that something was about to happen, sparkled encouragement through his eyes. My face registered "goal." There were red lights in my eyes.

The puck went from me to Phuc and back to me. I proceeded up the ice slowly, fluidly, concentrating on my body, conscious of the power in my legs. I was aware of nothing but me; like a true artist, I was all ego. There was no snack bar, no spectators, no Winfield, just me and the opposition's net. I did a prolonged version of the dance, lifting my knees and bouncing on my skates, before hurtling myself into a flurry of exertion. I exploded into overdrive, cutting to the left and to the right, digging in with my blades and leaving ruts in the ice like miniature railway tracks. I did a double crisscross with Phuc and broke between the defensemen. There was me and the goaltender. It was a waiting game, the first one who moves losing. The goalie went down and the puck went up. The red light went on.

Reality flooded into my life as I became conscious of tying the score, of Phuc putting his arms around me, of the noise from my cheering section. The spectators were standing. As the external world grew to a monstrous amplitude, I experienced a corresponding deflation. I was falling from a creative high, shrinking in size, but still slightly bloated. The act of becoming that huge required a lot of psychological energy. I was exhausted and welcomed the opportunity to wilt back to normalcy.

My father heralded in the second period with his famous whistling noises and bird calls. It was easy to identify Father in the crowd by the way his bald head, like a metallic dome, reflected the stadium lighting. Dad was notorious for making the same mistake twice, thrice, four times, multiples of ten. I harbored no ill will toward father for running away from home. "Living with eight women was too much for him," I reasoned compassionately. I couldn't understand, however, why he chose a girlfriend with as many as four daughters. Four may be an improvement from seven, but not much of one, especially since he bought a hairdressing salon and was surrounded by women all day. The original mistake was compounded. He was now interacting with over fifty women.

Instinct told me that it was bad luck for a bald man to be in the haircutting business. There was something hypocritical and mercenary about it. I didn't have the heart to discourage Father or dampen his enthusiasm when he was off on one of his incomprehensible schemes. He was already disillusioned with the hair industry and stealthily indulging in his real passion. On Saturday afternoons, he loved to ride the elevators at his girlfriend's apartment, pressing the buttons and gossiping with the passengers as they came and went. Father had a love-hate relationship with elevators. He couldn't live with them and he couldn't live without them. He tried everything from song writing to carpentry to doing paintings to plumbing, excelling in everything he touched, but always returning to the elevator trade. Elevators were a symbol of my father's life.

Bruno broke his stick over the back of someone's neck; the crowd was outraged that a penalty was called for such a minor indiscretion.

"Shake your head, ref, your eyeballs are stuck," shouted Father, "but watch you don't get sawdust on the ice." My father repeated the same mistakes and the same jokes. I had heard that line every game for three years.

Although it was uncomfortable for a while, my parents learned to tolerate each other. When Dad first brought Sara, his girlfriend, to one of my hockey games, Mom "accidentally" spilled a whole cup of coffee on his crotch. It happened between periods, and I could hear Dad screaming all the way from the dressing room. Mother was emphatic about claiming that it was an accident. I could understand a little spillage being an accident, but not a whole cup of coffee on the crotch. Fortunately, the accidents had stopped occurring.

Phuc and I had an effective system for killing penalties. Phuc forechecked and I waited until he passed me the puck. I'm the proverbial puck hog, refusing to pass unless hopelessly surrounded by the opposition. I've been known to rag the puck for the full two minutes of a penalty. Phuc didn't feel resentful or exploited by this game plan. It suited his personality to be the second man, getting the assists and letting me score the goals. We were both doing what we did best.

Phuc didn't so much as glance over his shoulder as he chased the puck into the Darlings' corner. There's nothing more intimidating in the game of hockey than feeling a hulking pursuer breathe hotly down your neck as you race into the corner. The secret is to commit yourself, to go full speed. It's when you hesitate, even slightly, that you end up being splattered headfirst against the boards. Phuc was a kamikaze pilot. "Orientals have no fear of dying," I said to myself admiringly, as I glided into the slot. Phuc dodged the onslaught of blue and drove a hard pass exactly to my stick. I felt the gap between the goalie's leg drawing me in, sucking me up with a gravitational force of its own.

The Dixie Queens didn't enjoy the short-handed goal for long. Steve Lawson, the captain of the Darlings and my handsome rival, tied the score shortly after the penalty was over and shortly before the second intermission. In the dressing room, Bruno did one of his assistant captain performances, loudly denouncing the team for costly lapses in concentration. He raised his voice to a shout and broke his stick against the wall in frustration, his second stick of the game. He apologized for letting emotion get the better of him and explained, with endearing modesty, that he was no superstar himself, just a hard-working guy with good intentions and a profound affection for the team.

"Shut up, Bruno," I said wearily, exercising my power as a superstar. "I'm trying to meditate and you're making it so I can't concentrate on my mantra."

Bruno sat down petulantly, giving me one of his unintelligible looks. My mother had a term for men like Bruno. "Glass cocks," she called them. "One knock and the cock shatters." A glass cock is a man who displays an exaggerated form of masculine pride to mask a quagmire of self-doubt. Bruno was mortally wounded. I closed my eyes and attempted to transcend the Brunos of the world through meditation.

"You're the captain," mumbled Bruno, interrupting me again, "you say something."

"My performance on the ice speaks for itself," I said somewhat pompously. I was struck with one of my ideas. "But since you ask for it Bruno, and I am captain, I'll share the secret of winning the game. It involves manipulation of the mind, ridding yourself of insecurity and negative thought. You must think golden. Did everyone hear that? Think golden. You must think of that championship cup of gold, fourteen-karat gold, like the number on my sweater, fourteen! I'm your leader, the captain, the queen of Queens. I'm your golden boy. Follow the golden boy. We must become one consciousness, one golden consciousness. Everyone close their eyes and think golden. Repeat the word in your mind over and over again. Golden. Golden. Golden."

The room filled with the silence of twenty reeking adolescent men lost in meditation, communing in the realm of infinity. There was no movement reflected in The Great Mirror, just a legion of armored buddhas and the invisible buzz of spiritual energy. Outside, the old Zambon ice groomer finished its job, coughed, and farted to a stop, increasing the resounding volume of quiet. Time passed unnoticed. Winfield was unnoticed too, as he entered the dressing room and glared confoundedly at his sleeping warriors.

"Fuck!" stammered Winfield. "What the hell is going on in here?"

"The name is Phuc, not fuck," said Phuc angrily, finally standing up and asserting himself. "Pronounce my name properly or not at all."

"Here! Here!" I said, supporting the rights of my linemate.

"The other team has been waiting for five minutes," responded Winfield distractedly. "If you don't get out there now, the game will be defaulted." I rose, grabbed my helmet, and marched out of the room. The team strutted behind me in an orderly procession. Winfield followed up the rear.

The Dixie Queens monopolized the third period. Red was dominant. Red was in the corners, along the boards, dashing around the opposition's net. We hit the post three times and the crossbar twice. The Darlings' goalie had never played better or luckier in his life. Even I missed opportunities. We couldn't score. Winfield had a negative presence which permeated the team, taking root in Bruno and spreading all the way to me. Winfield was the sour ingredient, the harbinger of bad luck. Man is a victim of subtle, unconscious forces that play in the atmosphere. Winfield corrupted the atmosphere.

I was on the bench, panting and observing my girlfriend Elizabeth Baldwin. Her unprecedented beauty was a tribute to nature, to nature's mysterious power of creating an aesthetically perfect construction. Brown hair hung in curls to her waist, accentuating a dark, immaculate complexion and classically feminine features. She was equally enchanting from behind. I almost fainted the first time I saw her buttocks. She had curves that I had never seen before and in the most interesting places. She walked down the hall in high school causing pubescent males to literally tear into the men's washroom and commit unutterable acts of sordid self-abuse. Her eyes were dark and emotional.

Elizabeth was an atrocious snob. Her little nose was forever vertical, like she was sniffing the air and enjoying a faint aroma that only a sensitive aristocrat could appreciate. She chattered almost exuberantly to Phil, which I found shocking, because she hardly opened her mouth around me. When you're young and falling in love, you do everything but talk. We had our own unique communication system. Phil was the middleman. Elizabeth confided her thoughts to Phil, who transmitted the message to me. I confided my response back to Phil, who transmitted the message to Elizabeth. It was like passing the baton in a relay race. The system worked. Phil felt included, and Elizabeth and I were saved the embarrassment of direct confrontation.

How did we get along when Phil wasn't there? Terrifically! Every moment we had alone was spent fumbling in the dark, exploring each other's bodies, discovering the mystical beauties of sex. I didn't get stimulating conversation from Elizabeth. "Let's face it, Ken," I whispered to myself, still on the bench and waiting for my shift, "few people can compete with you intellectually." Elizabeth and I had a gigantic, enormous, overpowering sexual attraction. Her parents went away one weekend, and we made love non-stop for forty-eight hours. We almost starved to death. If they had gone away the whole week, we could have died of starvation or permanently damaged our genitals!

Winfield crumbled under pressure. It was nearing the end of the third period and the game was tied. I was not surprised when Winfield was seized by epilepsy. It was one of his more violent fits. He cracked his already swollen head heavily on the cement floor a few times before the trainers were on the scene to hold him down. His eyes rolled white and his mouth made a gurgling noise. Winfield was a frightening mass of writhing anguish. The demon in his soul had taken possession of his whole being, wreaking vengeance on the other self, bent on destruction. There was something ominous about that suicidal beast, something that scared me. I was afraid it would get up and start chasing me.

Winfield's eyes unraveled and he began to regain consciousness. He may have damaged his head. The trainers hustled him off to the hospital before he had a chance to insist on staying; and he told me to act as coach. Winfield was embarrassed because everyone in the rink had a perfect view of his uncouth discharge of poisonous energy. It was over before it started. I was coach, ascending to the throne. I legislated a line change.

My line was on next. The face-off was in the Darlings' corner. I felt the atmosphere change, as if a curse had been lifted. There was no more Winfield, no more negativism, but a feeling of liberation and excitement. I decided to play defense and told Bruno to take my position at center. Bruno had grown compliant. If I had told him to get a shovelful of snow out of the Zamboni and stuff it in his jock, he would have done it. His glass cock was shattered; I didn't want to give him shriveled balls too.

Phuc could read my moods. He started doing my dance. The fever spread and all the Queens started dancing, including Bruno. I felt a wave of emotion as I joined the dance. The St. Charles Darlings never had a chance. Phuc was a blur of red. When he got the puck, his head was up and he was looking at me. I was given the puck as I maneuvered into open ice. My shot bounced off someone's stick and dropped into the net. "How revolting!" I exclaimed, when I realized that it was Bruno who deflected the puck. Bruno had scored the winning goal.

I wasn't shy in front of a camera. I loved having my picture taken. A reporter from a local newspaper snapped a flash at me as I came out of the dressing room, my hair still wet from showering. Bruno was too elated to shower. He left the dressing room early and followed the reporter around, elaborating on how he positioned himself in front of the net and calculated the velocity of my shot in order to make the deflection. The reporter couldn't stand still. He was searching for unpolluted air. Bruno was a foul-smelling person at the best of times. After having played three periods of hockey, his stench was unbearable.

"Congratulations," coughed the reporter, trying to turn away from Bruno and face me. "You had a good night tonight."

"The whole team had a good night tonight, not just me," I said modestly. Hockey fans can't get enough modesty. They consume modesty with gluttonous relish. If a player announced that he had won the game single-handedly, and that his teammates were a bunch of useless dolts, he would probably get hit by a car in the parking lot, even if what he said was true.

"To what do you attribute the team's success?" asked the reporter.

"The coach!" I answered convincingly, playing the part that was expected of a captain. "I adore Winfield! People with high foreheads are supposed to be intelligent. William Shakespeare had a high forehead. After a year with Mr. Winfield, I think that superstition has something to it. But it's more than intelligence. There's an air of tranquility about him. He has the calm of a man at peace with himself. I don't know how to express it exactly. He's . . . he's gentle. He's firm, mind you, and masculine, but he's gentle at the same time. He's a gifted speaker, too. The pre-game lectures are a work of art. They turn the whole team on. That's why we won the game. We won it for Winfield."

"How do you feel about the final game, Mr. Harrison?" asked the reporter.

"We were lucky tonight. We won by the skin of our teeth. We're playing a powerful team, perhaps the best junior B team in America. We had one good period tonight, the third. We're going to need three good periods next time. There'll be no relying on luck."

After dropping that ominous bit of foreshadowing, I left the reporter to the designs of the vulturous Bruno. My cheering section swarmed around me as I entered the snack bar area. Elizabeth, suspecting that I would be dehydrated from such a grueling game, had bought me a large coke. My father had bought me a large coke too. My sister Wendy had also bought me a large coke. My mother had bought me a large coke and a hot dog. I collected my bounty and thanked everyone gravely. I led my people out of the Dixie arena. I felt like Moses parting a carbonated sea of coca-cola with my followers trusting in the divinity of my confidence.

2. Virility

I knew Phil had arrived by the way my bowl of Raisin Bran vibrated on the kitchen table. Phil's car stereo was clearly audible from half a mile away and capable of shattering a bay window at three-quarters volume. The stereo was a useful piece of equipment. It gave us a feeling of power and territorial dominance. Phil, blessed with the family car, drove Paul, Ross and myself to school every morning. I barely distinguished the sound of the horn through the orchestrated roar of rock music. With Phil's stereo playing, the horn was redundant.

I ran out the door, down the stairs, and stopped on the driveway in front of the car. I dropped my books, started to dance, and worked myself into a rock 'n roll frenzy, limbs flailing, playing an imaginary guitar, jumping on and off the car fender, screaming along with the song in a grotesquely out-of-tune voice. My hair became a disheveled mess and my body contorted violently, coiling and uncoiling and striking like a cobra. Phil, Paul, and Ross were familiar with the morning ritual. They remained passive, witnessing my Dionysian revelry with patient forbearance.

The physical surroundings were congruous with my self-contained Bacchanalian orgy, the house and yard a pastoral haven in a den of suburban iniquity. It was a small, thick forest from the street; the house itself could not be seen. The only hint of civilization was a stone driveway, shrouded by lush vegetation and jungle-like overgrowth. Spring had blossomed early in the suburbs of Chicago. Trees were green, grass was tall, the air smelled of life. We didn't own a lawn mower or any kind of cutting utensil. Mother believed that nature should have full reign. It was as if nature had surrounded the house before invading and taking possession of the interior. Plants stood guard in every room. I was in the habit of escaping out the front door; you practically needed a machete to leave by the back.

Mr. Price lived next door. His property was well kept and sterile, with bristles for grass and a knee-high hedge composed of exactly straight lines—disciplined and orderly, not a twig out of place. He loved his lawn mower more than his wife. Cutting the lawn was Price's greatest passion and purpose in life. After his retirement, the love affair with the lawn mower became more serious and intense. He waged war against things that grow, as if by stopping growth he could obstruct the process of aging and stave off his own death. He looked at our wild yard with scathing disdain. Mr. Price had a swimming pool in the back which no one—including the Price family—was allowed to use. The vendetta with the Harrison family deepened because my dogs, Schultz, Whiskey, and Tanka, liked to hop the fence and go for a dip in their pool (Tanka was getting old and inclined to crawl under the fence). Price went insane over dog hairs in the water filter. It was unfortunate that two such different families happened to live beside each other.

"Let's go, you maniac," shouted Phil, leaning out the car window and interrupting my bestial celebration of life.

I was a born actor and pretended to notice them for the first time, feigning shock and embarrassment, like a shy person who had forgotten himself in his communion with the music. It was a routine act. I could never resist an audience or an opportunity to show off. I gathered my books with exaggerated nervousness and hung my head in shame as I walked to the car. The front seat was reserved for me. In a businesslike manner, Phil had explained that Paul and Ross must sit in the back seat because they were not as handsome as me. Phil argued that being seen with me would advance his own popularity. I turned down the music and used Phil's brush to fix my hair.

"Admit it," I demanded, as I preened myself in the rearview mirror. "I've got what it takes, stage presence. I'm going to be a rock star. Do you think being tone-deaf would hinder my music career?"

I swung around in the seat and winked at Ross. Ross was the latest addition to our circle of friends. He was Paul's friend, and I barely knew him. I reached back and pinched his testicles affectionately. "Hi cutie," I said, puckering my lips. I was acting another role.

"Keep your hands off me, queer," said Ross stridently, knocking my hand away.

"Playing hard to get? I like that," I said, sliding back into my seat and addressing Phil. "I love a challenge. It's sad though, Philip. Ross'll end up like all the others, just another conquest, another convert, another broken virgin. Then he'll be begging me for it, like a common slut."

Phil had an aggressive, protruding jaw and a strong face. He sported a fully matured mustache, making him appear older and more masculine than his peers. It was his tough, overbearing physical presence that made any display of homosexuality evoke fitful laughter. Phil puckered his lips and gave his rough voice an effeminate intonation. "Yes, Kenny-poo," giggled Phil coquettishly. Ross was beginning to enjoy the game.

"Look! Paulie-poo doesn't mind," I said, squeezing Paul's nipple through his shirt.

"Harder, you bitch," groaned Paul, who was notoriously responsive to any kind of sexual advance.

"I love it when you talk dirty," I said.

The music was returned to its usual deafening volume, causing every form of vehicle, car, truck, bike, to pull off the road and let us pass, as if an ambulance was flashing behind it. We were the center of the tornado, calm and expressionless in the midst of chaos. We commanded respect on the road, respect and awe. The last stretch, the stretch nearest the school, was dense with students, female students. We prepared for the girls by passing around the hairbrush. Phil and I were partners in crime. He was like the older brother I never had, loyal and supportive. We had the same interests, the same tastes, lusted after the same girls.

Together we were invincible. Together we feared nothing.

"Tell me I'm not as sexy as hell, and I just won't believe you," I said, checking myself in the rearview mirror one last time as we climbed out of the car.

"I'd give it to ya," said Phil. We forgot about Paul and Ross as we headed into the school. "I don't know who loves you more, me or Elizabeth. She didn't stop talking about you the whole game last night. 'Ken did this. Ken did that. Ken looks so cute when he sits on the bench. What does Ken say about me? Does Ken like me as much as I like him? I don't think his sisters like me. I hope his mother likes me. Don't you think his family is a bit weird?' Do you know what she said at one point? This really freaked me out! She said, 'I'd marry Ken tomorrow if he asked me.' I almost fell off my chair."

"You're kidding! Did she really say that?"

"Damn right. She's crazy about you. You've got it made. She's beautiful and crazy about you. What else could you ask for? I'd trade places with you any time. I'm picking up some tickets for the grade thirteen graduation. Do you want me to pick up some tickets for you and Elizabeth? They're twenty dollars each."

"Sure. When is it?" I asked.

"Thursday night. I'm off," said Phil, hurrying off to class.

Phil had a flagrant paternalism. He looked after Elizabeth and me, checking to see that all the arrangements were made and that everyone was happy. I was a lousy organizer; things happened spontaneously with me. Phil was the planner. If Elizabeth and I were irresponsible or bungled up the plans, Phil gave us a fatherly scolding. But he also had a knack for making a person feel good. He would give you a lift. You felt superior to the world because Phil was your friend. He bragged about his friends, used the most extravagant superlatives, and smashed his fist on the table if anyone disputed his compliments. Ken and Elizabeth were god and goddess, and I learned to depend on that kind of lift from Phil. Phil had a charm of his own.

Elizabeth wanted to marry me? Marriage?! It was like I had heard the word for the first time. What's marriage? Do people still take marriage seriously? When my parents divorced, I assumed everyone's parents divorced. The whole idea of marriage seemed vaguely ridiculous, an anachronism, a formality of the past. Although I was thrilled by her flattering comment, it was obvious that Elizabeth and I had different ideas on the subject. Moreover, Phil seemed to share Elizabeth's deference to marriage. I was the freak of the trio.

"Fuck marriage!" said my mother during the divorce.

"Fuck marriage!" said my father when he moved in with Sara.

"It's Phuc, not fuck!" was my latest response.

That was the attitude I was brought up with. Marriage was a standing joke in the Harrison family. Meanwhile, the Baldwins were looking at wedding pictures of the good old days, when the men looked like gangsters, and talking sentimentally about whatever it was they were supposed to be sentimental about. I could never understand the appeal of those pictures, but that was what Elizabeth was brought up to venerate. We were opposites in that way. It was strange that I lived beside someone like Mr. Price and was going out with someone like Elizabeth.

"Don't think with your penis," repeated Mother, ever since I was nine years old. She was afraid I would get a girl pregnant and have to get married. She knew it was impossible for this to happen to a nine-year-old boy, but wanted to warm me in advance. I sensed that the terrible thing was not getting a girl pregnant, but having to marry her afterwards. Sex wasn't sordid; marriage was! Mother knew everything about me. At the age of nine, Mother could see that I was dominated by my libido. My existence would be an endless search for sexual release. Sex was the center of my being, the source of my energy and creativity. Mother saw herself reflected in her son. "You're a lovely boy," repeated my mother, "but too preoccupied with your penis."

I literally stalked the halls of my school, a lascivious predator, burning with lust, foam collecting in the corners of my mouth. I pursued firm young breasts and tight adolescent bums. The pain and agony of flaming desire! My body was on fire. This physiological condition was not a mood or in any way transitory, but a permanent state of being. I was perpetually cloudy-eyed and horny, my brain consumed by images of sex. I hid the rock in my pants by carrying books in front of my crotch. I was up and down like one of Dad's elevators. I had a battering ram for a penis. I would thrust it against lockers, metal doors, walls, washroom cubicles.

Passion drove me from class to class. It was responsible for my education. In each class there were one or two girls with whom I was sincerely and profoundly in love. They were components of my fantasy harem. Whenever I was near one of them, I couldn't help leering down at her body, my heart pounding. I had what was called a reputation, a reputation that frightened and fascinated the opposite sex. I wasn't afraid "to do it." Elizabeth felt the magnetism of this reputation.

Although I was weak in sciences and practically retarded in mathematics, I got through school on very little work. I didn't worry or think about school. It was a place I went every day where there were lots of girls. I knew that I was destined for something artistic and intellectual and earthshaking, but I had no idea what it would be. I had been accepted at a large university in a small town and intended to star on the varsity hockey team and take a general arts degree. The university was a two-hour drive west of Chicago and called the University of Stockton.

I had a spare last period which I spent in the weightlifting room. I clad myself in white shorts and running shoes, no shirt. The weight lifters comprised a rigidly structured society, based on the individual's muscle bulk and the amount he bench-pressed. I was grudgingly accepted in the top echelon of the jock community, but not without some reservations. I wasn't big compared to some of the massive beasts on the football team, and I was suspected of being what they called a pretty boy. Although I was a little too pretty, I had a magic talent for the bench press which was solemnly revered by everyone, even the ugliest muscle-bound freak in the place. It was inexplicable. I could bench-press anything. I waited for some huge goon to finish his set, made a lot of noise about how the weight was far too light, and complained loudly about the lack of weights and poor facilities at the school. Once I had everyone's attention and twenty pounds were added to the bar, I tossed the bar around like a baby playing with a rattle. There was five minutes of silence after my set. Most of the guys could roll me into a snowball and throw me out the window, but no one could come near me on the bench press.

The dismissal bell was about to ring; it was time to make final preparations. I went to my locker, muscles pumped and swollen, and smeared a film of baby oil on my upper body. I was careful to put on the right amount, just enough to darken the color of my skin and accentuate the sinewy ripples of muscle that adorned my physique. The improvement was overwhelming. I looked sleek and powerful. I brushed my hair, tied on my sweaty red bandanna, and jogged out of the deserted hallway as the bell signaled the end of classes for the day.

The smoking area and race track, like incompatible lovers, slept together in the back of the school. I followed the track lazily until the smoking area began to fill with people; the bigger the audience, the faster I ran. The smoking area was bustling within five minutes and I was running at a pace slightly less than a sprint. If no one was watching, I would have crawled around the track twice and gone home. But since I had an audience, adrenalin pounded through my veins, inspiring me to awesome heights of athletic exertion. I didn't need to steal a glance to know that the females in the crowd were staring at me. I could feel their eyes on me, greedily consuming my body.

Elizabeth strolled to the side of the track, establishing her claim on me in front of her rivals. I ran full speed for the last hundred yards before collapsing to my knees. I had overdone it. With blood throbbing in my head, dizzy and delirious, I saw Elizabeth from the corner of my eye. She towered above me, the omnipotent image of sexuality, shimmering in the blur of exhaustion like a hallucination. Even in this painful condition, I noted that Elizabeth wasn't wearing a bra and that she had on a tight dress with a provocative slit up the side of her leg. I was afraid I was going to hyperventilate or faint, but eventually the pounding inside me subsided and I regained my equilibrium.

"You're an exhibitionist," accused Elizabeth with a grin. Periodically, Elizabeth displayed a perceptive awareness that surprised me. I didn't realize it was so obvious that I was showing off. She seemed older than me in some ways, in the things she thought about, like marriage, and in the books she read. I never read books and marriage entered my mind for the first time this morning, when Phil mentioned it. In another way she was a little child who would stomp her feet and cry when her lollipop was taken away. I was often the lollipop.

"It's my parents' twenty-fifth wedding anniversary party on Thursday, remember?" said Elizabeth, taking advantage of my defenselessness. "You promised to bartend."

"Yes," my voice squeaked, as I rolled painfully onto my back, closed my eyes, and felt the moisture flush out of my pores.

"Try to relax and get to know my parents," said Elizabeth. "They're nice people. You'd like each other if you'd give them a chance."

"I can't be myself around your parents," I whispered. "If I did, they'd think I was being rude. I'm not what they're used to."

"Of course you can be yourself."

"Can I swear?" I asked.

"Of course."

"Can I vomit?"

"If you want to."

"Can I call your mother Mrs. Ajax?"

I was supposed to call her Mrs. Baldwin, that was her real name, but I nicknamed her Mrs. Ajax because every time I came over she was washing the walls with Ajax. I would be kissing Elizabeth good night at two-thirty in the morning and see Mrs. Baldwin through the kitchen window. She would be there, scrubbing the walls. I had nightmares about being a germ in that household.

"Yes, you can call my mother Mrs. Ajax."

"OK. I'll come!"

Elizabeth was sensitive about her parents. I had seen Elizabeth crying and frustrated, but the only time she expressed anything near anger was when she was defending her parents. She insisted that everyone like each other. We pretended to like each other so that Elizabeth wouldn't get upset. Mr. and Mrs. Baldwin and I kept smiling at each other across the dinner table for Elizabeth's sake, but the underlying antipathy was clear from the start.

"Am I going to see you tonight?" asked Elizabeth.

"I'll be over after hockey practice." We kissed and went our separate ways.

I put my clothes in a bag and walked home in my shorts and running shoes. Spring was the season of energy. The bright sky and clean air made me feel twice as alive. As I arrived home and climbed the porch steps which headed to the front door, I heard rustling noises in the back yard. The noise moved from the back to the side of the house. Three silent dogs came tearing through the long grass into view, following each other with great precision and dexterity, like bomber airplanes. Although old Tanka was a little feeble on some of the turns, she managed to maintain her position in the rear.

I barked! Tanka and Whiskey stopped dead in their tracks. Shultz started to spring through the grass like he was on a pogo stick. Shultz was the one most like myself, intellectually astute, an articulate barker, and an obsessive show-off. I barked again. This time Shultz crouched in the grass too. I exploded with a short barking spree.

I have an esoteric relationship with dogs. I have a lot of dog traits. Dogs know how to have fun, sniffing, running around, and humping things. Dogs are natural and spontaneous, full of exuberance and love, but also capable of courage and self-sacrificing idealism. Shultz would defend me to the death. Shultz and I communicated through body language and eye contact. Shultz was a kindred spirit.

I pulled off my shorts and jock strap and ran naked through the long grass, dogs barking at my side. It was a thrilling feeling, wind and grass slapping my front and the clamor of dogs behind me. I could run forever. The presence of Shultz, Whiskey, and Tanka, a significantly smaller crowd than the smoking area audience, were enough to give me a resurgence of energy. We were a flurry of four, storming in circles, flying along the side of the house and into the backyard. I was the offensive player and they pursued me with gentle, harmless bites on the legs and rump. Shultz could have chomped off my penis and chewed it to shreds, but not once did he get carried away and bite me too hard. Dogs know how to shower a boy with love, jumping up and down and licking him everywhere. If only Elizabeth could love like that! We were having ourselves a party.

Panting, I dropped in the grass, and my three animal friends dropped on top of me, also panting. I spread my affection evenly, not wishing to cause friction or jealousies within the family. Shultz was the baby of the dogs, and I was the baby of the humans. We were both used to a generous supply of love. It was in this state of tranquil exhaustion and calm that I noticed the sudden silence of Mr. Price's lawn mower. It had been buzzing. I hadn't noticed it until it was shut off. I jumped up, knocked the mud off my knees, and headed for the back door, Shultz and Whiskey trailing behind me. Tanka didn't budge. She was either asleep or dead. Tanka was an old dog, probably older than Mr. Price, in dog years. Mr. Price was checking the oil, his shirt saturated with perspiration.

"Mr. Price," I shouted, barely visible in the dense greenery of my yard. "You missed a spot by the pool." I hoped he could see my bare buttocks as they disappeared into the house.

I had a bath, not for the sake of cleanliness, but for the sake of erotic pleasure. The door was locked, the shower curtain pulled, and I lolled in the steamy hot water. My body was flaccid, but my penis was erect. "Before you can love anyone, you've got to be able to love yourself," I said out loud, repeating one of my mother's slogans. There's a lot to say for masturbation. It was an opportunity to utilize my imagination. There was no fear of pregnancy or of the woman changing her mind at the last second. You didn't have to worry about pleasing your partner or whether you were doing a good job or lasting long enough or whether you were big enough or hard enough. You just enjoyed yourself.

The woman of my imagination fawned over me, muttered complimentary obscenities in my ear and orgasmed like an erupting volcano. Visions of the day's prowling flashed through my mind, a mangled assortment of body parts. My senses reeled. I was submerged in a pool of legs, breasts, shoulders, bums. I added soap for lubrication. Sperm floated on the water. I made waves and sent it to the other end of the bathtub. I fell asleep, but only for a few minutes.

Although my bike was made for a young kid and had high handle bars and a banana seat, it managed to get me to hockey practice before everyone else. Everyone, that is, except Winfield. Winfield was alone in the dressing room, reading the newspaper interview of me. He was reading the flattering lies I had made up about winning the game for the coach, and he was believing them. The article was taped to the great mirror and Winfield had probably been re-reading it for hours. He was red with embarrassment when I came in, as if I had thrown open the shower curtains and caught him abusing himself in the bathtub. He slunk out of the room. I read the article for the first time. My words had been accurately reproduced. Winfield and I were buddies again.

I put a sign on the front of the dressing room door, "Homosexual Disco," and turned the music up full blast. The music cracked and popped like an amplified bowl of Kellogg's Corn Flakes. I danced along the benches in my jock strap as my teammates entered, stripped down, and joined the gathering numbers on the dance floor in the center of the room. Bruno was doing the two step with his hairy defensive partner. Someone was turning the lights on and off to produce a strobe effect. The song ended and news came on. We silently returned to our places and dressed for the practice.

Winfield came in shyly, holding a shiny new hockey stick like a priest clutching a crucifix. He was coy. He wanted to make amends, in his awkward way, and show his humble appreciation for the crap I fed the reporter.

"I bought a new stick for the practice," he said to me. "It's a good one. Cost $11.50. Would you like to feel the whip?"

"Sure," I said. Winfield hadn't seemed to notice that everyone was watching us. At first I thought he was giving me the stick as a gift, but I realized that I was only supposed to lean on it, feel the bend, and pass it back like a peace pipe. "That's a good stick," I said.

"Cost $11.50," he repeated incredulously. The price tag was still on the stick.

The pathetic bastard was losing his mind. He had slammed his head against the cement floor once too often. Winfield made his exit, leaving his precious stick by the door. I was struck by another one of my ideas. Impulse was my master. The team owned a saw for altering the length of hockey sticks. I grabbed the saw and cut the blade of Winfield's eleven dollar and fifty cent stick in half. This pointless act of mischief hit a funny bone on the team, primarily because of its pointlessness, and the room filled with lengthy undulations of laughter. I taped the blade back on and returned the stick to its original spot. It appeared to be a perfectly intact eleven dollar and fifty cent stick.

Winfield's practices were exercises in futility. The Russians had made their dramatic impact on the American hockey scene and suddenly everyone was an apostle of the scientific method. The slogan "get back to basics" was popularized. According to the Russian ideal, practices had to be scientifically planned and organized to maximize training in the basics: skating, passing, stick handling, checking. Winfield interpreted these ideas as meaning that practices must be boring. They couldn't be boring enough. If the players weren't going out of their minds with boredom, it simply wasn't doing them any good. Winfield had a Presbyterian kind of practice, no fun and lots of suffering in the boring sense, not in the physical sense. We were instructed to line up and take turns leisurely carrying the puck to the other end of the rink and back. No one was allowed to pass the puck or shoot or do any checking. When you returned to the line, the next guy went. It was so easy and so boring that after a while you started making mistakes, tripping over your own feet and losing the puck. Winfield's scientific method was slowly eroding our skills as hockey players.

I lobbied for a scrimmage. I wanted to simulate a game situation and let Winfield blow the whistle whenever someone did something stupid. I argued that hockey is a spontaneous game and that this exercise would not only develop spontaneity and cohesion among players, it would be interesting and fun. Winfield adamantly refused. What I wanted was too pleasurable. I was being a self-indulgent, hedonistic pervert. I was being both unscientific and unAmerican. Winfield was programmed to suffer. He was too numb between the ears to change.

Winfield was teaching us one of his ludicrous drills. He took a slapshot and the end of his blade sailed clear across the rink, over the boards, and landed somewhere in the upper reaches of the bleachers. The look on his face haunts me. It wasn't his usual obnoxious expression, but a look that was sadly resigned, passive, self-deprecating. He softly placed the remainder of his stick in the garbage can. I don't know what that stick represented to Winfield, but it meant more than eleven dollars and fifty cents. It was a personal rejection. Perhaps he saw himself as sawed-off and incomplete. Perhaps the useless stick was a reflection of his impotence. Winfield tired too hard at life and was consumed by the frustration of never seeming to get anywhere. For a brief moment he had lost even his frustration, which made him pathetic. I didn't enjoy my role as the victor. I wasn't an evil person, just an impulsive one that tended to get carried away.

I skated with frantic enthusiasm. I wanted to draw the laughter away from Winfield, like trying to change the subject in a conversation, redirecting the center of attention. I asked him some meaningless questions as an excuse to call him Coach. His eyes glowed when he was called Coach.

"Don't forget," said Winfield, almost pleasantly, as the team headed into the homosexual disco for a shower. "The game is Thursday night at eight o'clock."

Thursday! Thursday! Thursday! It finally occurred to me that I had graduation, an anniversary party, and a hockey game on the same night. Could I do all three? That was too much of a challenge for someone with my retarded organizational skills. I needed eight mothers and a girlfriend to organize me. I decided not to worry about it. I was capable of forgetting about anything. I would rely on my natural instincts and decide what direction to go at the last minute. I would handle things my way: spontaneously.

I was in a sensitive mood that night because I was feeling guilty about sawing the blade off Winfield's hockey stick. Elizabeth loved my gentle moods. She was thrilled whenever I was quiet or feeling a little vulnerable and soft. She felt needed and reveled in the attention I gave her. I'm capable of gentleness. Anyone who's been brought up by eight women, a mother and seven sisters, is capable of gentleness. Although it made Elizabeth happy, I rarely behaved in a gentle way. I couldn't sustain it. On Elizabeth's birthday I planned this great magnanimous display of gentleness, but forgot after an hour and spent most of the evening barking at Shultz. My intentions were good, but my memory was lousy. At least Shultz enjoyed himself, although it wasn't his birthday.

"Hi, Mrs. Ajax," I said, as Elizabeth and I passed through the kitchen towards the basement stairs. Mrs. Baldwin was washing the refrigerator.

"Don't stay too late, Ken. It's a week night," said Mrs. Baldwin humorlessly. I knew she really meant to say, "Don't screw my daughter in the basement." The Baldwins made me feel as welcome as a herpes epidemic. I was a germ invading their household. I expected Mrs. Baldwin to attack me with the pail of Ajax.

Normally, I would have had Elizabeth's blouse off by the first landing, her pants off at the bottom of the stairs, and I would have ejaculated before reaching the couch. Tonight, I was in a gentle mood, I waited until we got the to couch before tearing into Elizabeth's clothing. Talk about virility! A Dionysian frenzy in the morning, a two-mile run at record speed in the afternoon, a session of masturbation in the bathtub, the homosexual disco, an hour hockey practice, and I was still desperately in need of sexual satisfaction. Would it ever stop?

Later, I climbed onto my banana seat and rode my bike home. I fidgeted in bed for what seemed an eternity; insomnia was an affliction that worsened with age. I masturbated twice before falling asleep.

3. Happy Anniversary

Thursday afternoon I was involved in a game of brick soccer. Brick soccer was like any other type of soccer, except you kick a brick instead of a ball and play in the teachers' parking lot. About forty years ago, when the school was nothing more than a hut in the wilderness, someone chased a ball across the street and almost got hit by a horse and buggy. As a safety precaution, the principal made the rule that no balls were allowed in the parking lot, so students began to play with a brick. No one seemed to think that a brick could be more hazardous than a soccer ball. The ancient rule was never disputed. Thus, the evolution of brick soccer, a tradition peculiar to my school, unconsciously passed down through generations of pubescent suburbanites. The sport had a history of casualties, from broken toes and bleeding thighs, to dislocated kneecaps and multiple fractures. There were also a number of smashed headlights and dented fenders. These injuries and accidents were tolerated, but not soccer balls. Soccer balls were dangerous.

Brick soccer was my favorite sport. I secretly preferred it over ice hockey. There was an atmosphere of warmth and camaraderie among the players, not merely among members of the same team, but between both teams. There were no scorekeepers, no winners or losers, just performers and survivors. It was the show, the style, and finesse of the performance that was important, not beating the other team. Nothing in life was more meaningful than brick soccer.

"Life is a game of brick soccer," I said to myself philosophically. "It doesn't matter who wins or loses, as long as you do it with style."

As is customary in real soccer, the opposition's goaltender got the brick and heaved it into the air. School was over for the day, but it was still early. There was plenty of light and plenty of time to clear out the way of the flying brick. I ran under it and stood transfixed, studied it in the air, watching it rise and arch, and when it came down I headed it, as though it was real soccer ball. I knew it was a brick, but I headed it anyway. I headed it for absolutely no reason, impulse again, like the desire to jump when staring at the ground from the top balcony of an apartment building. I succumbed to this self-destructive reflex because deep down I didn't believe it would hurt me. I believed it would bounce off my head like a beach ball. I believed it could only hurt other people, weaker people, mere mortals, not a mythical god like myself.

I can't remember much between getting hurt and arriving at the hospital. I was in a delirium. My brain was shortcircuiting, mixing up its signals, flashing a confused stream of images at me, numbers, sparks, colors, Winfield's head thudding against the cement floor. The thing that I remembered most vividly was what I thought to be a smell, but what was probably the sensation of nausea. The smell was unpleasantly familiar, like a disagreeable memory, like guilt, like the snapshot recall of a nightmare. My reaction to the smell was fear, fear of an intangible enemy.

Dear, faithful, reliable Phil stood beside my bed, the symbol of sanity. It was Phil whom my teammates had sought out when I dropped to the cement bleeding. It was Phil who drove me to the hospital. I thought my disorientation must have lasted for weeks, but it couldn't have been more than half an hour because the digital clock in the emergency ward read five p.m. The doctor, smiling jovially, told me that I had an inordinately hard head and that it wasn't serious. I was skeptical. As far as I was concerned, getting hit in the head with a brick was serious. He gave me fourteen stitches across the forehead, pain killers, and lots of patronizing advice on how heading a brick was not a sensible thing to do. I tried to explain that we used a brick because soccer balls were dangerous.

"Phil," I said cheerfully. "Phone Winfield. Tell him I got hit by a brick and won't be at the game tonight."

"I already did. He was angry. He'll hate you forever."

"I knew he would have nothing but concern for my well-being."

"I also phoned Elizabeth," said Phil. " She was upset and wanted to come to the hospital. I told her not to bother. I explained that it was a scratch on your forehead and you are as handsome as ever."

"That's no scratch. That's a gaping cavern." I sat up in order to look at myself in the mirror. I expected my face to be totally mutilated and disfigured, but, to my amazement, it was only a little swollen around the stitches.

"You're right! I'm as handsome as ever."

"Do you want me to call your mother?" asked Phil.

"No," I pronounced emphatically. "There's no need to."

Mother tended to overreact when she perceived her children to be in peril. Her battered Camaro would squeal into the hospital parking lot with five cop cars tailing it. She would storm past the front desk, bully the interns, tyrannize the nurses, and hurl the most outrageous threats imaginable at the doctors, castration, for example. She always threatened castration. She used the same threat on my father. I don't know any man who is not unnerved by the threat of castration. It took one glance at my mother's face to realize that she was, in fact, capable of such a primitive act of aggression. Once, I caught a high hockey stick on my upper lip and needed three stitches. Mother clutched a scalpel blade and said firmly to the doctor, "That boy's face is perfect. If you leave a scar, I'll come back here and cut your balls off." You don't reason with Mother. You do what you're told. I should mention, however, that the stitching job on my lip was excellent.

My problems were solved. Thursday night was mine. I had freed myself of responsibility, organized my life, and I had done it my way, spontaneously. My head was already feeling lighter. I was proud of myself. Phil drove me back to his house without the car stereo on and got his grandmother to cook us dinner.

Phil's parents were dead. He was the protector of the household, living alone with an ailing grandmother and an eleven-year-old sister. This family background had prematurely aged Phil, spurred his paternalistic leaning, and formulated his attitude towards women. If the instinct to protect me, a man, was strong, it was even stronger to protect a woman. Chivalry was not dead with Phil. I loved the opposite sex, but I was as rude and as disgusting in the company of women as I was with men. I was used to women who were completely capable of looking after themselves. There was nothing helpless about my mother. Phil had to look after a little girl and a frail old lady and he thought all women were that way.

Phil had a date for the graduation. He paid for the tickets, bought a corsage, put a full tank of gas in the car, rented a tuxedo. He told the girl exactly what time he would pick her up, promised to be prompt, and fully expected to talk to her parents for a few minutes before going out. Phil did everything right, and parents thought he was wonderful. I would pull into the girl's driveway, radio blasting, and honk my horn. If she didn't come out, I'd keep honking. I was indomitably cheerful, and, in my indomitably cheerful way, I'd get her to contribute a couple of dollars for gas and split the cost of the evening's entertainment. Despite my lack of dating etiquette, the girls were full of smiles and laughter and always came back for more.

Phil adorned himself in the appropriate garb, sprinkled on romantic smells, and assured me of getting a reimbursement for my graduation tickets. Phil left for his date, dropping me off at my place on his way. I was in a strangely morose mood as I climbed onto my banana seat and rode my bike to Elizabeth's house. I had gone from lightheaded and free to heavy-hearted and claustrophobic in a matter of minutes. I wanted to indulge in scorn, wallow in cynicism, harbor black thoughts about society and mankind. It may have been a result of the bump on the head or of the prospect of spending an evening at the Baldwins' anniversary party. My options had been spontaneously reduced to one. Fate was leading me to the anniversary party.

"Suburbia! Blah! It's destroying my mind," I said to myself, riding through a stop sign without even slowing down. I spat, and the wind sprayed it back into my face.

There was something wrong, something that bothered me about the Baldwins. I didn't believe them, not that they were telling me anything, but I didn't believe them anyway. It was their way of looking at the world I didn't like, a mentality that Elizabeth was committed to, brainwashed by, and wanted to honor and obey for the rest of her life. It was this mentality that was my rival, that competed for Elizabeth's affection, that created a distance between Elizabeth and me. I couldn't define it. I wasn't against materialism, or the unequal distribution of wealth in America, or the wasteful life-style of the bourgeoisie or anything to do with politics. It was something else.

The Baldwins were weird. They were so normal they were weird. What do you call a man who goes to Sears Automotive Center for a good time, who spends every waking moment either in a Sears store or playing with an automobile appliance or gadget? You call that man normal, with a capital "N." You call that man Mr. Baldwin! Mr. Baldwin got up early on Saturday mornings and stood at the door of the Sears Automotive Center, waiting until it opened, freezing his ass off in a lineup of other normal Americans. Fortunately for Mr. Baldwin, there were three Sears stores within driving distance, a suburbanite's vision of utopia. He knew everyone at these stores, employees and customers. I didn't trust anyone who spent that much time in an automotive center.

Elizabeth had an uncanny intuition for anticipating my arrival. I had my fist raised and positioned to knock at the door; it swung open and I almost punched Elizabeth in the forehead. She pressed her voluptuous body against mine and kissed me. The music throbbed in the basement like a swollen penis. It was an affectionate reception, almost too affectionate. Elizabeth had a way of not looking at me, of turning her head away. Something was bothering her, too.

"You're missing a wild party," said Elizabeth. "My parent's friends are going wild. The dance floor has been full all night. It's wild! My parents were asking about you. They'll be glad you came. It's wild down there. You don't have to stand behind the bar all night. You can go wild, too."

Elizabeth was trying to convince me about what great fun her parents were. She was challenging me. Am I man enough for that much wildness? A brick wall was separating Elizabeth and me, with a single brick missing around the crotch area for screwing purposes. We communicated through our genitals. The missing brick was the one that hit me on the head. We were full of adult emotion and passion, but the mechanisms necessary for dealing with these things were woefully infantile. The brick wall was getting bigger, bigger than us. It lacked supports and threatened to fall down, like a scene from TV commercials sponsored by Allstate Insurance. We would discover who really had the hardest head.

"Is it true you headed a brick?" asked Elizabeth.

"Look!" I said, pointing to my purple wound.

"Thank God it's just a scratch."

"That's no scratch. That's a gaping cavern," I protested.

"Why did you head it?" she asked.

"I was trying to commit suicide so that I wouldn't have to come to this wild party tonight," I said, trying to laugh as good-naturedly as possible. Elizabeth turned her head, pretending not to hear the comment.

Elizabeth inherited that trait. The Baldwins were forever pretending. They pretended to like me. They pretended there was nothing to life but Ajax, clean walls and auto parts stores. They pretended that Elizabeth was a virgin, that sex never existed in connection with their daughter, at least until marriage. They knew better, of course—no one could be that dense—but they pretended anyway. I was brought up differently. My mother, for example, kept condoms in a candy bowl by the front door for the use of the whole household. It was sad the Baldwins needed to pretend so much. It consumed a lot of energy.

Downstairs, boldly stretching across the dance floor, were the letters "Happy Anniversary." I recognized Elizabeth's workmanship. She contrasted primary colors and the effect was stunning. It made the room vibrant.

Elizabeth liked bold colors in dress, design, and boyfriends. I felt she had a knack for visual arts, but she didn't seem interested in anything except getting me to like her parents and her parents to like me, which was a losing battle and not even necessary. Elizabeth was desperate for harmony. She responded to disharmony by turning her head. Her pretty head wasn't hard enough.

Elizabeth's pudgy cousin stood dumbly behind the bar, looking like a prize pig in a butcher shop window. I had forgotten his name, so I made one up. "Hi, Porky," I said happily, patting his protruding tummy. "The women are taking some nice hot lasagna and garlic bread out of the oven. If you're hungry, you better get up there before it's gone." Porky fell for it. There was no lasagna or garlic bread, but I was confident he would find something to eat in the kitchen. I claimed the position of bartender.

Being separated behind the bar and elevated on a stool gave me a feeling of superiority. I hated jostling with the common people. The dance floor was packed, everyone bouncing to the disco beat and hanging themselves on Elizabeth's colorful "Happy Anniversary." They were Sears' auto patrons run amok. Everyone was best friends and had known each other since the beginning of time, since before the advent of Brick Soccer.

Middle-aged men smell horrible after a night's drinking. I pitied the women for what they would have to put up with in the morning. It wasn't just the inevitable gas. It wasn't just bad breath. Foul smells seemed to ooze through their skin and smear on the sheets. I was particularly sensitive to smells. If a girl stank, I wouldn't touch her, no matter how beautiful and willing she was. I would never be able to forgive her. The thought of getting a whiff of those men in the morning was making me nauseous again.

Mr. Simmons came to the bar with a smile on his face the size of a billboard. I didn't think of Mr. Simmons as a real person. He was the Friendly Neighbor, the personification of all neighbors, an archetype. He was immortal. You couldn't blast the smile off his face with a Sears store full of dynamite. Why did I have Mr. Price for a neighbor? Price didn't have a billboard smile. He dragged the dead weight of his misery around like a lawn mower through a wheat field.

"How they hanging, Ken?" said Mr. Simmons gamely.

"Down to my knees," I said, which was the stock reply, and, in my case, a gross exaggeration.

Mr. Simmons laughed as I gave him a cold beer. I watched his massive hand wrap the bottle. I noticed hands because I had heard that it was possible to judge the size of a man's penis by his hands. The friendly neighbor was hung down to his knees.

"I understand you'll be going to college next year," said Mr. Simmons, his face becoming serious and intent. "Good for you. It'll be the best years of your life. That's the place to sow your wild oats and prepare yourself for settling down with that little lady of yours. Elizabeth! She's lovely. I've watched her grow up."

Mr. Simmons acted like he was in the know, hinting about that exclusively male need for a stage of sexual experimentation and promiscuity. What he didn't realize was that little lady of mine was rather horny herself. Besides, there was no guarantee that I would want to return to my blushing virgin, which was what Elizabeth was supposed to be. Maybe I'd fall in love with one of the sluts. I wondered if college would be the best years of my life. ("If university is the best years of your life," I said to myself years later, after attaining my degree, "I've got fuck-all to look forward to.")

The song was finished and there was a rush for the bar. The next song was slow and romantic. I was serving a few people, but Mr. Simmons hung onto his position, and the dialogue continued.

"You think you're smart," said Mr. Simmons argumentatively, as though he could read my mind. "You want to know what life's about. I'll show you." His huge hand pointed to the dance floor, where Mr. and Mrs. Baldwin were locked in each other's arms, swaying to the music. "Need I say more? I rest my case." He gave me that billboard smile and went to mix with his friends.

After twenty-five years of marriage, Mr. and Mrs. Baldwin were a picture of love. I'm as sentimental as the next guy, and the scene moved me. I imagined them as the same age as Elizabeth and me. Mrs. Baldwin had sex appeal for a woman her age, but the old man needed some work, about forty pounds' worth. Was this the shadow of the future, of my future with Elizabeth?

"Blah! Suburbia! It's destroying my mind," I said to myself.

Elizabeth came down the stairs, leaned against the wall, and watched her parents on the dance floor. She was beaming. There was no one more thrilled about this happy anniversary than Elizabeth. It was an affirmation and celebration of her values, of Mr. Simmons' values, and her confidence was soaring. Her happiness was dependent on the level of cohesion in her parents' relationship, which made me jealous. I felt excluded. I had overcome that childish dependence when my parents divorced five years ago. Elizabeth was an only child, the focal point of the Baldwin universe, and perhaps it was more difficult for her.

Elizabeth looked like a little girl as she skipped towards me, got behind the bar, and sat on my stool. I was in the process of serving a rye and water. I could feel her playing with my testicles under the bar.

"On the rocks, sir?" I asked. Elizabeth giggled as the man walked away.

"Did you tell my cousin we had made lasagna and garlic bread?" asked Elizabeth.

"Yes."

"He was so upset I had to order him a pizza. How's your forehead? It's dangerous to sleep when you've had a bad bump on the head. You're supposed to have someone wake you up every few hours."

I loved it when Elizabeth took a maternal interest in me. I said, "The doctor told me I had to ejaculate every four hours or I'd die of a concussion." I studied the clock behind the bar. "I've seven minutes. If I go into a coma, give me a blow job and it'll bring me back to life."

"Don't be rude," said Elizabeth encouragingly, her hand on my testicles.

"Gin!" I looked up. It was Mr. Baldwin. Elizabeth's hand dropped from my crotch. "And tonic," he said.

It was as if Mr. Baldwin and I were from different planets. We could manage primitive hand signals, communicate "hello" and "good-bye," but anything beyond that was an impossibility. I had more sophisticated intellectual banter with Shultz than with Mr. Baldwin. There was no real hostility between us, nothing concrete, just a deep, unfathomable communication gap. I racked my brain for something to say, a topic that held a mutual interest. There was nothing. To my utter amazement, we didn't have a single thing in common except Elizabeth, but I couldn't very well discuss his daughter's wonderful technique at fellatio. Fathers are unreasonable about that type of thing.

"You two having a good time?" asked Mr. Baldwin.

"Great," answered Elizabeth, speaking for both of us.

I noticed that Mr. Baldwin's hands were the same size as mine. We had one thing in common, the size of our genitals.

"Have you seen that little lady of mine?" said Mr. Baldwin, referring to that little wife of his. "Every time we finish dancing she disappears somewhere."

"I'll go see if she's upstairs, Dad," said Elizabeth, who was hyper-cooperative when it came to getting her parents together. "Ken," she said, to placate me, "come upstairs in a while and we can sit together in the living room." Sex hint. I never missed a sex hint.

Alone with Mr. Baldwin! It was the silent moments that bothered me. I didn't mind him shouting at me, hitting me on the head with a brick, breathing fire through his nose, anything but silence. Tonight was monumental. Mr. Baldwin and I talked. We didn't communicate on a stupendously profound level, but there was a verbal exchange of some kind. Elizabeth was right. It was a wild night, beyond my wildest expectations.

"I grew up on the other side of the tracks," explained Mr. Baldwin. "There was no university for me. My education was on the street, the school of hard knocks. I was taught to work hard and use common sense. I'm damned happy with my life, the advancements I've made, what I've done for my family. My wife's family had money. They were sort of upper-class. She was such a snob! I always thought she deserved to be brought down a peg or two. She knew nothing about the real world, still doesn't. I've protected her from that."

Why was he justifying his life to me? Mr. Simmons did the same thing. Was my face broadcasting disapproval? Was I challenging him?

"You should be proud, Mr. Baldwin," I said sincerely. 'You've done very well for your family."

"Young people won't listen nowadays," continued Mr. Baldwin, visibly perking up and gaining confidence. I was getting bored already and having trouble listening. "They've had it too easy. Most of them are lazy and irresponsible. In my day you knew what you had to do. After you got married, you concentrated on your career, worked your butt off for the firm. The economy is getting bad in this country. Unemployment. B.A. Means Bugger-All. They're all unemployed too."

The conversation was getting me horny. I kept thinking of Elizabeth alone upstairs. Mr. Baldwin sounded like a broken record. As I said before, I didn't believe whatever it was he was trying to tell me, especially the bit about economics. I felt he was painting a bleak picture of the world to rationalize his own lack of initiative, to rationalize his paranoid security-conscious existence. He had an altered perception of reality: the loop strewn with starved carcasses of unemployed intellectuals. It wasn't true. Americans lived like kings, comparatively speaking, and yet they were perpetually moaning about being maltreated and hard-done-by. There's a two thousand-mile wheat field in the middle of our country, and we can't stop worrying about not having enough cereal for breakfast.

We were distracted by the sudden upsurge of the song, "Happy Anniversary." Mr. Simmons acted as conductor.

I took the opportunity to dash upstairs and seek refuge in the washroom. I opened my shirt, pulled down my pants and underwear, and stared at myself in the mirror. "If I had seven inches, I'd have everything," I said to myself sadly. Although it looked larger than usual, it was far short of the seven-inch ideal. When I didn't masturbate for a day or two it seemed to get bigger; now was the time to show it to Elizabeth. The mirror was well lit and vertical, making it possible to see from the head to the knees, for people like Mr. Simmons who were hung that low.

I imagined myself being photographed in different positions. With different facial expressions, for the front of an album cover, or a Marlboro ad, or the centerfold of a magazine. I had this fantasy about being a world-famous male stripteaser. I was given enormous amounts of money to expose my body. I contributed the money to wife-battery homes, rape-crisis and day-care centers around the country, and became a national hero among women. Feminists were breaking down my door to make love to me. I needed five bodyguards.

I marveled at the fact that that face, and that body and those hands belonged to me. I was convinced they belonged to someone else, a relation, a dear friend whom I had known all my life. The answer to my questions was directly in front of me. "That's me," I said in wonderment. My body was the fortress of my wisdom.

Elizabeth ambushed me in the hallway with a hug, laying siege to my fortress. "I heard you talking to yourself again," she said. "What were you saying?"

"Quick," I said. "I want to show you something."

I dragged her into the living room, which was roped off and quarantined with plastic footpaths on the rug and couch. The front room was for show, like Mr. Price's swimming pool. The room was unused for the obvious reason that it was covered in sheets of plastic and not particularly comfortable. I was strongly averse to covering furniture with plastic. Why not buy plastic furniture?

"Look at this," I said, pulling out my penis. Although the lights were out, there was enough light to see clearly. "Put it in your mouth before it gets hard."

"It's too late," said Elizabeth. "It's already hard."

"That's not hard. It gets way bigger than that."

Elizabeth bent down, put it in her mouth, and it was instantly harder. She made a gargling noise while it was in her mouth.

"What?" I said.

She pulled it out long enough to say, "I love you," and put it back in her mouth.

"I love you too, Elizabeth." It was the first time we had confessed to being in love. I felt a flood of excitement. The night was becoming wilder every minute.

That was a special night. That night I discovered the clitoris, and my life would never be the same. It was perhaps the single most important discovery of my life. Elizabeth stood up. Her mouth was red and, as we kissed, I slipped my hand into her panties. I knew that I was onto something good, a pleasure spot, because Elizabeth started making crying noises and repeatedly muttering, "I love you." She handled my penis with unprecedented aggressiveness. I had never seen a woman orgasm before, except in my imagination, and the reaction scared me. I thought she was in pain or even dying, the way her back arched and her face contorted. She was getting so loud I had to cover her mouth. The whole thing happened while on our feet.

The sound of sperm splattering on plastic was magical, a thing of extraordinary beauty. We fell against the wall hugging each other, my pants around my ankles and her dress up around her neck. It would have been awkward explaining this position to Elizabeth's father. "It's not what it looks like, Mr. Baldwin," I said to Elizabeth, teasing her. "I was tucking in my shirt and Elizabeth got a nasty itch in the small of her back. . ." Mr. Baldwin would pretend to believe me.

Elizabeth sprang into action. She produced a Kleenex out of thin air and scrubbed the floor. I finally realized the rationale behind the plastic floor coverings. I didn't think old Baldwin had it in him. For her next trick, I expected a bottle of Ajax to materialize. She gave me a kiss and disappeared into the washroom, no doubt to do a cleaning job on her private parts. I let whatever didn't make it to the floor dry in my underwear.

I was asleep on the couch. Elizabeth woke me by pushing softly on my chest, like a child wanting her father's attention.

"Are you sleeping?" she asked innocently.

"No," I whispered faintly. "I'm wide awake." My sisters complained bitterly about the type of man who falls asleep immediately after sex. They construed it as an insult, like eating and running after a dinner party. I never admitted to it, but, to be perfectly honest, I was exactly that type of guy. I tried to look chipper, but I could barely keep my eyes open.

"Let's talk," said Elizabeth spryly, sitting upright on the couch. Some guests were leaving by the front door which was around the corner from our plastic hideaway.

"Ok," I said. "You start and I'll follow right behind."

"Did you talk long with my father?" she asked.

"Too long. It was the longest conversation of my entire life."

Elizabeth turned her head. "Lovers are up and down like an elevator," my father once told me. Elizabeth was defensive when I expressed a lack of reverence towards her father. She didn't mind me being irreverent towards her mother. She even laughed occasionally at the nickname, Mrs. Ajax, but she wouldn't tolerate a similar comment applied to her father.

"What've you got against my parents?" asked Elizabeth.

"You want what they've got, don't you?" I accused.

"What's wrong with what they've got?" blurted Elizabeth, almost crying.

"There's nothing wrong with it, absolutely nothing, but for some reason it makes me nauseous."

"They're happy," continued Elizabeth dejectedly. "They love each other. They've a nice home and a nice daughter. They've got everything they want. You know what's wrong with you? You're all screwed up because you're from a divorced family. You don't believe that two people can live together twenty-five years and still be madly in love."

"You're screwed up because your parents aren't divorced," I said feebly, not able to think of anything else to say.

"I don't feel like talking anymore. I'm sleeping." Elizabeth slid down, put her head on my lap and immediately fell asleep. I was a hopeless insomniac; the swiftness with which Elizabeth fell asleep astounded me. She slept like a baby. She never snored. Her body twitched periodically, as if pinched by a ghost.

Maybe Elizabeth was right! Maybe I was a psychological mess and didn't even know it. But I felt all right. Is it possible to feel good and be screwed up? Elizabeth wasn't screwed up, born and bred in an ideal home, but she wasn't happy either. She couldn't help turning her head. I was screwed up and happy! Elizabeth was normal and unhappy. Who was better off? The logistics were mindboggling.

"Never forget one thing, Ken," I said to myself. "The whole world is wrong and you're right."

The basement door opened and music poured out. The door was shut and the music receded again. Two women were talking, coming up the stairs. The voices grew. It was Mrs. Baldwin talking to one of her guests. I knew the woman she was talking to, but couldn't remember her name. Elizabeth had explained to me that this woman was her mother's "divorced friend." She dressed well, I remembered. They were standing by the front door, a whisper away from me.

"I can't get away from him," Mrs. Baldwin complained. "He's driving me crazy. He's getting too old. Every night he comes home from work, drinks a beer, and falls asleep in front of the TV set. If my daughter wasn't here, I'd have gone crazy long ago. He's aging by the day. Men age so fast! I'm seriously considering leaving him. I can start working full-time, and I'll have enough money to support myself. I can't stand watching him get old."

"Be careful," warned the divorcee. "You go through bad times and you go through good times in a marriage. This might just be a bad time. It's not easy to change your life after twenty-five years. Besides, things may improve yet."

"If things don't change, I'm leaving him," said Mrs. Baldwin. "In the meantime, I'll keep trying. I appreciate you listening to me. I'm sorry, but I had to talk to someone."

Elizabeth twitched twice in her sleep. She looked incredibly beautiful, with incredibly tiny facial features and an incredibly alluring little body. I wanted to pick her up and squeeze her and say "I love you" a thousand times. I felt a surge of affection. I was tempted to wake her, just so that she'd know I was there and that I loved her. I reached down and kissed her softly on the temple.

I wanted to free her of worry. I felt the scar on my forehead and decided to let her sleep. From the basement I heard another faint chorus of "Happy Anniversary."

4. The Barren Room

The St. Charles Darlings, led by captain Steve Lawson, comfortably defeated the Dixie Queens four to zero. A picture of Lawson drinking champagne out of the big golden cup appeared in the paper the next day. Phil was right about Winfield hating me. Midway through summer I saw Winfield for the last time. I was picking up groceries at Kroger's for my mother. While I was at the counter paying the cashier, something whizzed past my forehead and splattered against the cash register. It was an egg. I looked up and saw what was Winfield's fat head rapidly disappearing into the crowded mall.

When mother discovered my stitches, and the reasoning behind not allowing balls in the parking lot, she went on a rampage. She kicked open the doors of the principal's office, heaved a brick onto his desk and said, "My son got fourteen stitches on the head. If you don't allow soccer balls in the parking lot so kids don't have to use a brick, I'm going to nail your testicles to a tree." The principal was no match for mother. He acquiesced.

Excluding these minor occurrences, it was a quiet, uneventful summer. For my birthday, Elizabeth gave me a blow-drier because she didn't think it was healthy for me to leave the dressing room at hockey games with wet hair. I loved the maternal side of her character. She got a good price for the hair-drier from Phil who had taken a well paying job selling kitchen and bathroom appliances. He planned on sticking at the job, at least for the time being. He worked hard and I didn't get to see him much.

I worked for the county as a surveyor's assistant, trying to save money for college in the fall. Paul and Ross, the backseat occupants of Phil's travelling music machine, were on the same crew as me. We worked with a friendly old man, a surveyor since the ice age, which made us a rather happy-go-lucky family of four.

The job was as futile as one of Winfield's hockey practices. There was nothing to do except listen to the old man tell stories of the past and to concentrate on our suntans. Suntanning became an all-consuming obsession. I didn't care about having a dark back, but I tanned my front with unflagging determination. If we had to walk away from the sun, I walked backwards. If I had to stop traffic, I held the sign in the appropriate direction and always faced the sun. Paul and Ross shook their heads in disgust, railed against my vanity, but after a month they were worse than I was. Paul refused to urinate indoors. He would run to the side of a building and do it facing the sun.

"You're just like women," squealed the old man with laughter.

My picture was taken by the *Chicago Sun Times* newspaper and I was christened, "Sunshine Boy." The caption read, "The sun always shines on today's sunshine boy, Ken Harrison. When Ken's not the surveyor, he's the surveyee. Nice contours!" I was in cut-off jeans, no shirt, and holding surveying equipment. It wasn't a flattering photograph, distorting the proportions of my body and elongating my head. Phil agreed that it didn't do me justice, but said he was proud I was his friend anyway.

Mother also had a photograph of me. It was a large action shot of me playing hockey and was hung respectfully above the fireplace in the living room at home, like a revered idol, like a picture of the beloved Mao Tse Tung on skates. A family council was in progress. The room was a crowded configuration of women, composed of my sisters, my mother, and Elizabeth. I sat on the couch, blissfully drowning in a sea of femininity. Tonight I would leave for the University of Stockton. They were discussing my future.

"I think the first thing Ken should do in Stockton is find himself a part-time job," suggested Ruth, my most vocal sister and closest to me in age. Ruth recently graduated from a university, majoring in English literature. Her marks were gigantic, which was no wonder to me. Ruth's nose never stopped sniffing the inner reaches of some great literary achievement. Ruth grew up with a book in her hand. I grew up holding my penis.

"No," said Mother. "He worked hard this summer and should spend his time studying. Hockey takes up enough time."

"I had two jobs when I went to school and paid for the whole thing myself," said June, sister number six.

"I worked full-time as a waitress," said Wendy, sister number four, "and still managed to stay in college."

"It will do him good to struggle for a change," said Mary, sister number three. Mary majored in Philosophy and married a minister, to the profound disappointment of my mother.

"Why marry him?" Mother had asked. "Why not just move in with him and try him out for a while?"

"A minister can't do that type of thing," said Mary.

Mother believed that religion was the opiate of the masses. "Keep away from those religious people," warned mother repeatedly as I was growing up. "They're a bad influence."

I awaited my fate with passive resignation. I totally trusted the decision of the family council. Mother was the leader, directing the discussion and maintaining veto power. Mother was relied upon for her instincts. Her instincts never lied. She dazzled us with her instincts.

"We can't afford to support Ken's education," said May, the oldest and most conservative sister. May seemed older than mother.

"Bullshit!" exclaimed Mother, swinging into action. When mother had something to say, she seemed to become energized. "You have to understand something about Ken. He's never been anything but perfect. When Ken was born, the doctor lifted him out of my stomach and he was perfect, not a wrinkle or an indentation or a birth mark. Nothing! A perfect baby without any struggle, and that's how he has gone through life. May came out arm first. They had to push her back inside me, and do a caesarean. Jane was just as bad. June and Ruth took a century to come out.

"Ken was the wonder of the hospital. No one had ever seen a more perfect child. The point is this; Ken's not like the rest of you. He's not a struggler, not a sufferer. He wasn't built for suffering. He doesn't know how to suffer. He's never been teased for having a big nose or big ears or for being fat. He's had nothing but adoration. A perfect child, a golden boy, has a longer way to fall than most people. Ken is not to work!"

"I don't know how you do it," said Ruth, looking at me with awe.

"When you're that perfect," repeated my mother, emphasizing her point, "you have a longer way to fall than most people. Don't worry about money, Ken."

"I love everyone," I said joyfully. "I love all woman-kind."

Elizabeth was silent. She was as silent around my family as I was around hers. "They're so aggressive," she would whisper to me occasionally. "They're the most aggressive women I've ever seen."

"Let's make love in the back yard," I suggested in her ear.

"I don't like the bugs," said Elizabeth.

Two of my sisters were missing, Jane the second oldest, and Candy, number five. They were co-partners in a home for battered women and worked downtown. Jane had worked as a prison guard for seven years, one of the first women to be hired at that position, before teaming up with her younger sister. She had the protective temperament of a lioness. When an irate husband went seeking his convalescing wife, he was confronted by

Jane. Jane had trained herself not to take her eyes off a man's crotch. She wore construction boots and her kick was famous for its unerring accuracy—a cute, feminine trick passed down from mother to daughter. Once I startled Jane in the dark. She flew around like a dueling cowboy drawing his gun and landed her foot exactly on the bullseye. Even in total darkness she never missed. I fell to the floor, struggling to regain my breath. She apologized profusely.

Ruth was closest to me in age and height. She was tall for a woman, a shade over five feet ten inches, and had a strange affinity for short men. The heels of her shoes kept getting higher and her boyfriends kept getting lower. Her latest man was five foot three. Mother unconsciously tended to patronize short people. When he was invited to dinner, mother referred to him as "Angel Pie" and insisted he eat his vegetables before he got dessert. Angel Pie was thirty-two years old.

"I hope you stick with this one," said Mother. "Soon you'll be bringing home midgets."

"I don't see what she sees in them," said Mary self-righteously.

"She likes little dinks," added Mother.

"Not true," I said. "Little people often have the biggest ones."

"Their dinks just look big," said May, the oldest, "because their bodies are so small." May seemed older than Mother.

"I've seen it," I said authoritatively. "And for a little guy, he has a big penis."

"When did you see it?" asked Ruth excitedly.

"A few weeks ago I was looking for you and called at his house," I said. "I must've gotten him out of bed because he answered the door in a black housecoat and his big red knob was poking through the front. Angel Pie is not so small."

"It just looked big," repeated May, "because his body is small."

"A big penis isn't everything," said Wendy sensibly, sister number four.

"I don't see what she sees in him," repeated Mary.

"I don't like a man to have power over me, intellectually, emotionally, or physically," said Ruth, defending herself. "I like an equal relationship."

"That's not equal. You like to tower over a man," said Wendy. "You're a glutton for power."

"You have to be able to give a man a good shot in the balls every once in a while," said Mother. "They love you afterwards."

"They're the most aggressive women I've ever met," whispered Elizabeth in my ear.

"How about the basement?" I whispered, still trying to find a hiding place to make love.

"It smells down there," said Elizabeth. The dogs defecated in the basement. I sympathized with that because I was sensitive to smells myself.

"Have you got everything you need, Ken?" asked Mother.

"Yes."

"Have you called Greyhound and found out what time the bus leaves?" asked Ruth.

"I don't need to. I'll just go to the station and a bus will be leaving," I said confidently. "I'm lucky that way."

I rode Elizabeth home on my banana seat and intended to go on to my father's apartment. I had yet to say goodbye to him. Elizabeth was in an insecure mood, which was another reason for her silence. She was afraid that she was losing me, that I was going off to a world of bigger and better things, that she was being left behind. I secretly thought the same thing, that perhaps I was leaving her behind, but I was wrong. It was already too late for me. I would never quite leave Elizabeth behind.

"Now that we're not having sex you're in a rush to get rid of me," said Elizabeth, turning her head and hiding her tears. Elizabeth was beautiful when she cried.

I exercised the patience of a martyr. I put my arms around her and hugged and kissed her all over her wet face. I told her that I loved her, that Stockton wasn't far, and that we could phone each other whenever we were lonely. I even went so far as to say that she didn't need to worry about me being unfaithful, that sex meant nothing to me, that it didn't even enter my mind unless it was with her. This made her cry again because she didn't believe me. She was reasonably calm by the time I left for Father's apartment.

The back door of his building was unlocked. I was ten paces inside when the elevator doors opened and Father's beaming face peeked into the lobby. He was joyriding again and greeted me with bubbling cheerfulness.

"Hop aboard, Ken," said Father, as I stepped onto the elevator. "What's the difference between pussy and parsley?"

"You don't eat parsley," I answered, as the doors closed. The joke was another of my father's repeats. "I haven't much time, Dad. I've got to catch a bus to Stockton."

"In that case, we can stay on the elevator. We can talk privately here. There's something I have to ask you, Ken, and it's appropriate that I ask you on an elevator. Besides, I don't get that much chance to be on an elevator these days because Sara doesn't like it. Women don't understand this type of thing, a man's love for an elevator. They get jealous."

"What do you want to ask me?" I said.

The elevator stopped and three elderly men joined us. Dad, who was never shy in a crowded elevator, acted like the host at a garden party. He smiled and shook their hands and pressed the button for the floor they wanted. Dad loved the social side of elevator riding, the short, friendly conversations. It was an ideal situation for his longstanding repertoire of funny lines.

"What do you give the man who has everything?" asked Dad.

The old men shrugged.

"Penicillin," I interrupted, proving that I had heard the joke before. Father looked disappointed.

Dad helped the bewildered old men into the lobby while I held the doors. They couldn't figure out why this strange person was so hospitable. Father gave them an elaborate good-bye, full of compliments and hand shakes. In a brief moment of senile confusion, one of the retired old gentlemen said loudly, "Thank you for the wonderful time. And your son is charming." Even in his disoriented state of mind, the old man intuitively deduced that he was dealing with father and son.

"Nice guys," concluded Dad, as he got back in the elevator and pressed another button. "What I want to ask you is simply this. I have an offer to get back into the elevator business, but I'd have to move to Florida. I was thinking about buying a condominium there. Sara wants to come and bring her daughters, but I was worried about leaving you alone with the women, you being my youngest child. If you want me to stay in Chicago, speak up, and I'll turn the job down with no questions asked."

The elevator stopped. No one got on and I pressed another button. It was obvious that Dad was thrilled by this new job opportunity, and I intended to give him unbridled support. I didn't believe in clinging to loved ones. I wanted love to be an unselfish emotion.

"I'd have to sell everything," he said, "my car and the hairdressing salon."

"Think of it as an adventure, Dad. I'm for it one hundred percent."

"I'll pay your way to come visit me after exams," said Father excitedly. "You'll need a place to unwind. You can get a suntan. There are lots of beautiful women in Florida."

He was appealing to my two great vices: women and suntanning. He pressed the button for his floor, number twelve, and let the tantalizing offer sink in.

"I can't wait" I said.

Both my parents liked the idea of me being single and free, unfettered by monogamy. They rarely mentioned Elizabeth. Mother once told me that I was the type of man who would be single for a large portion of my life, that it would be hard to find a woman who could keep up to me. I would never settle down in a relationship or marriage that was boring. Women would always be around me, and I was extremely vulnerable to whim, which was dangerous. "Don't think with your penis," warned mother again and again.

"Did you hear the one about the two baseball players?" asked Dad.

"I don't think so."

"These two baseball players had known each other for years and were best friends. They made a deal that if one of them died, he must return a message to the other and tell him if there is any baseball in heaven. One of them died and sure enough he came back with a message. "I've got good news and bad news," he said. "The good news is that you can play baseball as much as you want in heaven. The bad news is that you're scheduled to pitch tomorrow."

" 'Bye Dad," I said, as the elevator doors closed. I wondered if his joke had anything to do with the University of Stockton. Were there women and suntanning in heaven?

Instead of going down, I pressed the button for the top floor, the direction of heaven. I got an idea and wanted to try a trick my father had taught me. I flicked the "stop" switch, causing the elevator to halt between floors. I turned off the light and sat cross-legged on the floor. This would be my private meditation room, inherited from my father.

I meditated and the room seemed to become larger, empty and barren. It became the Barren Room which had persistently recurred in my dreams, which had always existed somewhere in the background of my mind. Through a rhythmic kind of chanting, my mind emptied of thought, became vacant, neutral, blandly masculine, gray and hollow, like the inside of a stripped army barrack. I had returned to the source of male consciousness where everything originated, to a world before color, a masculine womb. There were no sisters in my room, no hanging plants, and no girlfriend. No one stirred the blanket of dust on the floor and the plain-looking venetian blinds were never opened. The lighting was dull, but the visibility unobstructed with a black and white impersonality like a low-class motel.

My imagination was a utilitarian mechanism disclosing its own bleak atmosphere, an atmosphere of futile loneliness. I willfully banished myself from the land of plenty, indulged in the security of imprisonment. I locked myself in a vault, an austere coffin, where there was nothing to do but breathe, rhythmically. I existed to breathe. I didn't give the room meaning. I didn't have the energy or the inclination to give the room meaning. I retreated, descended to the bottom of the pit, as a form of protection and preparation. I did it willfully, but unconscious of my motives. It was instinctive.

I opened my pants, I was hard. My fist pumped up and down in time with my breathing, thumping consistently like the piston of an engine. I was still in the Barren Room, alone, no visions of body parts, nothing as concrete as an image. My mind was superfluous, impotent, fruitless, but my body was functioning, breathing, and pumping. I was exploring myself, exploring my male consciousness which I had inherited innocently and which owned me. I was covered in sticky warm fluid. I slept dreamlessly.

Meditation was supposed to make you feel tranquil and gentle and in harmony with the universe, but it had the opposite effect on me. It made me assertive, aggressive, almost violent. It made me fearless and alert. If a little thing bothered me, I wouldn't let it pass. I would jump on it. I would pound it into the ground. Consequently, I felt absolutely no hostility. My hostility was expressed, and when it was expressed, it evaporated. I was in tune with myself, expressing exactly what was inside me with appalling honesty, an honesty that grated on middle-class values.

I arrived home at dusk, poked my head into the basement and commenced an elaborate tirade of barking. Shultz, Whiskey and eventually Tanka came bounding after me into the backyard. I was naked except for my running shoes. We were four jubilant children of nature, jumping and rolling through the towering grass and shrubbery, energetic and free, abandoned to sensuality. It was a celebration. There was no presumption or intellectual abstraction to mar the purity of our love. We soared above mediocrity, heroic in our spontaneous enthusiasm. We were perfection, even pathetic old Tanka, who should have dropped dead years ago. Tanka was incapable of dying. I was panting like a dog, and my heart was pounding and I too felt incapable of dying, immortal.

Mr. Price made a grave mistake. He started his lawn mower! He revved the machine, warming it up, as if he intended to cut the lawn in the dark. The sun was setting when I jumped the fence and stood in front of Mr.

Price, naked and barking wildly, a full session of meditation under my belt. Shultz and Whiskey imitated me, leaping the fence and barking at Price. Poor old Tanka, resolutely refusing to be left out, found a place to squeeze under the metal fence, and joined us with her excited yelps. The savages had fled the jungle and were pillaging civilization. Mr. Price was wide-eyed, frozen to the spot.

Price must have thought I had gone insane and intended to kill him, but it was actually the lawn mower I was attacking. I felt no malice towards him. I yanked the hideous machine out of his hand and held it over my head. I took a hop, skip, and a jump and heaved the lawn mower into the swimming pool. It landed upright, treaded water for about ten seconds, shooting out spray in a panic-filled struggle for survival. Everyone was soaked, including Mr. Price. It finally sank to the bottom, leaving a surface of bubbles and gasoline. Shultz jumped in the water, swam through the turbulence, and climbed out again. I danced naked at the side of the pool, the happy assailant, barking madly with my three tail-wagging friends. On that note, I left town for the University of Stockton.

5. The University of Stockton

The classroom doors were shut and Philosophy 101 was in session. I arrived late and stood outside the class with a piece of paper in hand. It read, "Dr. Sterm, room 109." That was the professor's name. I tried the doorknob, but it seemed locked. I was puzzled and rechecked my piece of paper. It was definitely the right room. I didn't realize the doorknob was ornamental and not meant to be turned, but pulled. I rapped firmly on the windowpane, interrupting the lecture.

As Dr. Sterm was walking towards me, I figured it out. I simply pulled the door open.

"Sorry. I got confused about the doors," I said to the wrinkled brow of the professor.

"If you get confused over opening a door, you're going to have a rough time with this course," said Dr. Sterm.

I wanted to make up for my blunder, establish an atmosphere of congeniality and a positive rapport with the professor, but compounded the folly by mispronouncing his name. "Are you Dr. Sperm?" I asked with a hopeful smile, trying to make my way to a seat.

Phuc not fuck, I thought.

The class laughed for an unnecessarily long time, which pleased Sterm. He enjoyed my embarrassment, the deepening color in my face. He wrote down my name and handed me a syllabus.

"We've been debating the topic of afterlife. Do you know what I mean by afterlife, Mr. Harrison?" said Dr. Sterm patronizingly, trying to provoke more laughter at my expense.

"Isn't that the stuff that drains from a woman after she bears a child, Dr. Sperm?" I said.

"That's afterbirth," said Dr. Sterm redundantly.

I was the only one who laughed at my joke, and I laughed hysterically. I always laughed at my own jokes. No one enjoyed my jokes as much as me. I could entertain myself for hours with witty comments and humorously perceptive observations of humanity. In this particular instance, however, my perception of what was funny must have been completely altered. I was killing myself with laughter, and everyone else in the room was silent. Sterm had to wait a long time for me to calm down before carrying on with his lecture. Even after regaining control of myself, poorly suppressed snorts of laughter escaped my nose.

Dr. Sterm was a tiny man, skinny and short. He had tension in his facial muscles, as if he was in a constant state of irritation. Poor spelling and coffee stains on essays were gradually eroding his sanity. He could espy a grammatical error from twenty paces; he could sense it, taste it, smell its disgusting aroma. It made him want to spit and puke.

I believed that most intellectuals were frustrated jocks. As an adolescent, their physical ineptitude made them subject to ridicule on a sports field. They couldn't break into that athletic elite which was in every high school. Consequently, they sought status through other means, through learning big words and having all the answers in class. Sterm was an intellectual Bruno, an intellectual glass cock. He compensated for being short by being smart. The jock and the intellectual were not antithetical in my mind. Their differences were superficial. The underlying mentality was the same.

"This topic is my specialty," said Sterm. "My PhD thesis focused on philosophical arguments in favor of and against the existence of an afterlife. There are a number of philosophies we can touch on in this course. For example, the Judeo-Christian belief in heaven and hell. We've all been indoctrinated with this belief to some degree, whether or not we believe in it at face value, or metaphorically, or even if we reject it outright. Like it or not, Christian theology is implanted in our consciousness."

My consciousness was beginning to do unchristian-like things. My consciousness was dominated by my libido. I had a similar reaction listening to Mr. Baldwin discuss America's perilous economic situation. I got sexually excited. I converted negative into positive. The thing that struck me most intensely, even before I mispronounced Sterm's name, while I was in the hallway confounded by the ornamental doorknob, was that philosophy class had a higher proportion of men than women. Philosophy, history, and, to a lesser extent, political science, drew a predominantly male assemblage.

I was shopping for a major and needed a subject that appealed more to women. Fate had it that I was brought up in a family of eight women. I needed to be constantly surrounded by the opposite sex to be happy. Fine Arts, English Literature, and Drama had the largest female populations. These were my prime options.

I preferred to major in "Women," but no such course was offered. I was fascinated by women and wanted to study them. I was interested in whatever it was that a woman could give a man, that magic ingredient, that strength-giving force which was loosely referred to as love. I didn't need to sleep with a woman to get power from her. She just needed to be in the same room, the same building, and I could feed off her energy. I wanted to discover that woman inside me, to get closer to that creative core. I didn't want to learn about afterlife. I'd find out about that when I died. I wanted to learn about women.

Due to an unfortunate accident to the professor, Dr. Prigs, my creative writing course was cancelled. Prigs walked and talked and acted like a woman. He was more like a woman than any woman I knew. He took short quick steps, spoke with a lisp, and seemed to have no muscles in his wrists. Beneath this effeminate exterior, however, he was a man of steel. He had spent most of the first class reminiscing about the second world war, the trenches, wading through a sea of mud and dead bodies. He was fixated on wartime, and clearly thought of himself as tough and macho. He was a bit of a war hero, he admitted, but even heroes get afraid. I laughed at first, thinking he was kidding, but shut up when I realized he was serious. "It was so scary, I could have shit myself," said Professor Prigs naughtily, giggling as the naughty word slipped off his naughty little tongue.

Prigs read grammar books in his spare time—for pleasure! It was the challenge of finding grammatical errors in a grammar book that really aroused Prigs' enthusiasm, even more than masculine feats of heroism on the battlefield. It was perversity! He boasted of his sordid triumphs: "And on page ninety-seven, I was sure there was a mistake. I wrote the publishers and directed their attention to it. And you'll never guess. They wrote me back and said that I was correct, that they had made a mistake and would change it for the next edition. Imagine that! A grammatical error in a book that's supposed to teach students grammar!"

Prigs kept us in class the whole hour. There was one point that Prigs was adamant and unbending about, that brought the real man out in him. "We are here to study the rules and conventions of language, especially in relation to fiction," he said firmly. "Under absolutely no condition are you to write anything creative. If such an arrogant liberty is taken, an appropriate penalty against your marks will ensue."

I was mystified. I leaned to the guy beside me and asked, "Is this the creative writing course?"

"Of course," he said, irritated by the stupidity of my question.

"A creative writing course where you're forbidden to be creative?" I asked. I had a feeling it would be like Winfield's hockey practices.

It wasn't my idea to transfer into a novel course. Prigs taught the course in the morning and died of a heart attack in the afternoon. Thus, the deletion of the creative writing course. Prigs' death was reminiscent of his struggle in the trenches. He was chasing a runaway pussy cat through a wet and muddy football field during the first exhibition game of the University of Stockton. A stadium of spectators watched him charge, bent forward, along the fifty yard line after a cat, and suddenly fall down and die. The cat got squashed to death by a linebacker in the second half. It was an awful mess. Two deaths and Stockton still lost the game. Stockton never had a successful football team.

"If you believe in life after death," said Dr. Sterm, "it will influence the way you behave on a day-to-day basis. An existentialist believes death is the end of existence, that you're shoved into the ground and decompose into nothing. Life's passionate and precious because that's all we've got. There's no prize at the end of the tunnel for being a good boy. Christians more or less believe you put in time until death and don't start enjoying yourself until you're in heaven."

My Art History class was overflowing with women. It was a gold mine. There were so many attractive women that I became dizzy and disoriented and couldn't decide where to sit. I was deliriously happy and kept changing my seat. I sat beside the best-looking girl I could find and immediately noticed someone more beautiful a couple of rows up. I excused myself politely, complaining that I couldn't see the blackboard, and moved to a seat beside her. I saw an even lovelier girl ahead of me. I excused myself again, using the same excuse about not being able to see the blackboard, and moved next to my most recent find. I was preparing to move a third time because I noticed an absolute goddess about two seats ahead of me, but the professor arrived and began his lecture.

Dr. Ruta was totally unlike my other professors. He was a large man with an intimidating appearance and a forceful way of expressing himself. First impressions can be deceptive. It became apparent that beneath his rough exterior, Ruta was a man of warmth and sensitivity. He generated a lively discussion.

Each student was asked to name a favorite painting or artist. Someone mentioned Picasso's 'Old Man and Guitar,' which was a safe thing to choose. If you liked Picasso you were considered wise. A couple of illiterate dunces, wilting in their shame, admitted that the didn't know any painters. One naive young girl unwittingly acknowledged the work of Norman Rockwell. Everyone secretly liked Rockwell of course, but sophisticated people denied it. They were supposed to despise him for his commercialism. The girl beside me liked Marcel Duchamp, which incited a riot of vigorous monologue from Ruta, who also loved Duchamp. The class nodded approvingly, but I suspected they were like me. They had never heard of Marcel Duchamp.

"I identify with 'The Great Masturbator' by Salvador Dali," I said when it was my turn and broke into laughter. The girl beside me giggled, and the professor smiled, but the remainder of the class was quiet. I was beginning to realize that a university, at least in the classroom, was a humorless place. No one seemed willing to have a mindless, meaningless laugh.

"Do you masturbate often?" said the girl beside me, with an amused look on her face. We stood up and moved toward the exit.

"Not as much as I used to. I used to average three times a day," I said, smiling back. I motioned to shake hands. "Don't worry. I wash my hands afterwards. Besides, I usually don't even use my hands. I do it against a pillow. I'm Ken."

"I'm Barb," she said, shaking my hand. "I can imagine the stains on your pillowcase."

"I'm making a sculpture out of my pillow case. It's going to be a bust of Ronald Reagan as a tribute."

Dr. Sterm's philosophical exposition was ending, and the hour was drawing to a close. There was a guy sitting a few seats away who was staring at me. His eyes were lustful, signaling his homosexual desires. I ignored him, but spread my legs a little more to give him a better look. Winfield was right about me being a cock teaser. It wasn't until I was halfway out the door, my hand on the ornamental doorknob, that I felt a tug on my belt loop. It was Barb from art history. She was in the class the whole time, sitting near the back, and I hadn't noticed her.

"Do you want to go to the coffee shop?" she asked.

There was a coffee shop called 'The Artsie Fartsie' on campus, in the basement of an old dilapidated building. It was frequented by artists, criminals, and drug freaks, students with unconventional interests and sidelines. The place had a bohemian atmosphere, cluttered with a battered set of unmatching tables and chairs, dull lighting, and a low ceiling. Conversation never lagged. You could feel the probing of adventurous minds, young minds discovering the colorful world of the imagination, of literature, exploring the recesses of spiritual and metaphysical reality.

I felt a surge of excitement and fell in love with that filthy little coffee shop. It was like opening a door and stepping into the dilapidated basement of my mind. It was similar to the Barren Room, but it had a woman's touch. It was a place to discover yourself. The Artsie Fartsie had a seductive magic about it. It inspired my curiosity, animated my tongue, and gave me a quenchless thirst for mystery. Not the mystery of the spy novel, but the eternal mystery of the heart and mind. I wanted to acquaint myself with the demons and lovers of my soul.

Barb walked so quickly I had to jog to keep up. She paid for my tea and led me to an empty table. I was content to follow her anywhere, but realized that I had become spoiled and lazy from having a girlfriend. A single man had to work hard at meeting women or getting laid. He had to tune in to the woman, turn on the wit and charm. He had to assert his ideas without being a bully or coming on too strong. It was a precarious role, and I felt self-conscious and out of practice. I was used to grabbing Elizabeth and dragging her to the couch like a caveman. The single man had to be more subtle, and in some ways, more sensitive. Barb attracted and intimidated me at the same time.

"Sperm's a snarly bastard," stated Barb, initiating the conversation. She had long brown hair like Elizabeth, but her quick mannerisms were unlike Elizabeth. "Do you major in philosophy?"

"I haven't decided on a major yet," I said. "I'd like to major in Ken Harrison, me, but they don't offer that course."

"Do you think it would be very interesting?" asked Barb encouragingly.

"Fascinating," I said.

"Who would teach it?" asked Barb. Barb loved asking questions. I should have been able to guess her major.

"My mother," I said. "She knows me. What course are you in?"

"Philosophy."

We were interrupted by a friend of Barb's. The friend was a handsome guy with blond hair and sleepy blue eyes, very heavy eyelids. He stood there bobbing his head, his eyelids closing and opening like he was about to nod off to sleep, until Barb invited him to sit down. He reminded me of a beach bum from California who got lost and somehow ended up in Illinois.

"Ken Harrison," said Barb. "I'd like you to meet Henry Kissing-Balls."

"Right, right, right," said Henry, bobbing his head and shaking my hand. He sat down.

"Is that your real name?" I asked smiling.

"That's right," said Henry seriously. He was obviously used to the name and didn't find it amusing.

"Have you a class now, Henry?" asked Barb.

"Ya, right," he said, bobbing his head in total agreement. There was a look of absentmindedness about Henry which made you feel responsible for him. I couldn't fathom him getting through a day without some kind of practical assistance.

"What time's your class?" asked Barb. Barb asked questions compulsively.

Henry stopped bobbing and concentrated. He started bobbing slowly. "I think it's at two. . . or three. Maybe four. I'm sure I have a class at five some time this week."

"Do you have a schedule?" I asked.

Henry thought. "I think it's at home."

"You better get it," I said paternally.

Henry was in total agreement and bobbed frantically. "Ya right, right. But it doesn't really matter because I'm thinking, you know? You don't have to be in class to think. I do a lot of thinking. Sometimes I do nothing all day. I just sit in a chair, listen to music, smoke a joint, but I get a lot of thinking done."

"What do you think about?" I asked.

"Reality. Death. The universe. The existence of time," said Henry decisively.

Those were things that never entered my mind, like marriage. Henry traversed the mundane and trivial, embracing the ethereal. This was a friendship worth cultivating. His bobbing was hypnotic.

"I'm waiting for that first line," explained Henry obliquely. "It takes patience. I'm a poet, not that I've ever written any poetry before, but I feel it inside me. I'm waiting for that first line, that inspiration. Once it comes, I won't be able to stop."

A stranger walked up to our table and said, "Henry, coming to class?"

"Right, right," said Henry, bobbing his head. Henry managed to get through life without schedules. He stood up. "What I'm into now is cutting down on my sleep. I believe the human mind can do anything, even eliminate the need for sleep. I never sleep more than four hours a night."

"Maybe that's why you don't know when your classes are," suggested Barb.

"No. I've always forgotten things," said Henry, bobbing and looking at us through half closed eyelids. "When I started, I would get tired, but I enjoyed walking around tired. It was kind of mellow, like being stoned. Now I feel normal after four hours sleep."

Henry left a profound impression on me. Cutting down on sleep sounded like a sensible idea. If I could put the time I wasted sleeping to productive use, I could be ahead of everyone. Henry was obviously a regular at the Artsie Fartsie; several people nodded to him on his way out. He acknowledge them with a bob.

"Do you have a girlfriend?" asked Barb, taking me by surprise.

"Well . . . no . . . yes," I faltered. I couldn't deny Elizabeth. It seemed evil.

"Men are strange when it comes to sex," said Barb. "I think women are higher on the evolutionary scale. Sex is connected to a woman's emotions. Men will screw anything that looks nice and has a hole. They're apes sexually."

"I'm more like a dog sexually," I said, as if that was something to be proud of. I wasn't prepared for this sudden turn in the conversation. I decided to be the one asking the questions for a change. "What does it take for you to be sexually attracted to a man?"

"Time," said Barb.

"How much time?"

"I didn't make love with my last boyfriend until we were going out for six months," said Barb with great dignity.

"Six months!?"

"Maybe it was more like three or four or five months," said Barb, trying to remember.

"That long!?"

"I can't really remember," she admitted. "But I know it was at least three weeks. I've a lousy memory, like Henry Kissing-Balls."

I wasn't inclined to admire someone for abstaining from sex or for having a good memory. A bad memory and a high sex drive meant you were human. Computers can be used to remember things. Humans should spend their time doing something useful, like having sex.

The conversation skipped from sex to religion to death, which were Barb's three favorite subjects. Although I didn't realize it at the time, an extremely special relationship was germinating. It was my first asexual friendship with an eligible member of the opposite sex. Barb was an attractive, single woman whom I wasn't perpetually plotting to seduce. It was difficult at times, especially at first. Temptation knocked frantically at my door more than once. I came to respect her candor, compassion, and generous curiosity. I learned to ask questions. We loved each other, but it became a sisterly kind of love, love without sex.

Barb latched onto anything that had to do with death. Sterm's class engaged her passionately. I was shocked to discover that almost every one of her blood relations was dead. A few years ago her father was warming up alone on a squash court when he managed to hit himself on the head with the racket. It was an unlucky blow and ended his life. Her mother was an excellent swimmer and did a lot of diving off olympic size diving boards. The pool was closed one day, but she was a strong-minded woman and hopped the fence. She climbed to the lofty height of the diving board, took a run, kicked into the air, arched gracefully, only to realize that every drop of water had been drained from the pool. Barb had other death stories to tell about her brother, cousins, aunts, and uncles. The stories were all related to sports. She came from an athletic family.

It was in a mood of optimism and goodwill that I left the Artsie Fartsie and headed for the athletic center. The coach had posted a list of those players on his door that he wanted to see. I was on the list and figured the coach was just feeling self-important. Coaches love having private and mysterious gatherings where they impart top secret information, like who kills the penalties. I humored coaches. They were like children playing war games.

I got an unpleasant sensation as I watched the players swarm around the coach's door. During our workouts, I had noticed they were the unpopular sector of the team, players who were shy and quiet and easily passed over. I noticed the veteran players were not around. I stood a short distance from the group because, for some reason, I didn't like to be associated with them.

"I suppose you've figured out why I called you here," said the coach guiltily, standing in the doorway of his office. "It's not a fun job having to make cuts, to tell players to hand in their equipment, but someone has to do it. There were some difficult decisions to make.

You are good hockey players, but the competition is stiff, and I'm looking for players who fit a certain style. I'd like to thank you for trying out, but I'm afraid I won't be able to use you. Sorry!"

It was a gently executed guillotine act, except it was my balls that dropped into the basket, not my head. I was convinced that a mistake had been made, that my name was placed on the list erroneously, that I had been confused with someone else. I didn't belong in this group. I belonged with the winners. I waited to speak to the coach and clear up the misunderstanding. He would be surprised to see me, scratch my name off the list, and tell me to wear a tie to the exhibition game on Sunday. I would joke that I didn't own a tie.

"Am I being cut, Sir?" I asked. "I was the highest scorer in Junior B for three consecutive years."

"It was a difficult decision, especially with regards to you, Ken," said the coach. "We're strong up the center. Center is our strongest position. The choice was between you and Steve Lawson—you know Steve, he used to be captain of the St. Charles Darlings. We decided Steve was more of a team player. We can't use you this year. Keep in shape and try next year."

"You don't sit out a year and play hockey again," I said, stating what both of us were well aware of. "I'm finished as a hockey player."

Steve Lawson was my conscience, haunting me. He triggered the memory of Winfield's epileptic fit. I could tell Lawson had been weight-lifting during the summer because his neck looked like a tree trunk and his legs were thick and sturdy. He wasn't like Bruno, brash and brainless. Bruno was better suited to the game of brick soccer. Lawson was fast, coordinated, and intelligent. He didn't have nearly as much style as me on the ice, but he was consistent and dependable.

The hallway was deserted and the door was shut. I checked to make sure my name was truly on the list. "Ken Harrison," I read aloud. The name was unfamiliar, a stranger's name. I couldn't remember how to leave the athletic center, which direction to walk in, where I wanted to go. There was too much open ground, too many decisions to make. I walked around in a circle. Playing hockey was something I had always done, like breathing. I played hockey before I could talk. I came out of my mother's womb wearing a pair of skates. Hockey was in my soul. It was the quintessence of my being. I walked in one direction, changed my mind, walked in the other direction, changed my mind, and finally left in the original direction.

I took the long way home. I wanted to talk to myself. I often talked to myself, but this time I was talking in an unusually full voice, like I was communicating to someone on the other side of the street. It felt good to talk that loudly and I didn't stop myself, keeping watch for passersby who might overhear me.

"I still love you, Ken," I said to myself. "You've got two powerful legs, Ken, and an exciting mind, and the rest of your life ahead of you. Embrace your freedom, Ken, sweetheart. Become the sex king of the intellectual crowd, of the English Literature and Drama Society. Those intellectuals are scrawny, sickly looking things; you could be a sexual god with both beauty and brains."

Ahead of me on the right, was the old university stone church with a huge steeple and clock, and beyond that was the dorm. There was activity and laughing on top of the clock tower. I couldn't bring it into focus. "You must be going blind," I said to myself, as I gradually moved closer.

A mob of engineering students were holding a rope. Tied to the end of the rope and dangling against the wall was their friend, who clung to a dripping can of paint and was painting the massive clock pink. It was three-quarters finished. This kind of practical joke was characteristic of engineers. I felt sorry for engineers because they didn't have women in their classes and didn't know how to interact with the opposite sex. They didn't know how to go about getting laid and committed puerile acts of mischief through sexual frustration. They moved in gangs, got drunk together, and were rude to artsies, calling them 'fags'. A lot of artsies were in fact gay, but at least they weren't sexually frustrated.

"Self," I said to myself. "Not all's bad. At least you're not an engineer." The truth of the matter was that painting a church clock pink was exactly the kind of thing I would do.

I passed directly under the precariously perched engineer and marveled at the looming heights of the clock tower, stretching to the heavens. The rope slipped from around his waist to under his arms. I was laughing and sort of waving my hand, trying to act like one of the engineering boys. It happened behind me. I felt a sensation inside me, a cracking thump, as if something in my chest had exploded. The sound was astonishing, the sound of a human body dropping a great distance, hitting concrete. The whole world could feel and hear the shattering force of the fall. It was a heavy sound and startlingly loud, like splintering wood, but deeper and louder. I thought of Barb's mother, pirouetting gracefully in the sky and splattering against the floor of the swimming pool.

There was silence, a scream, someone yelled, "Call an ambulance!"

I ran into the church, shouting and swearing. The place was empty, lonely pews, and a solemnly decorated altar, prepared for the sacrificial goat. It felt like I was being chased through the aisle, as if I was the goat. I was looking for something, help, a phone, an ambulance. I was shouting, swearing at the air. My voice echoed. The preacher was in the back wearing his black robe. He had beaten me to a phone and was calling the hospital.

The panic was spent and I calmly left the church. A crowd circled the broken engineer, and I headed in the direction of the dorm. Help was on the way and there was nothing else to do.

"Welcome to the University of Stockton," I said to myself loudly. "Nothing like a liberal education."

6. I Don't Know

Henry Kissing-Balls put life in perspective. Through the implementation of the philosophical method, Henry induced and deduced a cogent argument that my reaction to four hours of sleep a night was normal, even admirable. Although I didn't quite follow his line of thinking—logic never seemed logical to me—his self-assured way of expressing himself was convincing enough. It would take time for the lethargy, disorientation, and general anomie to disappear, he explained sensibly, bobbing his head. Staying up late was not difficult for me. It was getting up early in the morning that was painful.

I awoke with an upset feeling in my stomach. I dreamt I had only one hundred and seventeen dollars in the bank to last me the whole academic year. I was no mathematical wizard, but I managed to induce and deduce that I would run short of money within the month. It was a financial crisis. I was in a panic to get to the bank and check my balance. If my dream was accurate I would have to get a job. Perhaps, I could make bran muffins at the Artsie Fartsie coffee shop. I used to be able to make good bran muffins.

My mind was obsessed by a novella called the *Double* by Fyodor Dostoevski which kept me awake most of the night. It was like acid on my brain, shattering my structured view of the world. I was still under its spell in the morning. Dostoevski was fascinated with paranoia. His characters were completely self-absorbed and existed in a subjective reality, boundless and incomprehensible, on the fringe of sanity. I was a plodding, inexperienced reader, but once I tasted the power of Dostoevski's writing, felt his iron grip, the ceaseless probing of his will, I couldn't put the book down. I enjoyed literature, but my marks were too poor to make English a major.

I didn't read to relax. Reading was exhausting business for me, a spur to insomnia. I didn't read a novel; I experienced it. If the protagonist ran seven miles, my calves swelled and my heart started pounding. If someone got his leg cut off, I'd walk with a limp for a few days. If there was a deaf character in the story, I'd repeat "pardon" to everyone who talked to me. I could never become one of those ferocious readers tackling *War and Peace, Women in Love*, and *Crime and Punishment* in the same week. It would overstimulate my brain and dangerously alter my personality.

The men's bathroom in the dorm was across the hall from my room. I stepped out of the shower and discovered Chuck concentrating on the arduous process of shaving himself. Chuck was blind and had to find the bristles with his fingers before using the razor. The University of Stockton was conscientious about accommodating the handicapped, providing specialized facilities whenever possible, such as a highly technical reading machine in the library for people who can't see. I had a happy relationship with Chuck's seeing-eye dog. We barked at each other as I passed Chuck's room in the morning. Chuck wasn't pleased about me provoking his dog to bark, especially in public places like the library.

I considered faking blindness and bringing Shultz in as my seeing eye dog, but was afraid I'd become blind for real. Also, it would be placing Shultz in a servile and demeaning role. I couldn't stand watching Shultz being treated like a dog, strangers telling him to sit and give paw. He had been sheltered from that kind of treatment, Shultz wasn't aware that there was any difference between a human and a dog.

"Hi! It's Ken," I whispered, drying myself with a towel. I always mentioned my name when I said 'hi' to Chuck. It made it easier for him to recognize my voice. I wasn't shy about exposing my private parts because Chuck couldn't see them anyway.

"Hi, Ken. It's Chuck," he whispered back, mentioning his name as if I was blind too. There was no reason for it, but we always whispered in the bathroom. The bathroom was like a house of prayer. It was heretical to speak loudly, especially while someone was taking a shit.

Chuck had given me the idea that I was going blind. His presence made me conscious of my own eyesight. After talking to him for a few minutes I got this burning sensation in my eyes, my peripheral vision began to narrow, and everything seemed blurry. I was in a rush and didn't bother to blow-dry my hair. I hurried into my clothes and raced to the bank, practicing my eye exercises on the way. My eye exercises involved keeping the head stationary and straining the eye muscles to the left, right, up and down, and around in circles. I focused on a point in the distance. I was staring at the three-quarters pink clock on top of the church steeple and sprinting full speed to the bank. As I got closer to the clock, my head cocked upwards, vertically, until I was looking straight up at the sky.

Needless to say, I wasn't looking where I was going. A plump girl, with her back to me, was drinking coffee from a styrofoam cup and talking to three girlfriends. She was standing on the spot where the engineer had fallen. My eyes were riveted on the clock above me, and I was finally managing to bring it into focus. I could distinguish the individual stones, the pink clock, the unpainted metal. I bulldozed into the plump girl at full speed—an explosion of coffee and papers—and flattened her against the sidewalk. It was like breaking through the offensive line and demolishing the quarterback, sacking him for a loss of ten. It was a perfect tackle, something that would be shown on the instant replay for the instruction of youngsters. I rolled and bounced a few yards, miraculously landing on my feet.

"What happened?" exclaimed the girl, lying on her back in a state of shock. I expected it to be a fatal blow and was amazed that she was capable of speaking after such a collision.

"I saw him coming," said one of her plain-looking friends. "He wasn't watching where he was going."

"Are you blind or what!" said the other girl.

"As a matter of fact . . ." I said, unable to finish my sentence. I was about to tell her that, in fact, I was afraid of going blind, and that I didn't see her because I was practicing my eye exercises, but the explanation seemed too complicated. Her books and papers covered the sidewalk, and I was picking them up.

"Leave them alone," said the plump girl in disgust, as if I had a disease that was transmitted through books. Her back was still on the pavement. She had an awfully lively tongue for someone who should have been dead. She said, "Get out of here, you pig."

"Get out of here, you pig," echoed her friend ruthlessly.

That type of comment upset me first thing in the morning before breakfast. They didn't have to call me a pig, anything but a pig. They didn't have to go that far. "It was an accident," I said, which was, I suppose, a rather lame statement after nearly killing someone. Nevertheless, I couldn't understand their anger toward me. I couldn't understand why they hated me. I didn't hate them. I wanted them to like me. I almost started crying, but I fought back the tears and the urge disappeared.

I probably interrupted one of those heated discussions about men, about how all men are the same, about the ruthless tactics men use in the subjugation of women. They were inflamed over the issue of rape, or wife battering, or the impediments to women entering the work force. My timing was unlucky; I confirmed their latest suspicion, their latest revelation on the violent intentions of men. I didn't know much about that kind of women's stuff, except what I heard from my sisters. I wanted everyone to be friendly.

"I'm in sympathy with the feminist cause," I blurted out absurdly. They looked stunned. It was the same look Mr. Price gave me when I threw his lawn mower into the swimming pool.

The bank was in the university center, a short run from the scene of my humiliation. The bank was closed, of course, because it was eight o'clock in the morning. I felt embarrassed for forgetting that banks don't open until nine. Everything was locked up in the university center, except a room with a coffee machine, tables, and chairs. Orientals were scattered around doing homework. Coffee from machines was too strong and tended to give me diarrhea, but I had one anyway and sat with the Orientals. The reverent tapping of calculators, like termites nibbling on my conscience, was making me feel guilty for not doing my schoolwork. I wondered what good old Phuc Wildfong was doing these days.

I decided to pass the time by doing my eye exercises. I stretched my eye balls to the left, right, up and down, around in circles. There was a clock on the wall and I stared at it, trying to bring it into focus. My heartbeat was accelerating with each sip of coffee. I could feel a great deal of acidic activity in my bowels, a loosening process, a breaking down of enzymes. I had had no sleep, no breakfast, and a heavy dose of caffeine. My body trembled slightly; I kept drinking the coffee.

"I have to drop a load of mud," I said to myself tenderly. The Orientals stopped and looked to see who I was talking to. I smiled at them and blushed. The tapping of the calculators recommenced.

That coffee machine was insidious. The problem was that I hated using public toilets. It wasn't that I had anything against Orientals—I sincerely liked Orientals—but the thought of strangers, filthy old men, and perverts sitting on the same toilet seat as me was revolting. I could actually see the germs swarming over the toilet seat, swimming in the water, crawling up the side of the bowl. I would often take the time to cover the seat with toilet paper, but felt that germs had a way of pole-vaulting onto me. Sometimes, I would crouch down without touching the seat, my rump hovering in the air like a flying saucer, but that was extremely painful in the legs and caused too big a splash. Although I got a lot of pleasure from dropping mud, I had to be at home to fully enjoy it. It was especially satisfying when I had to hold it for a long time. Holding it made me contemplative and philosophical.

"I get my best ideas when I'm holding back a load of mud," I said to myself, and smiled at the Orientals again.

I suddenly remembered that I had saved my money the whole summer, and it was impossible for me to have only a hundred and seventeen dollars in the bank. Mother specifically told me not to worry about money. There was never much extra money around in a family of nine, but everyone was grown up and working now. They would have no qualms about helping me through school. Furthermore, Father had a job in Florida and would be happy to give me money. I realized that I had it made. The bank was opening in fifteen minutes, but my money problems were solved, and there was no reason for me to stay.

"What a relief!" I exclaimed, and smiled at the multiplying numbers of Orientals occupying the tables. It was an arcade of calculators.

Speaking of relief, I decided to make my way to that familiar toilet across from my room in the dorm. It was a treacherous journey home, fraught with danger at every turn. In order to avoid seepage, I had to move slowly, take short steps, and tightly pinch my buttocks together, like Charlie Chaplin. The first obstruction to my progress was a set of stairs. Climbing stairs would surely result in a natural disaster; fortunately, there was a bicycle ramp for me to use. Students who were late for class were bounding like deer up three stairs at a time. I tiptoed past the three-quarters pink clock and arrived home with unmarked underwear.

I didn't go straight to the bathroom. I hid in my bedroom and stared out of the window, determined to hold onto it even longer. My ass muscles were swollen in knots, ached painfully, yet the pain was indescribably pleasing. I wanted the feeling to last forever. I had never been in a more philosophical mood in my life. I thought that a university was a wonderful place for a young person to find himself, to experiment with ideas and people, and discover where he fits into the world. It was a great place to grow and self-actualize.

"Oops!" I said to myself, self-actualizing a small turd in my pants.

I braced myself on the toilet seat. The grand finale was an intense combination of pleasure and pain, like an orgasm. The eruption came in spasms, causing shivers to reverberate through my body. My mood shifted immediately, from philosophical to practical. I had wasted the morning, I was suddenly intent upon getting things accomplished. I showered, my second shower of the day. I always showered after dropping a load of mud, even if I was at a stranger's house or a party, especially at a party. I would ask politely to use the bathroom, lock myself in, and make myself comfortable. I was keenly aware of unclean smells.

My phone rang. Forgetting my towel, I had to dash naked across the hall into my room, leaving behind a trail of water. Chuck's dog barked sportively, thinking I wanted to play. I instantly recognized the babyish intonation of Elizabeth's voice. She was as impetuous and whimsical as a child, not hesitating to phone at prime time when the rates for a long distance call were at the highest.

"Are you coming to Chicago this weekend?" asked Elizabeth.

"This is costing you a fortune," I said, standing in a puddle of water, my penis shriveling in the cold.

"Are you coming to Chicago?" she repeated.

"I don't know," I said. I resented being forced into making a promise. Elizabeth made a big thing about breaking promises.

"If not this weekend, when are you coming?" she asked.

"I don't know."

"Why haven't you come home? What's keeping you in Stockton?" asked Elizabeth, implying subtly that I was seeing another woman.

"I don't know," I answered.

"Do you miss me?" she asked.

"I don't know," I said. Perhaps it was cruel of me not to give her some kind of reassurance, but I answered truthfully. I honestly didn't know.

"If you say 'I don't know' one more time, I'm going to hang up," threatened Elizabeth.

"I don't know."

Click!

Barb was with a girlfriend when I met her for lunch at the Artsie Fartsie. The girlfriend's name was Penny, a strict-looking woman, with rigid features and an abrasive personality. It was an unfair assumption, but I figured that Penny was suffering from sexual frustration. She would be an ideal public school teacher. I pictured her secretly getting turned on over giving little boys the strap. I felt she wanted to give me the strap too. She didn't have the kind of physical appeal to attract someone of my sexual stature, but I was generous with my time. I talked to anybody, even the ugly ones. Penny was eating grapes. Fruit was missing from my diet and I was worried that I was deficient in vitamin C. I remembered that fruit was once used to ward off scurvy. I was afraid that I had scurvy, that my teeth were loosening from rotting gums.

"The story kept me awake most of the night," I said, chewing a banquet-burger and gulping a glass of milk. I was starving because I had forgotten breakfast. "Dostoevski does something weird to me, upsets my stomach. He scares me. He tinkers with something inside me, my sanity, fucks up my sense of reality, like a nightmare."

Barb was a captivated listener. When something sparked her interest, she leaned forward and beamed enthusiasm. Penny was solely interested in stuffing her face with grapes. I wanted a couple of grapes myself because my gums felt kind of spongy, but she didn't offer me any, and I was afraid to ask. She wasn't the type of person to give grapes away. She wasn't the type of person to give anything away. Her stinginess with grapes was symbolic of her willful frigidity.

"What was it about?' asked Barb, who loved asking questions.

"This guy gets kicked out of a party because he's drunk and making an ass of himself," I said. "It's winter, the kind of winter you get in the midwest, and he's walking home, listening to the snow crunch under his feet. Someone passes him in the night. There's something familiar about this stranger, but the guy who's a bit drunk can't remember where he's seem him before. The familiar stranger somehow passes him a second time. How could the same guy, walking in the opposite direction, pass him twice? It happens again. The same man passes him a third time, with the same incredibly familiar face.

"Suddenly, he sees the stranger ahead of him walking in the same direction as himself. The stranger turns down the drunk's street and goes into the drunk's house. The drunk follows him right into his own bedroom. The stranger finally turns and confronts him. It was himself he was following, his double."

"Then what happens?" exclaimed Barb.

"I'm not telling you because I don't want to ruin the story," I said, like the cock teaser I was.

"The story is sold, Ken," said Barb. "You should get a job selling literature."

"That's exactly what I plan to do. That's exactly why I'm going to major in Drama. As an actor, I can sell literature."

"It should have been obvious from the beginning. You're a born actor."

"My drama professor said the most important thing an actor needs, besides talent, is a huge ego."

"You'll have no trouble there," said Penny. I was surprised she could talk. I thought she was only capable of eating grapes: a grape-eating machine.

It took a few minutes to realize I had been given a subtle feminine shot in the balls. If you had good looks, vitality, and a lively spirit, everyone was shooting for your balls. People resent a winner. I lived in the age of the anti-hero, the Holden Caulfield, the Woody Allen, the wimpy neurotic who was quick-witted and perceptive, but far from a tragic hero. A tragic hero has to be a powerful man, larger than life, or else his fall couldn't be tragic. A great man has a longer way to fall. When a great man hits the ground, he makes a resounding crash. There was a prevailing misconception in the air that you had to act like a mouse to be considered sensitive. I believed that strength combined with sensitivity was what made a great man, a man capable of asserting his sensitivity, of affecting the world positively, heroically. It was my experience that most wimps were sleazy, underhanded, cowardly bastards.

Everyone wanted to crucify a golden boy. Jesus Christ was a golden boy, a big-mouth like me, crunched under the stampeding feet of mediocrity. I was usually prepared for a shot in the balls, but today my defenses were down. I hadn't had much sleep, I was called a pig before breakfast, I was worried about going blind, and my gums felt like sponges from not eating grapes. I felt that Penny had unfairly classified me. Admittedly, I indeed had a somewhat egotistical side to my character, but I wasn't excessively indulging in egotism at the particular time she gave me the shot in the balls. I was genuinely excited about a book I had read and about my decision to become an actor. Why did she trample on my enthusiasm? Why did she bring me down to her depressed level?

"Got classes today, Ken?" asked Barb congenially, standing up and gathering her books. Penny was also on her feet.

"I'm not going to my classes because I've got an appointment at the eye doctor's. I think I'm going blind."

"Me, too," said Barb. "It's from masturbating."

"If that wives' tale is true, I'm a goner. Salvador Dali's not blind and he beats off like crazy. It affected him differently. It made him go insane."

"You'll have to kick the habit."

"I tried that before," I said. "I only lasted a few days. Then I locked myself in my bedroom with a library of pornographic novels and went on a bout of self-abuse that lasted three weeks. That was the beginning of my interest in literature."

It was a relief to discover that I was not going blind, that I was only experiencing the symptoms of eyestrain. The eye doctor patiently assured me that it was impossible to catch blindness. My eye problems were from reading too much, not from sharing a bathroom with a blind person. I was afraid I had caught a disease from Chuck, transmitted through toilet seats, which caused blindness.

He gave me a prescription for a pair of glasses that would help me see distances. I threw the prescription away because seeing distances wasn't important to me. I only wanted to see the person in front of me, the person I was talking to or making love with. I wasn't interested in anything beyond that range. I liked the idea of people seeing me and me not seeing them. It would have been a crime against nature, an unpardonable waste, to cover my face with anything, glasses or a beard. Like a Michelangelo sculpture, like classical art, my face belonged to humanity as an inspiration, as setting the standard for the ideal. I had a moral responsibility to keep my face unveiled.

"Your eyes look like two piss-holes in the snow," I said to Henry Kissing-Balls. It was a regional maxim.

Henry and I were at the stand-up bar in Ring Stadium. Ring Stadium was the most popular drinking establishment on campus. It was a circular building with a large round dance floor surrounded by tables and chairs and a bar at one end. Henry was wearing a brilliant Hawaiian shirt which flashed phosphorescent colors like neon lights. The shirt was congruous with his blond-haired, beachbum image, but contrasted sharply with his sleepy face. It was as if the shirt was the only thing keeping him awake.

"I've got eyes like Jim Morrison of the Doors," said Henry.

"Morrison's eyes were like two piss-holes in the snow," I said.

Henry disappeared into the crowd, searching for a dance partner. He returned empty-handed a few seconds later, a look of rejection on his sleepy face. I noticed an attractive dark-haired girl sitting across from this doltish looking character with a moustache. I was convinced that she was staring at me, gazing at me seductively. The Italian with the moustache was probably a brother or a cousin or some guy following her around who she wanted to get rid of. I decided to ask her to dance. If she was having a bad date with a jerk, she would appreciate the opportunity to be free of him for a couple of dances. If she was friendly and responsive, I'd discreetly ask for her name and phone number. I could even arrange a late night rendezvous. It would have to be done so the Italian with the moustache was oblivious to the transaction.

"Excuse me," I said. "Would you like to . . ."

"No," she snapped, interrupting me. She turned away, giving me no further acknowledgment.

I was baffled by the hostility of her reaction. I had no intention of being persistent; a simple 'no thank you' would have been sufficient. She had spent most of the evening staring at me; yet she rebuffed me with absolute vehemence. It was as if she did everything in her power to arouse my attention and utterly scorned me when this attention was attained. Perhaps she was angry at the mustached Italian and using me as an outlet for her frustration. Perhaps she was frustrated with men in general.

A white cane whacked against my ankle. It was Chuck from the dorm, forcing his way past the congested bar. I stopped him, told him it was Ken, and introduced him to Henry. Blind Chuck loved Ring Stadium. He asked girls to dance by wading through the tables until he heard an appealing female voice. He explained that when he got drunk, he had this illusion that he could see and never failed to find the prettiest girl in the place. We had slits for eyes, piss-holes in the snow. We looked like three blind drug freaks, strung out on a depressant aphrodisiac.

We wandered off in separate directions, each pursuing a private course. Henry and I returned to the same spot thirty seconds later, without much to talk about, another bruise on our tender egos. Chuck had disappeared. The more refusals I got, the more determined and desperate I became to get someone to dance with. After being turned down about fifteen times it didn't bother me so much any more. I became numb, even getting a perverse pleasure from it. It was an unlucky night, with one nominal success hardly worth mentioning.

"Please dance with me?" my voice pleaded pathetically.

The girl I begged to dance was not half as attractive as Elizabeth, and I wouldn't have looked twice at her in the light of day. It was ladies' night at Ring Stadium. She didn't answer my plea for a long time, looked me over carefully, thought a little longer, looked me over again. I got down on one knee and tried to look as wholesome as possible. I was beginning to think she would never answer, that she hadn't heard my question or didn't speak English. Finally, grudgingly, she consented, but not without casting a warning glance at me. Her eyes said, "Keep your hands behind your back, you filthy pig."

I coaxed and nodded and bobbed all the way to the dance floor, keeping my disgusting hands safely behind my back.

"Are you a student?" I asked. It was an unoriginal conversation starter.

"Obviously," she said. In a student pub, it was indeed likely that she would be a student.

"Do you like Stockton?"

"No," she answered, without volunteering a further explanation.

"Why not?" I pressed.

"I don't know," she said hauntingly. That was the line I used on Elizabeth.

The women of the world were in league together, plotting my fall.

"What's your major?" I asked undauntedly.

"I don't know," she said. "I was in Political Science, but my parents want me to take French. So I don't know."

"Major in the subject you enjoy most," I suggested, advocating my beautifully simplistic golden boy philosophy. "Make up your own mind."

"My parents will let me major in whatever I want," she said defensively, as if I was implying that she had no mind of her own.

"As long as it's French?" I said. Her perception was accurate. I was implying that she had no mind of her own. This small slice of petty vindictiveness was unfair—the result of a sour feeling I had about myself—and I regretted making the jab.

"My parents won't influence my decision," she said vehemently, although I didn't believe her.

I was usually a good dancer. I thought of dancing as a primitive mating ritual, like a peacock strutting his irridescent plumage, but I couldn't seem to feel the music. It was extra difficult to feel the music when I had my hands held awkwardly behind my back. The town of Stockton must have recently been scorched by roving bands of rapists and sex maniacs. It was the only possible explanation for the impenetrable reticence of the women. The song couldn't end soon enough for my quiet dancing partner, and she hurriedly retreated to her seat.

There must have been something wrong with my approach. I was making a negative first impression. I had to be nicer or wittier or sexier or more profound. Henry wasn't doing any better than me. He got so despondent that he started dancing to a slow song with a chair, but the manager came by and told him to return the chair to its original spot. Dancing with chairs was not allowed at Ring Stadium.

"I took this Psychology course and learned that if you have six beers in a night you're a third degree alcoholic," said Henry, pushing his half-filled bottle away. "This is my cutoff point."

"That's how many I've had," I said, "five or six."

"Don't worry about it," continued Henry. "Most people are third degree alcoholics. It's when you're a first degree alcoholic that you have to worry. Could you go to a party and not have a drink?"

"I always drink when I go to a party," I said.

"I think that means you're a second degree alcoholic, but I'm not sure. It doesn't matter because it creeps up on you. People who start out as third degree end up as first degree alcoholics."

I lost my thirst and pushed my beer away. A white cane whacked against my ankle. Blind Chuck was passing, a voluptuous blonde holding on to his arm. I watched in agony as she moved towards the exit, a burning sexuality oozing out of every pore of her body. My throat felt parched and I took one more gulp of beer.

"I don't feel depressed when I get turned down by a woman," said Henry mournfully. "I feel normal."

The next girl I asked to dance responded with a curt, "No."

"You mean no thank you," I said. It was as if I had insulted her. It was as if I was being rude by asking her to dance. It was as if I had marched up to her, slapped my penis on the table and said, "Suck it!" You give a curt "no" to a dog when it tries to hump your leg or sniff your crotch. I didn't deserve to be treated like that.

I resolved never to say "no" to any woman who asked me to dance. I would be willing to dance with the ugliest thing on the face of the earth, with a face covered in snot and pimples and an ass like the back of a bus. I would bounce onto my feet enthusiastically and escort her to the dance floor like she was a princess from a fairy tale. I would swoon and adore her and do everything in my power to make her feel good about herself. I would make this hideous-looking creature feel attractive for the first time in her life. I would make love to her, martyring myself.

It was in this mood of generosity that I began my search for the ugliest woman in the bar. There were a lot of ugly girls to choose from, but I wanted the absolute ugliest. There was a shadow in the distance that appeared to be four people sitting extremely close together, but upon closer inspection proved to be only one person sitting alone, one enormous woman, like a transport truck idling in the night. The legs of her chair were bent and strained and on the verge of snapping under her mammoth weight. She could have eaten me, swallowed me whole. This was undoubtedly the girl for me.

"Hi," I said charmingly. "Do you feel like dancing?"

"No thank you," she said politely. I expected someone that size to have a man's voice, but her voice had a very feminine quality.

I decided to unceremoniously bail out. I left the weather-beaten hulk in the darkness, picked up my jacket, and slid out the back door into the cold night air. I felt the ominous approach of winter causing my testicles to shrivel and tighten. It was a chilly evening, but the sky was clear and vast and starry. The naked moon was my dancing partner, my only real partner that night, shimmering and vibrating with color like a Vincent Van Gogh painting. I was skipping home. Skipping was more practical than dancing because you can maintain a forward progression. It was not a particularly masculine movement, and I never did it in the daylight, but it was faster and more fun than walking.

I scoured the community refrigerators at the dorm, trying to find some fruit so that my teeth wouldn't fall out while I was sleeping. My teeth seemed loose, but I suspected that my imagination was carrying me away, especially since I had discovered that I was wrong about going blind. I missed the good old days, the Golden Age, dancing in the grass with Shultz, the days before I had become a third degree drunk. I got this idea that my spine was crooked. I didn't know for sure, but I felt it was important for me to go to a chiropractor and get my back straightened. The fruit expedition was unsuccessful. I retired to my bedroom with the feeling that my whole body was falling apart.

"No more reading Dostoevski," I said to myself, pulling the covers over my head.

7. Shriveled Genitals

I returned to the Barren Room. It was an accident this time, happening in a vacant bedroom of a student boardinghouse for men. The party was on the bottom floor and I imagined myself in an elevator as I ascended the stairs, searching for a bathroom. I wandered into an unoccupied room, plastic sheets covering the floor and bed, like the Baldwins' living room. I leaned against the windowsill clutching a magnum of wine, which caused the vein in my right bicep to swell and protrude. I wore a tight-fitting t-shirt and my muscles seemed to be bursting out of it. The world was insulated in a layer of plastic, a lifeless void, shades of black and white! There was no sign of creation, no color, no evidence of womankind.

It was the unethereal, mundanely physical need to urinate that saved me from the abyss, that brought me back to Stockton, Illinois. The bed had been shoved into the middle of the room. I held the plastic sheet in one hand, my penis in the other, and relieved myself directly on the mattress, like a naughty boy. The freedom of the deed gave me a kind of thrill, and I delighted as the yellow stream splashed and foamed into puddles. It was Penny, Barb's strict-looking friend from the Artsie Fartsie, who caught me in the act. Penny was standing in the hallway, watching me with critical curiosity.

"I'm creating art," I explained with laughter.

Penny disappeared hurriedly.

My body felt strong as I pushed through the crowd of strangers in the kitchen, the nucleus of the party. I was lugging my magnum of wine. The atmosphere was desperate, vibrating with the reckless release of pent-up energy, like the tumultuous outpouring of a broken dam. November meant exams and pressure, working hard and playing even harder. The air was alive, racing with nervous tension, with the purging of evil spirits. It was the pandemonium of Milton's *Paradise Lost*, a satanic revelry, an exorcism of chaos.

A finger encircled my belt loop and dragged me into a corner. I expected it to be Barb, but I was greeted by an unfamiliar face. She was a slightly squat, not particularly attractive woman. She had a drunken sexuality. Feeling my arms and chest, she rubbed herself against my body.

"Where do you think you're going?" she said threateningly, pushing her breasts against me and holding my ass.

"I was coming over to introduce myself," I said charmingly, with a swelling erection.

There was an awkward silence as we studied each other, more awkward for me than for her. She looked me straight in the eye, unafraid, challenging me. We kissed frantically, probing with our tongues, grinding our crotches together. She was an uninhibited woman, by no means self-conscious about having sex with an interloper in the kitchen at a party, masses of students bustling past to get a cold beer out of the refrigerator. I'm not unreasonably shy, but when she started yanking her dress up I had to do something fast.

"Do you want to go upstairs?" I asked, trying to sound casual.

Everything was happening so quickly. I felt like an elevator again, as we climbed to the top floor of the dilapidated old house, fondling each other impetuously on each landing. We discovered the kingdom of heaven, an oasis. It was an apartment with the door left open, complete with bathroom, kitchen, stereo, and bed. I shut the door behind me and put an album on the turntable.

"The bathroom's over there," I said, as if I had lived in the place my whole life.

"Come in with me," she said.

"What for?" I asked warily, hesitating before following her into the bathroom.

She lured me into the sacred abode of bodily functions, locked the door, dropped her panties and planted her rump on the toilet seat. She had no reservations about using unknown toilet seats. In accordance with standard etiquette, I waited for my lady to be seated before modestly positioning myself on the edge of the bathtub, like a courtier attending his queen. There was an eternity of silence, except for the gentle drone of music in the next room. I was convinced that my presence was making it difficult for her to get the flow started. It was not easy to pee under pressure. I was incapable of letting loose in a public washroom if I knew there was a line for my urinal. I would give up, return to the end of the line, try again, return to the end of the line, et cetera. I felt like a pervert, getting my kicks from hanging out in men's washrooms. We sat in silence. There was nothing happening.

"Have you ever done this before?" she asked.

"What?" I responded stupidly, as if meeting a woman for the first time and being invited to watch her urinate was an everyday occurrence.

"Have you ever done what we're doing?"

"Yes," I lied. "Lots of times."

Although it was a new experience, watching a woman pee was not one of my great ambitions or fantasies in life. If I went my entire life without ever seeing a woman use a toilet, it wouldn't have bothered me in the least. I wouldn't undergo symptoms of deprivation. I stared at the wall and wished for the ordeal to be over, but nothing was happening. Silence reigned.

"You don't seem to be having any luck," I observed tactfully.

She reached over the sink and turned the tap on. I noticed a hollow whistling noise from the depths of the toilet bowl. I could tell the trick had worked by the look of satisfied calm on her face.

Once in bed, I prepared to give her my best moves. I would proudly display my sexual prowess, mesmerize her with my resilience, my unconquerable will, my supernatural capacity to get an erection after thirty-seven consecutive orgasms. I would defile the worth of the Guinness Book of World Records, rise triumphant from the battle with Soviet domination and take my place as the American Gigolo, the most sought-after stud on the continent. My business was giving women pleasure. I combined intense sexual vitality with the finer points of artistic self-expression. It was a winning combination, the dualism of a Golden Boy.

I had a foolproof system. I spent a few minutes tonguing the left nipple, shifted to the right nipple, and worked my way towards her belly button with tormenting slowness. Her pelvis began to heave as I lightly kissed her clitoris. I stabbed her with tongue licks and my face was bathed in lubrication. The action accumulated momentum and intensity, until my head was bouncing up and down with the fierceness of a woodpecker chipping a hole into a tree trunk. Her feet kicked, her back arched, and she clutched the sheets in her fists. It was after I climbed on top and penetrated her that I heard a bizarre gagging noise in the back of her throat. I distinctly recognized the sound. It was the exact kind of sound that a person made before throwing up.

I leaped out of bed, ejaculating in mid-air, and scrambled across the floor in search of a garbage pail. I found a plastic bag, but by the time I noticed a pair of shoes in the bottom, it was too late. My erection pumped sperm in rhythm with her spasmodic retching, flooding the shoes with lumpy purple liquid. She fell backwards onto the bed, and my penis drooped towards the floor like an actor making a final bow. I figured the sex was over for the evening, flipped the album, took a gulp from the magnum of wine, and settled into bed. I thought about visiting my father in Florida, no exams, only suntanning and chasing women.

She came at me again with her mouth open and her tongue wagging. It would have been selfish and rude to rebuke her, to cut her off merely because of an accidental bout of sickness. She tasted sour and I returned to the infallible system, nibbled on the left nipple, moved to the right, worked down to the belly button, and zeroed in on the clitoris, softly at first, and gradually more reckless. When the squirming and moaning began, I hopped on top and flailed away like a broncobuster on a wild steed. "Oh, no!" I exclaimed, recognizing the gagging noise in her throat again.

Once more I shot out of bed, spraying sperm around the room like a fertilizing machine, and retrieved the plastic bag with the shoes in it. She spewed forth more purple liquid, submerging the shoes and causing the bag to bloat like a water bomb. I felt drunk as I tied up the end of the bag and opened the window, the cold air slapping my naked body. There were no people to heave it at, so I tossed it at a parked car but missed. It splattered the road. The shoes tumbled in opposite directions. I took a few swigs of wine and investigated the refrigerator. To my delight, I discovered nine plums, gobbling them down with a ravenous appetite, envisioning myself as a pirate stricken with scurvy. I nestled back into bed, anxious for sleep.

She attacked me a third time, ruthlessly crawling over me, and taking my spent penis into her cavernous mouth. She was remarkably tenacious, like the German army. I was sleepy, full of cheap wine and plums, and positive my penis was incapable of coming back to life, but I was wrong. It was miraculously resurrected from the dead. Though only a semi, half as hard as usual, that was enough to do the job. I worked fast, rolling her onto her stomach, aware that a wasted second could result in total flaccidity. I entered from behind, rocked gingerly, slowly gaining confidence in the feeling that I could finish what was started, what she started. There was a word tattooed to the cheek of her ass. Without a delay in the procedure, I looked closer and realized it was her name.

"Julia," I said aloud, as I was rising to the climax. It was the first time I used her name and felt introductions were in order. "My name's Ken!"

Everything happened on cue, the gagging, the hectic search for a garbage container, the erratic trail of sperm across the room. I backed away from the bed, watched her with vigilance, guzzled wine. She looked harmless, but I knew she was waiting, stalking her prey with the patience of a tarantula. I finally regained my courage and slipped cautiously onto the bed. She immediately sensed my presence and pounced on me again, taking my battered appendage into her mouth. I was amazed to find my penis respond, thicken slightly, painfully. It didn't seem to grow, just harden. I climbed on top.

"I don't think we should do this," she said. "I hardly know you."

"What? We've already done it three times," I exclaimed, although it seemed like a hundred. I was baffled and she was incoherent.

"Have we?" she asked, genuinely surprised.

"Maybe you're right," I said, backtracking, hoping she'd forget the whole thing. "We hardly know each other."

"What have we done?"

"Nothing, oral sex. . . we made love three times, once from behind."

"Sounds great," she panted. "Do it again."

"We hardly know each other," I said, but it was too late. She had spent the pure white image of holy maidenhood and intended to get her money's worth. There was no stopping her now, no refunds on chastity.

I lost count of the number of times we made love, but we were still locked in intercourse when the morning sun began to creep over the red horizon, like the chafed knob of an overly worn penis. I didn't ejaculate; I drooled. My genitals shriveled into little red knots, and my penis felt brittle, like it would fall off if someone knocked it. The crotch area was a large rash and painfully sore to touch.

"Again!" she ordered.

"I can't," I cried. The magnum of wine was empty. I lifted it over my head and threatened to club her if she came near me.

I felt my insides heave and the taste of sour plums in my mouth. I ran, locked myself in the bathroom, and embraced the toilet bowl. I had never been as intimate with an unfamiliar toilet bowl. Half-digested plums slid out of my mouth and splashed in the water. Although I was drunk and incapable of movement, my mind worked clearly and I was aware of what was happening in the bedroom. I heard a man and woman enter, then angry words. Julia fumbled for her clothes and stumbled out the door. They tried to get into the bathroom, but it was locked.

"Who's in there?" a man asked.

"Fuck off, I'm dying," I said.

I was a wet rag, draped helplessly over the toilet. The slightest shift in position would evoke a violent burst of vomit. I remained motionless. I was struck by the realization that I was not wearing any clothing, but too sick to care.

"You have to do something," said the girl on the other side of the door. She was doing most of the talking. "I'm not sleeping with a weirdo pervert in the bathroom. Are you afraid of him? I'm sure he's too drunk to hurt you."

"Open the door!" shouted the man.

I didn't budge. The girl was becoming frantic, pushing and bullying her boyfriend.

"Get him out," she said. "I want him out now."

"We need something in the bathroom," he said, somewhat reasonably. "My girlfriend needs something for her contact lenses. If you unlock the door, we'll get it and leave you alone."

"Promise?" I asked suspiciously. "You'll leave me alone afterwards?"

"Promise!" he said reassuringly.

I dragged my naked body across the floor and unlocked the door. I had been fooled. If I was sober he would have been frightened of a person with my muscular build, but since I was in a completely harmless state, he became super-courageous. He was a bony character and obviously enjoyed this opportunity to manhandle someone stronger than himself. He could live out a personal fantasy and impress his girlfriend.

"You asshole," he said, roughly grabbing me under the arms and bouncing me along the floor. I was being pulled backwards, my legs stretched out in front of me and my arms dangling limply at my sides. He was the king of the jungle, and I was his slain victim, displayed like a trophy for his swooning mistress, a tribute to his fearless protective instincts. He was boldly rattling off a string of profanities, stopping occasionally to slap me on the back of the head.

I didn't seem to have power over my body, but my mind was alert. I thought about what a shock he would get if I sprung back to life, jumped spryly to my feet, and confronted him. The fantasy became a reality. Discovering a latent resource of energy, I bounded to a fighting stance and watched his face drop. I took advantage of that interval of astonishment and landed three rather weak blows on his jaw before collapsing on the bed, utterly debilitated. He could have capitalized on my infirmity and killed me, but the hysterical screaming of his girlfriend brought half a dozen people into the room. They converged on him. He didn't get a chance to throw one punch.

The atmosphere was hostile. I didn't understand what everyone was angry about, except they had to wake up a little earlier than usual. At least they were dressed even if it was only underwear or a blanket. I was naked and ashamed of my nakedness, of my ugly bent penis; an inflamed wart. I did my best to hide it, floundering off the bed and onto the floor, searching for my pants. I didn't look up and couldn't put voices and sounds in order. It was chaos.

"He threw a pair of shoes out the window."

"His puke looks like plums."

"The sheets are covered in sperm."

"He's been playing the stereo."

"He's puked everywhere."

Once my shoes and pants were on, my confidence returned. I decided to grab my t-shirt and exit as quickly as possible. They didn't conduct a unified attack against me since they were snarling and shrieking amongst themselves. I was only a catalyst. The real enemy was less tangible. I hesitated at the doorway fascinated by the confusion.

"There's a lot of hate in this room," I sighed, feeling a comment on human imperfection was in order.

There was frost on the ground. It was not the kind of morning to be wandering around without a jacket. My first stop was the dry cleaners in the university center. Mother had the foresight to insist that I take my winter coat to Stockton and warned me emphatically to have it cleaned before putting it on. I was superstitious about anything my mother said. I knew something terrible would happen if I wore my coat before it was cleaned.

"My coat!" I demanded.

"Do you have your ticket!" asked the young man. He was probably a student.

"No," I shouted, banging my fist on the counter, my muscles bulging threateningly. "I lost the useless fuckin' thing. My coat is long and black and has pockets. I brought it in a long time ago.

The skinny counter boy disappeared into the back. I again began fantasizing about finishing exams and visiting Dad in Florida—beaches, sun, women. I got it into my head that I could take Shultz. The airlines had a special arrangement for accommodating pets. I was lonely for Shultz.

"Hurry up, for fuck sakes," I shouted. The store was beginning to fill up with customers.

"Is that it?" he murmured, turning red.

"That's it. Give it here," I said in a bullying manner. He hung it on a hook by the cash register. "How much?"

"$7.50, sir."

"$7.50," I roared. "Holy Fuck! Do you think I'm made of money? For $7.50 you should throw in a blow job or a steam job on one of those machines." The thought gave me a sharp pain in my groin. I slammed the money on the table and walked out, forgetting my coat on the hook by the cash register.

"Why don't you employ a few more tellers," I said, "instead of having a fuckin' lineup three miles long?"

"I'm only a teller," the woman explained patiently. "I'm not in a position to do any hiring, but if you want to complain to the manager, I'd by happy to get him."

"Give me my money. I haven't got time to chat with your manager, but you can give him a message. Tell him I think he's a fuckin' asshole."

I snatched up my bankbook and strode out the door, forgetting my money on the counter. She probably called me, tried to draw my attention to the unattended pile of money, but I was consumed by self-righteous anger and heard nothing.

"Hamburger, french fries with gravy, and a coke," I said, ordering my breakfast. "I don't know how you guys get that much grease on a hamburger. Do you add extra grease?" I yelled to the chef in the back. "Easy on the fuckin' grease." I pushed my way to the cash register, "How much is that?"

"$3.25, sir."

"$3.25!" I shouted. "I'm a student for fuck sakes! How the hell can students be expected to pay that kind of money." I slammed the money on the counter. I was late and hurried to class, forgetting to eat my greasy breakfast.

Class was in session and Dr. Sterm gave me an unfriendly glare. I returned a glare that was twice as unfriendly, challenging him with my eyes. I borrowed a pen and paper from Barb, which lengthened the interruption. I was an inordinately cheerful person, but when I was hungry and tired and humiliated, I tended to be short-tempered. Mother used to feed me when I was irritable. She stuffed my face with my favorite food, hot dogs and spaghetti. As my stomach expanded, my mood changed. I became full of smiles, laughter, and benevolence. I wanted to spread the wealth, expound upon my generous love of humanity, divide the spoils of the bourgeoisie amongst the multitudes. The more I ate, the more I aligned myself with virtues of Jesus Christ.

"The unfortunate aspect of a semester system is that learning is too rushed. There's not enough time for extensive philosophical thought. You can only scratch the surface. Of course, this is a first-year course and perhaps I shouldn't have such high expectations. We've studied a broad range of philosophies, unified by a common theme, death. In advanced philosophy courses, there is more of a concentrated focus, more specialization. For example, you may spend a whole semester on a phenomenological perspective of death. Today is the final day of classes and I don't want to lecture. I don't want to do any talking. I want to listen, let you people do the talking."

"It's about time," I interrupted, provoking a fight, an intellectual boxing match. "I doubt you're capable of keeping your mouth shut."

"I'm the professor here," said Dr. Sterm, with controlled paternal anger. "I get paid to open my mouth, to share my knowledge with students. Students are interested in learning what the great masters of the past thought, and my job is to impart that wisdom. You, Mr. Harrison, are too self-absorbed to be interested in what the greatest minds in the world have to say. You are interested in yourself and not everyone finds himself that fascinating."

"Then they should stop listening to you, because everyone is that fascinating," I countered. "Even illiterate morons like myself, even first-year students. Everyone is fascinating because they contain a personal philosophy, a philosophy that's an innate part of their character. You don't need a thousand years of education to have a philosophy. A truck driver may live by a sophisticated, even heroic philosophy, a philosophy that's morally superior to yours or mine or Descartes, and not know it."

"I bow to your superior knowledge," said Dr. Sterm snobbishly. He had underestimated me. He had to be careful. "Enlighten the class, Mr. Harrison. What's your personal philosophy?"

"Turd," I said in a conversational tone. "You're a turd; I'm a turd. This room is full of a whole bunch of turds. I'm not talking about the shit that comes out of your brain, Dr. Sperm, I'm talkin' about your being, your soul. Your purpose in life is to decompose in a field and make the grass greener, like cow dung. Everyone spends their lives refuting that fact, blindly denying it, struggling to rise above the status of a turd. You spend your life getting things, accumulating things, trying to make yourself feel important. You get God, a woman, a car, a PhD in Philosophy. It's self-deception. You can become a fat turd or a well-dressed turd, but a turd you will remain. The irony, Dr. Sperm, is that you accuse me of being vain. If you look at my personal philosophy, I'm the least vain person in the world."

"You're an existentialist," said Dr. Sterm with unbending academic precision.

My stomach growled. The dormant side of my brain, the side responsible for organizing and remembering details in my physical surroundings, stirred restlessly in its sleep. That side of my brain was suddenly struck with panic and leaped uncharacteristically out of bed, prompting a flood of recall. My mind's eye flashed a picture of a fat greasy hamburger, a snapshot of a forlorn bank teller, and a black winter coat hung on a hook by a cash register. I was hungry enough to eat the whole university and found myself on my feet.

"You fuckin' asshole pile of shit fuckin' turd," I screamed. Everything poured out of me in one violent explosion, sparks and fire, tears and rage, frustration and self-pity. I was crying and swearing; not only was Sterm shocked and the class shocked, and I suppose Barb, but I was shocked at myself. I felt outside my body, elevated on a stool behind me, watching the whole ordeal from a comfortable distance with shock and dismay.

Despite my fitful hysteria, I maintained an eloquent, even poetic, stream of dialogue. In a storm of obscenities, I explained the story of the engineer falling off the clock tower while painting it pink as an allegory of life. I gave an emphatic demonstration of the sound of his body hitting the pavement. Then I took an imaginative departure from the truth. I constructed an outrageous lie, wailing and gesticulating about how my mother had recently committed suicide by jumping from the twelfth floor of an apartment building. They found fragments of her skull fifty yards from her body. I saw it all and ran to embrace the shattered remains of my mother's body. Thus ended the description. There was a deathly hush. Sterm's mouth was open, but nothing came out. I took that as my cue to pick up my piece of paper and march out of class.

"Ken," said a voice, chasing me down the hall. I waited for Barb to catch up. "That was the most horrible thing I've ever heard."

"What?" I said. My eyes were dry. I had that refreshed feeling you get after a good cry.

"About your mother jumping off that apartment building."

"I made it up," I said. "My mother's not the type to commit suicide. She loves sex too much. She thinks of herself as the best piece of ass in America."

"How could you make a story like that up?"

"It came to me out of the blue, spontaneously," I said. "My drama professor tells us to practice acting in our day-to-day lives, at a bar or the library or the registrar's office. Go berserk in the university center for no reason; act angry or upset. Pretend you're a homosexual, a football player, or a retarded person. He says it's not only fun, it's a good way of getting what you want out of certain situations. My professor gets on the bus for free by pretending he's blind. He makes himself look like an old man to get into the movies cheaper. He has unconventional teaching methods, and he's totally unscrupulous, but there's something sensible about everything he says. I'm his pet student, his protégé. I wanted an excuse to get out of class early because I was hungry.

"Sterm was stunned," said Barb. "He'll never attempt a class discussion again."

There was no need to verbalize the destination. We headed directly to the Artsie Fartsie. The exciting thing about acting is that a good actor never really acts, not on the inside. He doesn't fake it, or behave like someone else, but finds the character he's portraying within himself; the homosexual or football player or retarded person. I have all kinds of people inside me and, as an actor, I can discover them. Through acting I can be more me, more aware of me. The story about my mother's death was fictitious, but the emotion I expressed was real. I was acting, but I wasn't acting.

I had my first taste of power as an artist. Art is power, real power, internal power, power of the heart and soul. The artist is a spiritual muscle-man. As an academic, Sterm spent his life studying and idealizing artists. Although the academic deifies the artist, when he meets someone with an artistic temperament, someone with the instincts of an artist, but not the successful reputation, someone like myself, he has an instant negative reaction. The academic is status-conscious. He humbles himself to the artist and expects his students to humble themselves to him. An artistic person is often vain, arrogant, and obnoxiously outspoken, and the academic is affronted by the audacity of such a student. The academic seeks out his own kind, warms up to the burgeoning young scholars, and treats the potential artist with cool distrust.

"Fantastic!" said Barb, shaking her head in amazement. "Especially the part about kissing the shattered remains of your mother's skull."

I drooled over my lunch, growled, and snapped at anyone that came near my hamburger. It felt good to have food inside me. I burped quietly and blew in the opposite direction, so Barb couldn't smell it. While my head was turned, I recognized a familiar face. At a nearby table was my fighting partner from the night before, and he noticed me at the same time. We looked away in unison. I bent my head and whispered a condensed version of the story to Barb, about getting laid in the bedroom of "that guy over there" and being sick and getting dragged by him out of the bathroom. When I told her it was embarrassing because my penis was sore and shrivelled from too much sex, she was on her feet.

"You big prick," she yelled at the guy two tables away. The guy didn't know what to do, but his girlfriend responded immediately. Barb and his girlfriend were shouting at each other. I had to hold Barb back and calm her. The stranger was doing the same thing with his girlfriend. I had had enough for the day and took the earliest opportunity to leave for my secure little room in the dorm.

It was cold outside without a coat. I was passionate for sleep, for the warmth of my bed. I had satisfied my lust for food and needed to satisfy my lust for sleep. The craving was urgent so everything had to wait, the dry cleaners, the bank line, exams.

"Hi, Ken!" said a voice.

"Hi, Henry," I said.

"Where's your coat?" asked Henry. Henry Kissing-Balls, who didn't know if his class was at two or three or four or five, was giving me advice on how to look after myself. I ignored the question.

"You wouldn't believe what happened to me last night," I said, shivering, "I met this girl at a party. We went upstairs. . ."

"Hi, Julia," interrupted Henry.

It was none other than the Vomiter. A pain shot through my groin. Crossing my arms in front of my crotch, I walked backwards, fending off Dracula with a crucifix. She smiled sinisterly, two devilish fangs protruding from her lips. Henry was about to make the introductions, unaware that we had already met. I turned and sprinted for safety as Henry called after me, but I didn't look back.

8. On the Roof

I was spreadeagled on the roof of Phil's car, barely gripping the three-quarter inch rim above the front window. I held on with aching fingertips, the cold wind hammering my forehead. Phil was driving down a snowpacked residential street while Paul and Ross guzzled beer in the back seat. The car was insane, reckless, speeding on inclines, braking on declines, sliding into snow banks. Phil's foot danced on the gas and brake pedals, throwing the car into spins. We twirled in one direction and then in the other. The purpose of the game was to throw me off the roof.

"Ken," shouted Phil, opening the window and bringing the car to a standstill. Heat and music poured out. "Why don't you get a normal girl, like Elizabeth?"

"That's all I want, a normal girl," I shouted back. "Honest!"

The car lurched forward, resuming its erratic course. I didn't resent being on the roof while Phil was at the controls, warm and surrounded by music. I was there by choice, a perverse desire to expose myself to the elements. I was an American cowboy, graduating from wild broncos to this mechanical monster. I was primitive man, a tragic hero, King Lear writhing on the heath.

My position was tenuous and my voice was hoarse as I roared theatrically.

"Blow, winds, and crack your cheeks! Rage! Blow!
You cataracts and hurricanoes, spout
Till you have drench'd out steeples, drown'd the cocks!
You sulphurous and thought-executing fires,
Vaunt-couriers to oak-cleaving thunderbolts,
Singe my white head!. . ."

Paul and Ross applauded my soliloquy and tossed an empty beer bottle out of the window. They were the commoners in the pit of my imaginary Elizabethan theater. I had dazzled my Drama professor with that rendition of King Lear and marveled at the relevance of Shakespeare to my life in twentieth-century suburbia. Shakespeare had a feel for atmosphere, black overcast skies, threatening storms, the eerie violence of nature paralleling the violence of man's actions. Nature was as temperamental as man, capable of sublime beauty and gentleness, but subject to harsh moods and fits of rage. In this context, the violent propensities of man were almost forgivable. Man was the beneficiary and victim of this energy force, this spirit inside himself.

I had been ravaged by exams, raped and pillaged by the masked marauders of academia. I was naked, legs spread, waiting for the next assailant with fatalistic resolve. But tomorrow Shultz and I would fly to Florida for a week's reprieve with my father: sun, women, sleep.

I was lonely for sleep! When pressure invaded my life, sleep slipped away like an elusive lover.

There was a stairway that sloped towards a school yard, each step about three inches high. It had been shoveled and salted and was wide enough for the car. Phil drove down it with me on the roof, digging in with my fingers and toes, jittering around like a sack of jumping beans. Although it was night and the sky was dark and stormy, the pathway was well lit. I felt a murder was being enacted in a nearby castle.

I whispered to myself with histrionic weariness.

"Sleep that knits up the ravell'd sleave of care,
The death of each day's life, sore labour's bath,
Balm of hurt minds, great nature's second course,
Chief nourisher in life's feast."

The car reached the bottom and moved fast and smooth along the path, finding its way back to the street. Phil laughed boisterously. He rolled down the window and began to throw things out of the car. Pieces of garbage caught the wind. A full bottle of beer bounced along the street into a snow bank. Phil kept a box of kitchen and bathroom appliances for sales purposes in my usual seat. His laughter increased as a hair-drier and a plastic shelving unit flew out the window. Paul and Ross joined in the laughter. There was lots of laughter. Even the wind was cackling, but I had missed the joke. I was excluded; my fingers were numb.

Paul was too drunk to face his parents and slept at my house. The basement was concrete, and pipes stretched the length of the ceiling. Mother must have cleaned up the hardened mountain of dog shit which usually covered the basement floor. There were two single beds, one on each side of the room. I was semi-conscious, vaguely aware of the encroachment of morning, of the brightening room, of Shultz curled up at the foot of my bed. I drifted in and out of a dream. There was a snake in the Barren Room. I was running around the basement, looking for a gun to shoot the snake.

Paul farted and giggled. Judging from the smell of the room, he had been farting all night. I was irritated. Sleep had become a precious commodity. I wanted to shout angrily at Paul, but that would have completely awakened me, and I was hoping for a few more hours of sleep. I concentrated on oblivion, blackness, the Barren Room, and gradually drifted into a drowsy fog. I submerged myself in a warm, soothing pool of water, the balm of hurt minds.

Paul farted again, longer and louder than the last one. He thought it was hilarious and fought painfully to suppress his laughter.

"You fuckin' pig," I roared, which sent Paul into an uncontrollable fit of hysterics. "It stinks in here! One more time and I'll . . . ram a plug up your ass."

It took a great effort for Paul to regain his composure. There must have been a serious malfunction in his bowels to produce a smell with that kind of density. The air was as thick as syrup. A green mist hung stubbornly over the room, unmovable, a poisonous wall of gas between me and freedom. If Paul's insides were that decayed at his age, that foul, imagine what they would be like when he got older! Beer eventually causes your internal organs to rot and putrefy. That is why fifty-year-old men are so disgusting the morning after a night of drinking. Paul had the farting capacity of a middle-aged man.

I sought safety under the blankets where the air was stuffy, but unpolluted. I couldn't sleep, kept anticipating the next explosion, waiting for it, my wrath steadily building. I resented being woken by Paul's puerility and was too healthy to be of any challenge to Paul in a game of chemical warfare. I started playing footsie with Shultz at the bottom of the bed, letting him bite my foot through the blankets.

Paul farted a third time. His anus made a deep bass sound like a trombone. "A wet one," snorted Paul jubilantly.

I was on my feet, naked and growling, bent on retrieving the plug from the upstairs bathtub and shoving it up Paul's ass. En route I noticed a can of Lysol disinfectant spray and got an idea. I felt the weight of the can and realized it was full, a loaded weapon.

Paul was sitting up in bed when I yanked off the sheets, threw him on his stomach, and sat on his back. Shultz was barking and dancing and I could hear Whiskey and Tanka charging down the stairs to join the excitement. Paul had a skinny build and it was easy for me to overpower him. I sprayed through his underwear until the material was soaking wet. I held up the elastic waistband and sprayed directly onto his ass. He kicked and fought at first, but eventually gave up and resigned himself to the punishment. Everything was wet and sticky. I didn't climb off until the can of spray was empty. Paul wiped himself with a dry corner of a sheet.

"You lunatic! My asshole is burning," said Paul with a painful expression.

Later, at the airport, Shultz was frightened. He didn't like airports, too much noise, cement, confusion. Shultz belonged to long grass, to nakedness and spontaneity, to the sensual world of nature. The bustling crowds of businessmen made him self-conscious and unsure of himself. He lost touch with his confidence, his natural instincts, cringing away from people and clinging to my side for protection. I provided motherly security, the only island of familiarity.

The leash upset Shultz. It was a humiliating experience for him. Shultz was more than a dog; he was even more than a kindred spirit; he was inside me, part of my personality. I know that everyone loves his dog, but the love is tainted by an attitude of superiority and condescension. Shultz and I loved each other as equals. I didn't believe in the hierarchy of life, with man on the top. I was arrogant, but not that arrogant. In my opinion, Shultz surpassed the average citizen of the human race. He transcended the mediocrity of suburbia.

Shultz was Shultz. He was himself, free of the pressure to fit a prescription or mold. He didn't care what professors thought or why a girl wouldn't dance with him or if he could go the distance in bed. He didn't need an exterior stamp to be legitimized. He had an unintellectual wisdom, a closeness to the energy of nature, and would leap through a field of grass, humping everyone and loving everything. Few humans achieve such unbounded purity of expression, except perhaps musicians. If reincarnation exists, I want to be reborn as a dog, aspiring to no higher level of consciousness.

I picked Shultz up and he clung to me like a scared child, wrapping his paws around my neck and his legs around my waist. He dug in with his nails, fearful of being torn away and separated from me. He stuck his head under my chin, hiding his face.

"It's OK, baby," I whispered, kissing him on the snout and between the eyes. He looked at me occasionally and licked my face. It was an act of forgiveness.

I brought a cage for forty dollars. Shultz was to be caged and stored in a remote section of the plane. I tried to convince the lady in the uniform that Shultz was a polite, sensitive dog and should be allowed to sit on my lap for the flight. Apparently my request was outrageous and went against every regulation in the world. She was angry at me for holding up the line. Although Shultz yelped and cried, it never occurred to him to bite the miserable bitch who was handling him so roughly. I wished he would. I held Shultz until he calmed down and placed him without resistance into the cage. Shultz had absolute faith in me.

"I love you, Shultz," I said through the bars. I noticed his limbs shivering as he disappeared down the conveyor belt.

The plane ride was long and uncomfortable. I was nowhere near a window, and the seating arrangement was designed for midgets, perfect for my sister's boyfriends like Angel Pie. If I was an inch taller I would have had to stand on my seat and I was sure seat-standing was also against regulations. The regulations were not accommodating to dogs or people above average height.

When I thought of Shultz shivering in a cage, I felt sick to my stomach. A million things irritated me, the cramped sitting space, the fat slob beside me hogging the arm rest, the crying of a baby. It smelt like the infant had shit its diaper. I fantasized about putting the filthy brat in a cage and heaving it out the window like Phil did with the hair-drier and shelving unit. The flight home wouldn't be as bad. Shultz would be familiar with the routine.

At the airport, a conveyor belt carried the luggage to a revolving disc. I waved to my father who was waiting behind a pane of glass, his bald head shining, and muscled into the crowd at the luggage area. I helped old ladies with their suitcases. It wasn't an expression of benevolence, but of a desire to get rid of the old biddies. They were irritating me and Shultz would be intimidated by this mob. I wanted him to have a clear passage.

There was lots of elbow room by the time my suitcase dropped to the carousel. The interval between one bag of luggage and the next became greater until only a couple of people were left. Finally, I was alone.

"Shultz," I shouted up the belt.

I tried to imagine Shultz gliding down the belt, tail wagging, but I couldn't do it. I grabbed an attendant and demanded to know the whereabouts of my dog. I kept glancing at the conveyor belt, trying to create Shultz with my imagination. The attendant promised to investigate the problem. I began circling the carousel.

"Shultz!" I shouted.

My father dodged the security guard and made his way into the luggage area, breaking another regulation. He was concerned about me. I was concerned about Schultz. I was running around the carousel and Father was chasing me, like children playing tag. I belonged in the wilderness and cursed the body politic, the world of regulations.

"Shultz!" I screamed, falling over my suitcase.

The attendant stood above me. Her uniform gleamed like the cold blade of a guillotine. I rolled onto my back, panting. She was inverted. We studied each other upside down. Her eyes were shy and hesitant. She had a cat in her arms.

"Would you like a cat, Sir?" she asked.

"What!?" I exclaimed, unbelievingly.

"It's a lovely cat."

"But I don't like cats."

"They make lovely pets, sir."

The handle of my suitcase was greasy, like a bar of soap slipping out of my hand. Twice! Thrice! Four times! I only advanced a few yards. I got down on my knees and wrapped my arms around it, but I couldn't lift it. It was solid rock, a boulder. I tried to push it, but it didn't move. I was crying because it didn't move. I was crawling along the floor, feeling my way like a blind man, trying to find my suitcase. My suitcase was lost. Tears came in a flood, splashing on the floor, blurring my vision. The floor dissolved into liquid.

It was a baptism that lasted a week, seven days and seven nights of fervent purgation. Once the tears started, they couldn't be stopped. They gushed forth with the hearty eloquence of a Shakespearean sonnet and the passionate crescendos of a Mozart symphony. I shuddered until my stomach muscles felt like the taut sinews of a racked animal. The skin under my nose was red and chafed. My eyes were swollen. I cried enough to flush away five months of abstruse hurt, of disorientation and frustration.

Father swooped me off the floor and carried me to his nest in the darkness of a cave where I found more than emotional release. I found sleep. Real sleep. Deep sleep. Not the unsettling delirium of a troubled insomniac. I slept and cried and cried and slept. The drapes were pulled and I remained concealed from the light, no sun, no beaches, no women. I didn't even masturbate very often. It was a ritual of mourning, presided over by my dad.

My father scurried among the shadows bearing ceremonial paraphernalia such as boxes of Kleenex and trayloads of food. We had short meaningless conversations on a variety of inane subjects. These conversations were immensely satisfying to both of us, and Father never got insulted if I fell asleep in the middle of an exposition about elevators or the weather. It's curious the way a father and son express their love. It's done covertly, on the sly, without direct eye contact. Men are inhibited creatures when it comes to expressing love for each other. Father and I had a lengthy discussion about the box of Kleenex on the table, the colorful design, the philosophical intention of the advertiser, the soft texture of the tissue. The subject matter was superficial. The transfer of affection was profound.

I was haunted by a dream, a collage of images and sounds. The engineer was painting the clock tower pink. I heard the horrible thud of his body hitting concrete, like the thunderclap of an apocalypse. I turned to discover Shultz standing on four healthy limbs. Relief! Shultz became Elizabeth. She was an oasis in the desert. I ran to embrace her, but she disappeared in my arms like a hallucination. She was nothing more than air, a ghost, a tremor on ether.

I awoke with a burning sensation inside me. I cried for Schultz, for myself, for Elizabeth. Where was Elizabeth? Who was Elizabeth? Did she exist in reality or was she a figment of my imagination, a sexual fantasy? There was a person inside that beautiful body of hers! I wanted to explore that person. I wanted to light a candle and study her in the flame. I wanted to seduce her imagination, discover her fantasies and fears, share in her vision. I wanted to make love in slow motion. I wanted to hear her voice in the early morning before the cars get out of bed, and factories light up their first cigarette. I wanted to show her the hole in my armor, the secret spot where there was no protective padding. And I wanted to make her concrete, alive, not just a tremor of ether or a passing fragrance.

It was this renewed passion for Elizabeth which inspired me to occasionally venture out of my bedroom. It helped regenerate my enthusiasm for sunlight. Sara and her daughters were kind, but reticent. They thought I overreacted. Shultz was only a dog, and although a dog is man's best friend; a dog is not a brother, a sister, or a parent. How would I survive the death of a human being, a family member? They responded to me in the same way they responded to Father. We were excluded from the circle of women, isolated in camps according to sex and blood ties. The intimacy between father and son was intensified.

"This guy had a beautiful German Shepherd," said Father. "It was an award-winning dog and his central interest in life. He went on a month-long holiday in Europe and got his most trusted friend to look after his dog. He wasn't gone a week when he received a letter from his friend saying, 'Your dog is dead,' with no explanation and no condolences. He was appalled by the insensitivity of the letter and wrote his friend back saying, 'You don't say something that point blank. You ease into it with a little gentleness, prepare the person. You should have written, for example, that my dog is on the roof and you're worried because you haven't been able to get him down. In the next letter you could warn me that my dog had an unfortunate accident, but he's receiving the best possible medical attention. Then say you're extremely sorry, but my dog has passed away.' A week later he got another letter from his friend saying simply, 'Your mother is on the roof.' "

I laughed for the first time in a week or more. I participated in the sanity of humor. Strength returned to my finger tips and I regained my grip on mental health.

I would lobby Elizabeth for forgiveness, profess my devotion, announce that I was finally ready for love. I would take her for a drink, let the conversation and emotion pour out. I had drunk with lots of women, but not with the woman I loved. I had attempted to woo and seduce lots of women, but not the woman I loved. Does love have to be cramped by domesticity? Does love exclude the verbal activity of a bar? I would give Elizabeth more than love. I would give her a good time, adventure, music. It was through these things that I'd get to know the person inside Elizabeth's body. She was a stranger to me. It would be a crime if we could never be anything but strangers to each other.

I hurriedly said good-bye to Dad and Sara and hurriedly said hello to Mother. Dad must have phoned Mother because she didn't mention Shultz. I was anxious. I didn't want to stand around talking. I wanted Mother to drive faster on the highway, and I didn't bother to put my suitcase in the house. I put it in the garage and got my bike. It was a sudden mild spell and the roads were wet, not icy. I stopped off at a mall to buy Elizabeth flowers and an album. The bike seemed to pedal itself the rest of the way. I rode with one hand.

There were no cars in the driveway, and no cars meant no parents—an encouraging sign. I expected Elizabeth to intuitively sense my arrival, throw open the door as I was about to knock, and press her voluptuous body against mine. The door had been left open a crack, and I stepped quietly into the house. Elizabeth's bedroom was at the end of the hall. I heard two familiar voices, laughter. I followed the voices and stood in the doorway, flowers in one hand and an album in the other. Phil was sitting up in bed, a hairy leg protruding from the sheets. Elizabeth was at the base of the bed, partially naked, modelling an apron. The apron exposed her backside and perhaps that was the joke. There was a picture of Charlie Brown on the apron trying to kick a field goal. Lucy had pulled the ball away and Charlie

Brown landed flat on his back. Phil noticed me first. The laughter ceased.

"What's so funny," I whispered. Phil bowed his head. Elizabeth stood her ground and looked me boldly in the eye.

"If my parents could only see your face now!" said Elizabeth.

The cruelty of her response frightened me. I didn't like her parents and gave them no reason to like me; but, strangely, it hurt to know that the feeling was mutual. I hated the feeling of being excluded from the Baldwin family or from the warmth of a joke. I walked backwards down the hall. Elizabeth pursued me, stalked me. I stumbled over a fold in the plastic footpath. She was zeroing in for the kill.

"How was your holiday?" asked Elizabeth sarcastically.

"I don't like airports," I said.

"You don't have much of a tan."

"It rained," I said.

"You're going bald," said Elizabeth. This was the cruelest blow of all, a direct hit in the genital area. I had noticed my hair thinning, but up to that point I hadn't admitted it to myself.

"My father is bald," I said. "I guess it's hereditary."

Phil's car was parked on the street. How could I have missed it? I dropped the flowers and album at the end of the driveway. There was something wrong with my bike. The wheel was rubbing against something. I had to stand on the pedal and pull with my arms to achieve forward momentum. The wet roads, mixed with dirt, contributed to the stickiness. I jumped off, kicked the wheel, and jumped on again, but it didn't stop the rubbing. I made it to the main street. The traffic was backed up for some reason, probably an accident. It was downhill, but seemed like the steepest incline I had ever climbed. I was barely moving, like the traffic. I hopped off, ran with the bike, hopped on. Nothing unclogged. I slowed to a snail's pace. I pushed and pushed and pushed and kept on pushing.

9. Gay by Default

I stood naked in front of a mirror in the dorm bathroom frantically massaging my head. Baldness! The primordial male fear, a major crisis point in the life of a golden boy. Massaging loosens the scalp and provides a nourishing supply of blood to the hair follicles. I jerked the skin below the hairline. Intellectual masturbation. My hair was thinning. There was hair on my pillow in the morning, hair collected in the drain after a shower, hair was in my food. I was confronted by the degeneration of my own body, death, mortality.

"I hate you, February," I said to my reflection. "February, you're a miserable bastard."

I slapped my penis to make it hang better and look bigger and returned to massaging my scalp. I practiced my eye exercises, left-right, up-down, around in circles. I farted and waited for the aroma to rise to nostril level. Beer! Now it was rotting my insides. Fortunately, there were no exterior signs of second degree alcoholism, no purple veins on my nose, no bloating, no fat. I had lost weight. My body was thinning like my hair.

I made my towel into a cushion, placed it on the bench, and used it to stand on my head. Blood rushed to the rescue of the hair follicles. I could see my genitals in the mirror, topsy-turvy, and I giggled with affection. They looked like a caricature of the pudgy head of a Jewish baker, with wispy hair and a big nose. Blind Chuck came in and urinated, but I was quiet and he didn't notice me.

I lolled in the shower. Showering, one of the most heightened experiences in daily life, appeals to my sensual nature. I was covered in suds from head to foot when I heard my phone ringing across the hall. God had contrived a plot to interrupt my showers as punishment for my sins. God is a vindictive bastard! I streaked to my room, feeling like Mr. Bubble, caught in the act of fondling babies in a bathtub, exposed as a pervert and a child molester. The mother and father were right behind me armed with garden shears. Chuck's dog barked, but I didn't bark back because I wasn't feeling playful towards dogs. Dogs were dumb, unclean animals. I didn't like the way they pissed and shit everywhere.

"It's Elizabeth," said a voice on the phone. She sounded soft and nervous.

"Elizabeth who?" I responded caustically. "The Queen?"

"Elizabeth Baldwin."

"Fuck off and die," I said.

"Please!" pleaded Elizabeth. "Listen to me. If you hang up I don't know what I'll do."

"I have a few suggestions. . ." I said, but I didn't make them. The fact was that I didn't know what Elizabeth would do either, and sometimes she scared me. I didn't really want her to fuck off and die. She was a mystery to me, not a woman. She was something that defined me, with her beauty and her poise, but she wasn't a separate being. I couldn't detach her from my ego. I couldn't even guess what was going on inside her.

"I want you to know, Ken, that I didn't make love to Phil. We just slept together. I was lonely and missing you and needed to be close to someone. You seemed to have dropped me cold, for no reason and without a word of explanation. You forgot about me just like you forgot about hockey, like I wasn't a person."

"I've got a good memory, but it's short," I said meaninglessly.

"Do you believe me?" asked Elizabeth.

"It's a technicality. If you didn't fuck around in fact, you certainly fucked around in spirit. I'm sure there was lots of fondling under the cover."

There were voices inside my head screaming at me: 'hypocrite.' They were the voices of my sisters, a chorus of seven betrayed females. I was unfaithful to Elizabeth from the moment I set foot in Stockton, in fact and in spirit. I was sure Elizabeth's experience with Phil was more human and less sordid than my experience with the Vomiter. I recognized the proverbial double standard and struggled to pacify my jealous anger.

"Suddenly you're at my door, all humble and flowers in your hand," continued Elizabeth. "I have to wait upon your mood, which is about as consistent as the weather. I felt angry, destructive. Let's stop hurting each other. Let's help each other, love each other. It could be so nice! I think of you putting your arms around me and hugging me, and it makes me cry. I love you, Ken

Harrison. I love you more now than I ever have. You have to see me again, at least once, and soon, Saturday at the latest. You have to! Please!"

"Well," I said, my defenses beginning to crumble like the first tumbling rock of an avalanche. It was the sound of my name, pronounced in full, that burned down my throat and warmed my stomach. The sound of my name was intoxicating. "Maybe once," I said. "But it doesn't necessarily mean anything. And we're not going anywhere near a bed. No screwing. We'll sit on the plastic in the living room, drink and talk and I'll go home early."

Ring Stadium was like any other bar on Friday night: crowded, loud, feverish, irascible, passionate. It was an intensified world, a world of back alley fights, sadness and rejection, boisterous optimism. I loved the crazed, primitive atmosphere. I loved the contagious excitement. I loved the raw emotion which was visible on every face. Bars aren't evil or superficial. They are profoundly sincere, a place where self-deceivers confront their own loneliness and brave men find freedom. Ring Stadium was sacred, a spiritual haven, a prison, heaven and hell rolled into one.

Henry Kissing-Balls, my partner at the stand-up bar, looked characteristically handsome, dopey, and sleepy-eyed. He had a cosmic consciousness, a mental affinity for metaphysical and abstract thought. It was his leaning towards abstraction that made the practical struggle of daily life so complicated and insurmountable. If only Henry didn't have to contend with the society that whirled around him! If only he could break his Promethean chains and soar into the universe.

Henry was respected by his fellow earthlings. He bobbed aimlessly, and everyone who passed him returned the bob. This nervous gesture made him seem friendly and approachable. The bob was interpreted as both a gallant salutation and an esoteric signal between two higher minds. It was flattering to be greeted by Henry's bob. It was as if this stranger understood you. Consequently, there was no one who didn't know Henry or who didn't feel a deep, telepathic bond with him. Henry was unconscious of his appeal and popularity. He was unconscious of his own bobbing. He rarely knew the names of his spiritual brothers and sisters.

"I finally got over my existential crisis," said Henry, raising his voice above the music. "Now I'm in the middle of an identity crisis."

"If it's not one thing it's another," I sympathized. "You're supposed to have the identity crisis first. You should try getting more sleep at night."

He briefly considered this option and replied, "I wish it was that easy. Sleep won't increase my self-knowledge. I have to wait for that first line of poetry. That's when the answers will come."

Stockton was alive at the beginning of a semester. It was a fresh start, complete with a brand new slate of classes and highlighted by enthusiastic reunions with friends. I had an animated meeting with Barb at the Artsie Fartsie. It was the first day back and we had a lot to talk about. Before I could tell her what happened with Elizabeth, that I considered myself single, available, free to date and screw with a clear conscience, that I was ripe for the picking, Barb began to talk about some guy she met from another university. Apparently, her new boyfriend was a wonderful person, intelligent, articulate, artistic. I was happy for her. Fate conspired to make us friends, not lovers. Arguing with fate is like pissing into the wind.

Steve Lawson pissed with the wind at his back. He had an uninhibited confidence, the type of guy who farts at a crowded urinal. He stepped out of the men's room at Ring Stadium and looked in my direction. Lawson had earned a widespread popularity for his expertise as a hockey player, his good looks, and his lively sense of humor. It was Henry he recognized, not me. Lawson smiled. Henry bobbed.

"Pressed shirt, with seam along the shoulder," said Lawson, without an introduction. He stopped in front of Henry and pointed to the seam with his finger. Lawson had the temperament of an actor, and his eyes sparkled with common sense and wit. "Pressed pants with seam down the front. New shoes, cost $95.00. Seiko watch, also very expensive." He put the watch to his ear and listened for the tick. "Rings are gold, fourteen-karat gold, my favorite number. I can't lose tonight." Lawson didn't bother with a formal au revoir. He imitated the clownish strut of a macho disco playboy—the type that drives a Trans-Am and leaves his shirt open to the navel—and sat at a table with two girls.

Lawson was right. He couldn't lose. The magic blood of a golden boy pumped through his veins. Henry laughed for an inordinately long period of time. I didn't find it that funny.

GOLDENROD

I had survived a day of desperate horniness in the library. There was something about being in a library that gave me an instant erection; it made my whole body burn with lust. I regularly reached under the desk and squeezed my hard-on, rubbed it up and down, and went back to writing my essay. It was a nagging itch that wouldn't leave me alone. I stood up and circled my desk, restless and frustrated. I was plagued by mental images of female anatomy appearing all over the pages in front of me. Women passed my desk on the way to the bathroom, and I couldn't help glaring at their body parts. I drooled on the desk once, which was shameful and embarrassing. I considered masturbating in the bathroom, but decided against it because of my aversion to unpleasant smells. A girl had fallen asleep in one of the lounge chairs in the smoking area, unaware that her legs were spread as wide as the prairies. I looked at her crotch every thirty seconds.

Ironically, bars tended to cool my eagerness for sex. The flame of desire is reduced to a burning coal. It was with a clear head that I noticed an attractive girl who, I was convinced, was staring at me. It was an encouraging look, a look of sexual curiosity. I racked my brains for something to say, an original approach, an intelligent or humorous introduction. I would have to gain her trust, establish a comfortable, harmonious rapport, let her know that I wasn't a pervert, a rapist, or an obnoxiously persistent sex hound. Everything hinged on the first line. I was looking for that first line of poetry.

I could have borrowed a cigarette, but that was as unimaginative as "haven't I seen you somewhere before?" or "do you come here often?" Some cheapskates get nasty about handing over a cigarette, especially if they haven't got many left. I could ask to buy a cigarette from her, and she would probably insist that I take one for free, but I remembered that I didn't smoke. I would look awkward trying to act like an experienced smoker. I was beginning to realize that meeting a woman in a bar was not easy. It never occurred to me to simply walk over and say, "hello."

I created mock conversations in my head and attempted to predict the outcome. "Do you know what the population of the world is?" I imagined myself saying with playful seriousness, like a child asking why the sky is blue.

She would laugh at my unconventional question, cast an amused smile at her girlfriend, and look back at me with parental concern. She would have a sense of humor herself, play along with the game, and answer in good faith, "About thirty-five billion, Dear."

"That's a lonely number," I would say.

I contemplated various scenarios like asking her opinion of the seal hunt atrocities. If she was majoring in social work or had liberal political leanings or some other manifestation of middle-class guilt, I would give her an irresistible offer. I would offer her a martyrdom, "Fuck me or I'll kill myself." That was not my style, too crude and unsophisticated! If she was incapable of guilt, void of compassion, or had conservative political leanings, I would take a more domineering approach. I would take her for a ride in my mammoth yacht and when we were in the middle of the lake I would give her that infamous, right-wing ultimatum, "Hump or jump." Unfortunately, I didn't have a yacht handy or a large body of water. In the arena of sexual politics, I was a liberal by default.

Henry Kissing-Balls was gay by default. He was talking to Chris, the homosexual I used to cock-tease in philosophy class last semester. Chris monopolized Henry's attention and profoundly empathized with his identity crisis. Chris was throwing resentful vibes in my direction, afraid that I intended to steal his man. I needed empathy too, but I hadn't given up on women yet.

My heart pounded in my chest as I decided to make my move. It was an order from that heterosexual commander in my brain. I zigged and zagged through the crowd until I was standing directly behind the object of my aspiration, this unconquered territory. There was no turning back. I was frightened by my own nervousness. It was absurd to feel such anxiety just because I wanted to talk to a member of the opposite sex.

"Excuse me, member of the opposite sex," I croaked. She turned and looked at me with an expression of impatience. "Do you know what the population of the world is?"

She stared at me blankly, and looked away without answering. I contemplated the back of her head, unsure of my next move. Questions raced through my mind. Had she misheard me? Had she heard me at all? Should I repeat the line? Jokes aren't funny when you have to repeat them to someone who didn't get it the first time. They lose the illusion of spontaneity. No! I didn't need to repeat it. There was no doubt she had heard me.

I skulked back to Henry and Chris with a limp dick, my tail between my legs. Why the provocative eyes and the zombie face when I confronted her? It was possible to get rid of me without being rude. She could have explained that she didn't come to Ring Stadium, and hang around the standup bar with the single people and stare down men across from her because she wanted to talk to anyone. She could have explained that she came to a bar to stare into thin air, like a vegetable, like a cow grazing in a pasture, not to talk. She could have explained that she was too dead between the ears or too bored with herself to be capable of responding to what I had to say. I would have understood. I would have been happy to leave her alone.

It was a difficult role a man had a play in a bar, difficult not to fall into the stereotype of the insensitive cock chasing a quick pickup. The man was in the position of dreaming up an opening line, and the woman was the judge. The Queen says, "We are not amused," and off goes the head. Women may get trodden on and abused within a relationship, but they have the power at a singles bar. I wanted a more balanced power structure. I wanted to be the one asked to dance, to be the judge of the opening line. I wanted to be the critic instead of always having to perform.

I stood on my toes because I felt short. I should have worn my shoes with the heels. I tried to forgive the girl who had jilted me. She was as lost and as lonely and as horny as the rest of us, but she had been conditioned to deny it, as if there was something disgusting about being lost and lonely and horny, as if it was something to conceal, something like closet homosexuality. Chuck passed me with a beautiful woman on his arm, someone I had never seen before. I marveled quietly without interrupting his progress out the door, and, no doubt, to a bed large enough for two. Why did a blind man need such an attractive girl? He couldn't see her! He should have had a girl who felt nice, not one who looked beautiful.

"Do you recognize me from the dorm?" said a girl beside me, catching me by surprise.

"You're familiar," I lied. I had never seen her before in my life. My eyes were drawn to the crucifix suspended between two well-propped breasts.

"You're an artsie, aren't you?"

"How did you guess?" I asked. "Do I look like an artsie?"

"You came into the cafeteria once, and I overheard some girls talking about you."

"What did they say?" I asked, flattered and seeking comfort for my wounded ego.

"That you're. . ."

"That I'm what?"

"Forget it," she said. "You'll get angry."

"No I won't," I said, raising my voice angrily. Henry and Chris looked at us. "That I'm what?"

"That you're bisexual."

Henry laughed. I was the only one of the three who didn't bend in both directions. I followed cue, slumped one shoulder forward, puckered my lips slightly, and let my wrist go limp. The transformation was made with acute subtlety and finesse. I had an immaculate gay act, assuming the classical gestures of feminine sexuality without overdoing it or making it too obvious. I was so convincing that I almost convinced myself. I would have liked to be gay, free of the need for a woman, but it wouldn't have worked. My basic metal was formed. I was eternally committed to the opposite sex, loathingly straight.

"My girlfriend says the best looking guys are gay," she said, placatingly.

"I went gay out of revenge against women," I said.

The gay act is a liberal method of seduction, a cross between the pathetic "Fuck me or I'll kill myself" and the ruthless "Hump or jump." The idea is not to plead with or threaten the object of your affection, but to swindle her. You appeal to her womanly ego, present yourself as a challenge, as if few women are capable of turning you on sexually—when in fact you'd fuck anything: bird nests, stuffed animals, vacuum cleaners, rattlesnakes. You have to convince her you're unattainable. The more unattainable you appear, the more she'll want you. In order to sustain your reserve, sometimes it's helpful to slip off to the men's room, hide in the cubicle, and masturbate, smell or no smell. Once she is teased to the point of no return, you are free to pounce on top of her, without resistance or qualification.

"Why are you standing on your toes?" asked Henry.

"Because I feel short," I answered honestly. Henry accepted this response with a bob. I pursued the gay act with stubborn flamboyance and pronounced loudly to Henry and Chris, "Let's dance!"

There wasn't a free seat in the place, not enough elbow room for an anorexic midget to brush his teeth, but the dance floor was, as usual, like a graveyard. Inhibition lorded over the children of the middle class, a malevolent dictator. We were alone on the dance floor, center stage. Henry was too sleepy-eyed to care;

Chris was too gay to care; I loved an audience anytime. I danced with a vengeance, heaving and contorting my body with a snake-like sensuality. Chris did a bizarre, mystical kind of dance with his hands, like he was plucking an imaginary harp. Henry bobbed.

Three Weirdo Artsies. It was a one-act play. The next song was too slow for anything but hugs and kisses. Henry and Chris left together, and I didn't see them for the rest of the night. Dancing was a curious phenomenon. It was a prelude to sex. A primitive mating ritual, a mock orgy. There was an empty chair nearby. I picked it up and danced with my arms around it. The owner asked for it back. I returned to the stand-up bar. In Ring Stadium, you can't even dance with a chair.

I felt a tug on my belt loop. It was the girl I was talking to earlier. She said, "I've got a table with some friends. Come join us."

"Are bisexuals allowed?" I asked, following her through the crowd. She held my hand. She had an interesting bum, very small and very interesting.

"I'm Kim," she said. She was younger than I.

"Ken," I said.

"You're a sexy dancer," she giggled.

Kim's table proved to be less than hospitable. Penny was the first person I recognized, and she looked as disappointed to see me as I was to see her. She had a sarcastic smirk on her face. She had sized me up and knew exactly what kind of man I really was. She was wise enough not to trust good-looking men who are sexy dancers. She saw through me and beyond, beyond the superficial and the physical, beyond the comprehension of a golden boy. I was incensed by her patronizing arrogance. There were two other girls at the table, but no one bothered with introductions. Kim did a lot of giggling at nothing.

"Have you been creating art lately?" asked Penny.

"I've matured. I don't wet the bed or create anything."

There was a plump girl across from me. "Haven't we met before?" I asked.

"You ran into me under the clock tower last semester," she said. "Almost broke my ribs."

"Sorry about that," I said, apologizing, apologizing, apologizing.

"I hear you were dancing with a chair," said the third girl. She had no personal grudge against me, but was eager to participate in the crucifixion.

"Fuck this silly shit," I said, standing up and facing Penny. I was enraged. When a golden boy is enraged at a woman, he doesn't hit her or make a big scene; he does something worse. He walks away, depriving her of his sparking company—a far crueler blow. "Listen, scuzface," I said to Penny. "I don't know what you have against me. Maybe I represent something you can't have, but I haven't got time for your verbal war games."

I did the famous golden boy walk, out the back door and home for a good night's sleep. I masturbated to the image of Kim's crucifix and her interesting little bum.

I didn't stop off at my place when I arrived in Chicago, but headed directly to Elizabeth's house. I had a pillowcase thrown over my shoulder stuffed with underwear, a pair of jeans, a couple of books. I used a pillowcase because a suitcase was too awkward to carry.

There was a strange bounce in my step, as if my boots had springs in the soles, as if I was walking on a trampoline. I started skipping. I was aware of how ridiculous I looked skipping down the street with a pillowcase over my shoulder, like a satire of Santa Claus in drag, but I couldn't help it. I couldn't control my feet. My feet, hands, and sex organs had a mind of their own.

It was dark and I was about three blocks from Elizabeth's when there was a piercing eruption inside me, somewhere around the solar plexus area. It was like I had pulled the pin and swallowed a grenade. It was an internal explosion. I needed Elizabeth to save my life. Everything looked like Elizabeth, tasted like Elizabeth, smelt like Elizabeth. The skip shifted into a full sprint. I barreled through back yards, slid around corners, hopped fences. I kicked up enough snow to look like a sandstorm in a desert.

I was driven by a supernatural force, something larger than the human race, deeper than the Atlantic Ocean, more awesome than the atom bomb. A dog chased me for a short distance, barking, but was too slow and soon gave up. The years I spent as a hockey player and athlete culminated in that sprint. It was the consummate achievement of my youth.

Elizabeth anticipated my arrival, throwing open the door as I charged up the driveway. I dropped my pillowcase as we collided into each other's arms and fell to the floor. We scrambled along the floor to the front vestibule, tearing off my coat, her blouse, opening my pants, pulling up her dress, crying and panting and laughing and whimpering. We croaked out our love in panicked tones, desperate confessions of loneliness, hushed pledges of everlasting devotion. I had the end of my penis inside her.

"Are your parents home?" I asked.

"No," said Elizabeth, crying and laughing. "I thought we weren't supposed to have sex."

"I held off as long as I could," I said, pulling out. I had one boot on and one boot off. "Let's go to bed and feel it, save the discussion for later."

Elizabeth was radiant, a tower of jewels, a fountain of eternal youth. She was perfection. Her ravishing mane of hair was teased into cascading curls. Her little breasts were topped with beautiful big brown nipples. Her body was supple, curved, and petite, without an ounce of fat. There was too much for my senses to take in at once, too much to see and smell and touch. It felt so good it hurt. It felt so good I needed to pull away briefly. I needed a second to salvage my sanity.

Elizabeth hurriedly did up her clothes and hurried down the hall into her bedroom. I hurried after her. We dove into bed and started over again. Clothes sailed into the air, settled gently on the dressing table, the back of a chair, and dropped to the floor. Elizabeth's panties ricocheted off the mirror and landed on her nail polish collection, causing a few bottles to fall behind the desk. We were children playing leapfrog in bed, hopping up and down on a flannelette lily pad. The mattress bounced off the boxspring, landing on the floor. We tumbled against the closet door, but managed to remain attached at the crotch. I accidentally kicked the chair which flew against the desk, knocking over a vase and more bottles of nail polish. Elizabeth's pretty little arm swung out and hit a plant stand, sending a philodendron crashing against the wall.

"You're my ideal of a woman, Elizabeth," I said passionately.

We climaxed simultaneously, squawking and scratching like angry cats. The bedroom was magnificent, chaotic, the crumbling remains of an ancient temple. We crawled through the rubble and onto the dismantled mattress, the sacrificial altar, pulled the thick white comforter over us, like a blanket of snow, entwined our limbs and bodies, and slept. I awoke frequently in the night, felt rushes of love through my body. I squeezed her and she squeezed me. The electricity flowed through both of us.

When morning came, I was physically sick to my stomach. I went to the bathroom, vomited, brushed my teeth, and went back to bed. I had gorged myself at the feast of love, drunk too deeply from the cup of desire. I was no longer a rock of independence. I needed Elizabeth, if not to survive, to flourish. I lived with a fantasy inside my head of a woman, of a poetic kind of love, of a courageous and passionate relationship between a man and a woman. I didn't want to exist on the lifeless plane of a suburban couple where you eat together and sleep together, but never really talk to each other, never see the woman you love for who she really is. I wanted to be alive, aware, one hundred percent.

"I hear voices inside my head," I said. "They tell me things."

"That's the first sign of going crazy," said Elizabeth, and she left it at that. She lay on my arm complacently, but it wasn't important who owned the arm. It could have been Phil's arm or anyone who happened to be playing the role of boyfriend. An arm is an arm and a boyfriend is a boyfriend. I resented her lack of curiosity.

"Aren't you interested in what those voices tell me, for fuck sakes?" I said. My blood boiled.

"Yes? What?" she said, responding to my anger. I was silent. I wouldn't share my visions, not now. You shouldn't have to ask for someone's curiosity, any more than you should ask for a compliment.

"It used to bother me that we're not close," I said, testingly, probingly. "Or do you prefer it the way it was?"

"I like it the way it was," she said with a naive honesty. "At least until you marry me."

"What the fuck has marriage got to do with anything?"

I wanted to discuss pure love, Mount Olympus, immortality, and she was only interested in an institution. She wanted the institution more than she wanted to be close to a man. What did she think an institution could possibly give her? As if an institution could be a safeguard against loneliness; as if anything but courage and honesty and a lot of talking and listening could dispel loneliness; as if an institution could protect her from any of the real threats. It was a childish attachment, an attachment to the idea of playing house permanently, suntanning in the backyard, buying curtains and maternity clothes, asking for her husband at the reservation desk of a posh restaurant.

I was a young man, at an age when callow, delusive attitudes on life enraged me, instead of simply making me sad. I vaguely remember shouting, shouting incoherently and dressing incoherently, pulling on my pants, hopping on one foot to regain my balance. I put my shirt on inside out, took it off, put it on again the right way, ripping it in the act. I couldn't understand what was happening inside me, my violent swings of emotion like a giant pendulum. Passion is a double-edged sword. Rage flowed out of me with a force of its own. Elizabeth's mouth was open. She had never seen me angry before.

I left in the same flurry that I had arrived.

10. Up the Bum

Loneliness was the theme of the summer semester. The normal cycle of night and day didn't exist. The summer was one long uninterrupted, very humid day, so humid my sticky clothing and bed sheets clung to my body like a straitjacket and the air was oppressively thick, like breathing through a pillow. Loneliness is the most debilitating torture that God, in all his vengeful glory, inflicted on the human race. I couldn't sleep. I couldn't concentrate on school work. I couldn't hoist my spirits up high enough to enjoy a party. My confidence was eroded to a molehill. I couldn't talk in class without shaking and trembling with nervousness. I drifted in limbo and stared at nothing, frightened that I might never wake up.

It was difficult to believe that someone with my obvious physical advantages would have any experience with loneliness. You didn't expect a sex symbol like myself to be lonely. You expected to find me at the hub of a party, exchanging witty observations of humanity with vampish female guests, or at the nucleus of an orgy, at the bottom of the pile, a panting heap of insatiable women fighting over my undying erection. I was in foreign territory, voyaging into a different time zone. I had one prop to lean on, a solitary buoy floating in a desolate sea: Barb. When I talked to Barb, I felt like Ken Harrison again.

I did my best to talk to Kim—the girl with the interesting bum who thought I was bisexual—but the conversation couldn't get off the ground. She lived on the floor above me in the dorm and approached me at every opportunity: When my door was open, when I was eating alone in the cafeteria, when I was jerking off under my desk in the library. She had this distracting habit of giggling. Every time I talked to her or asked her a question, she giggled. I said, "How are you, Kim?" and she giggled. I said, "Got any classes today?" and she giggled. "What's on special for lunch?" Giggle giggle. If she was with a friend, she'd keep looking away and giggling with her friend. It got to the point where I started giggling with them. Kim and her friend would stop me in the hall, and the three of us would giggle together for five minutes before walking on. I didn't know at the time that when a young girl is constantly giggling around you, it means she wants to have sex.

Kim had unintentionally propagated the myth that I was bisexual. I was flattered that rumors of my sexual activities generated such interest in the dorm. Every male, from the macho football player to the wimpy bookworm, literally ran from my company. The reaction didn't bother me. It made feel powerful, frightening away fully grown adults like cockroaches scrambling across a cupboard shelf. I carried myself with an air of superiority and detachment.

In order to clear my name, all I had to do was make an overt display of masculinity, kick over garbage cans, spit on the sidewalk, shout "fag" at passing strangers. I preferred to wallow in isolation. I preferred the role of the misunderstood poet; Byronic and melancholy with solitary walks late at night. I maintained a defiant pride in the face of ostracism. "Fuck 'em all," I decided, with an uncompromising vehemence which was strikingly reminiscent of my mother. I had taken to slipping on women's clothing, high heels and a pair of frilly panties and skipping across the hall to the bathroom. I made sure someone caught a glimpse of me. There was only one exterior link between me and the man I once was: the bench press. I began a moderate weight-lifting schedule for the chief purpose of humiliating my narrow-minded neighbors. They disliked being outdone on the bench press by a fag.

Barb and I went for a marathon jog at dusk every day. We ran lazily into the night for two whole hours, although we moved so slowly it was more like a fast walk. Barb usually quit before me and I topped off the jog with a climactic sprint. The emphasis was on conversation, not physical drudgery. Tired limbs and gasping lungs didn't interfere with the two-way chatter.

"I heard somewhere that if you put sperm on your scalp once a day, it'll stop hair loss," I said. "I doubt that I could consistently ejaculate that high, but I could masturbate into a jar and use it as shampoo."

"Every day!" exclaimed Barb. "That's a lot of sperm. You couldn't do it without help. You'd need a girlfriend, unless you put an ad in the university paper and collected other people's sperm."

"That's disgusting! I'd never use someone else's sperm."

"It'd smell horrible after a while," concluded Barb. "Are you really worried about losing your hair?"

"I've considered suicide."

"Vanity, thy name is Ken Harrison," laughed Barb good naturedly.

"Wouldn't you be worried about it?" I said. "Can't men be vain too?"

"You still have lots left," reassured Barb sweetly.

We skirted a farmer's field and turned onto a dark path that cut under a clump of trees. I was wearing my famous white shorts, running shoes, and bandana, no shirt. Barb wore a pair of shorts pulled over a purple leotard. The humid air loosened my muscles and provoked a bathing flood of perspiration, an ideal physiological state for exercise. Insects collided with my torso and drowned in the moisture. The odd bug flew into my open mouth, and I swallowed it. My background as an all-star jock athlete gave me an appetite for physical labor, a perverse desire to inflict pain on my own body. Barb's presence prevented me from running myself into the ground.

"Loneliness! Fuck!" I confessed. "It's destroying my mind. I need an army of women to fill the gap Elizabeth left, and I can't find one. The spirit of loneliness is chewing on my testicles. My balls feel like bubble gum."

"What about Kim?"

"Kim couldn't come close to comprehending the complicated workings of my brain," I said magnificently. "And I hear she has a boyfriend out of town."

"That doesn't matter," said Barb with superior female wisdom. "She wants you. A fling might do you good."

"To tell you the truth, I often lie in bed fantasizing about her interesting little ass. She brags about being a virgin. I like the way virgins yell and scream in pain when you make love to them, as if your penis is ten inches long."

"Believe me," said Barb. "That virginity trip is bullshit."

"She'll probably giggle through the whole thing, killing both my concentration and my confidence."

"It'll be a break from masturbating."

"Masturbation keeps me in practice," I explained. "As my father always says, use it or lose it."

"You were well brought up," said Barb.

Barb was a cure for misogyny. Loneliness reduced many a man to a woman-hater, but my friendship with Barb made it impossible to project internal feelings of cynicism on womankind. She had a cheerful confidence that mystified and fascinated me. Her support system was blighted by a bizarre history of bereavement, from a mother's deathly pirouette into a dry swimming pool to a father who butchered himself with his own squash racket, yet there was nothing maudlin or self-pitying in her attitude towards life. Her heroic courage made me feel ashamed. I was forced to swallow my bitterness, not shoot it at extraneous targets or innocent bystanders.

"I'm tired of myself," I said quietly. "For the first time in my life, I'm tired of myself. I'm sick of my silly little middle-class traumas, agonizing over the fact that I haven't been laid for two months, suffering because I haven't got a woman around to tell me I'm wonderful." I shouted with theatrical exaggeration, "Do you hear that, World? Ken Harrison hasn't been laid for two months! Shut down the factories! Board up the classrooms! Sound the alarm! Someone fuck Ken Harrison before his burning ego consumes the universe!"

I lowered my voice. "It boggles my mind to think that some people have it even worse than me, such as cripples and rape victims and mongoloids and amputees and drug freaks and starving Biafrans and eunuchs and hospital-ridden cancer patients and fat people with glandular problems. What right have I to complain? What is there for me to bitch about? I'm not in the Vietnam War dodging snipers in the jungle. I eat well, brush my teeth twice a day, lie in the sun and read, buy dirty magazines, and beat off. I have a healthy body and an alert mind. I have more choices in life than most people. Why don't I feel good? We arts students glorify depression. I think depression is petty and bourgeois. It's boring and pretentious, as if I'm suffering for the good of humanity. The truth of the matter is I'm sulking. I'm sulking because I can't always have my own way. I'm a spoiled brat!"

"You're being unfair to yourself," said Barb. "You are going through changes for the better."

"Let's not talk about me," I said. "I'm tired of the subject. Let's talk about you. How's it going with your boyfriend? What's his name again? It sounds like anus."

"Hannes."

"What is he, Greek?"

"Estonian," said Barb. "I think it's a beautiful name. His sister is called Annaliisa."

"Anal Ingus? I'd like to meet her. Must be an interesting country, Estonia."

"It's Annaliisa. Not Anal Ingus."

It was Phuc not fuck, Sterm not sperm. Annaliisa not Anal Ingus.

Barb told me her friends were deserting her because she had a boyfriend. They rarely phoned and when they did phone it was a one-way conversation. They talked about what they saw and who they'd met without bothering to inquire into Barb's life. It was as if a single person, by her very nature, was more alive than someone with a mate. It was as if couples were necessarily dull and uninteresting. It was as if the only things that occupied her mind were domestic chores and sexual fidelity.

"We single people are self-obsessed bastards," I said.

"I hate being thought of as having settled down," said Barb, "just because I've met a man who I like to be with. I still like to go to a bar, stay up late, get drunk, swear. I'm a bohemian at heart. I enjoy roaming around discussing art, being spontaneous, and doing something different every day."

"I solemnly swear never to desert you because you have a boyfriend."

"I blame it on suburbia," said Barb. "It's a suburban stereotype, this crap about being wild and having fun when you're single, then getting a man and settling down to routine and monotony. I'm expected to cut off the world and focus my attention on my man and my career. No fuckin' way!"

"Fuck suburbia!" I exclaimed excitedly. Barb and I had a common enemy: suburbia. This private war gave us a feeling of camaraderie. We had great fun saying filthy obscene things about "suburban people." We blamed everything on suburbia.

"Fuck 'em all," she said. We both suffered ostracism in one sphere or another; yet we were united in our friendship.

"Sometimes you remind me of my mother," I said. "It's the way you pronounce 'fuck.' "

"I like our friendship, you make me feel good."

"I love you Barb, in a friendly kind of way."

Barb veered to the left and headed home alone. I accelerated my pace, sprinting the final stretch to the athletic center. There was a solitary tree on an island in the parking lot directly outside the front doors which I used for my ritualistic baldness treatment. I stood on my head, maintained my balance by placing my feet on the tree trunk, and let my pounding heart pump blood into the hair follicles. My head was swimming. I opened my dizzy eyes and the athletic center was upside down spinning around me. I got on my knees, raised my head about an inch off the ground, and massaged my scalp.

"Are you OK?" said a voice. I looked up and saw a woman staring at me with an expression of concern and bewilderment.

"Fine, thanks!" I said. "Just massaging. It helps prevent baldness."

I carried my towel modestly in front of my crotch as I walked towards the showers. Suspended on the horizon of naked bodies was the most grotesque monstrosity I had ever seen. It was none other than Steve Lawson's big, fleshy, uncircumcised penis, dangling halfway to his knees like the snout of a bloated anteater. Lawson was obviously proud of the awesome weapon between his legs because he danced around the change room flinging it rudely in people's faces. Someone was drying his toes, innocently minding his own business. Lawson thumped the knob of his giant penis on the back of the guy's head a couple of times and exploded with laughter. If he'd had done that to me, I'd have bitten his cock off.

"Is that thing ever ugly!" I said disgustedly to Lawson as I marched past him into the showers. He didn't have a chance to get the last word. It probably took him a couple of seconds to realize what "thing" I was referring to.

My penis has a distinctly Anglo-Saxon appearance with a circumcised crown and handsome contours. It is clean-cut and respectable. Admittedly it's not the biggest organ on the face of the earth, but it's efficient and reliable. Elizabeth once referred to it as cute. I'm not sure I like that particular adjective—too harmless, not menacing enough. At least you could depend on my erection. I was shocked if I couldn't get it up after the third time.

"Men tend to be highly critical of their own penises," I whispered to myself perceptively.

The person at the shower-head across from me had a penis that stuck out in a crowd. He had a ghostly frame, knobby knees, anemic skin, toothpick arms, but swaying between his skinny legs was a limp edifice of gigantic proportions. It was a foot long, curving up at the end like a ski jump and swerving to the right. He could have used it to kick field goals. I recognized the owner.

It belonged to Chris, which made me fearful for Henry. Henry couldn't take a tree trunk like that up his ass. It would rupture his sphincter muscle. I placed the towel on my crotch and dried my balls distractedly all the way to my locker.

In my room I prepared to stage the seduction scene on Kim. A run and a shower made me feel sexy. I wore baggy sweat pants, no underwear, and no shirt. I held a bottle of wine in one hand and a corkscrew in the other as I listened at the door for the hall to be silent. My head popped out, then the rest of my body. I heard a noise and jumped back into the room. It was a false alarm, Chuck's dog wagging his tail against a garbage bin in the next room. I tiptoed down the hall, heart pounding, flew up the stairs and stopped at the landing outside Kim's door. I peeked under the door and noticed the light was on and a clock radio was playing. I heard the slow tapping of a typewriter.

A stampede was approaching. I ducked into the women's room and listened to six or seven, perhaps more, female voices charging past, all talking at once. The coast was clear. I slipped out and wasted no time knocking on Kim's door. It opened. Kim flashed a breast as she was doing up her housecoat.

"It's your bisexual neighbor," I said, checking to see that she was alone. "I thought you could use a break."

She giggled, noticed my bottle of wine, and giggled again. I let myself in and shut the door. There were posters of puppy dogs and pussy cats on the wall which was depressingly indicative of Kim's preadolescent aesthetic maturity. It was almost enough to make me leave, but the crucifix accentuating the cleft between her breasts enraptured me in a spiritual trance. I pushed the face of the desk light against the wall, darkening the room, and poured a couple of glasses of wine.

"Thank the lord for what you are about to receive," I said, handing her a glass of wine and sitting beside her on the bed.

By an unfortunate coincidence, Kim was writing a philosophy essay on the existence of God. Page four bent backwards out of the typewriter. Kim swooned and glowed in a mood of passionate religious ecstasy. Suddenly spitting with disgust, she launched into a graphic description of aborted babies in garbage cans, which she had seen in a propaganda film by something like the Christian Fellowship Society. She denounced premarital sex as responsible for the degeneration of traditional value systems and bragged that she had the only intact hymen on campus. With my luck, her hymen was probably four inches thick and as impenetrable as granite. I decided to monopolize the bottle of wine, get drunk, not even try to seduce her. She was becoming so excited about God that I started to get nervous. She was ranting about the throbbing power of his paternal love, feeling his omnipotent presence entering her, probing her, etc., etc. When I noticed her hand inside her robe caressing her crotch, I was thoroughly frightened. She lunged at me, knocked the glass out of my hand, pulled me on top of her, and began thrusting up and down with her pelvis.

After a momentary fit of disorientation, I regained my composure and assimilated the rhythm of her heaving groin. I opened her housecoat. She was naked and I was wearing thin cotton sweat pants which were soft against my erection. Her legs were spread as wide as they could go, one foot dangling over the side of the bed, I kissed and licked all the way to her clitoris. My face was between her legs. The lower I went, the more excited she became, until I was rocking back and forth from one hole to the next with my tongue, and she was tearing and scratching at the mattress with her deadly talons. She jumped away when I poled at her hymen with my finger, but gave various squawks of encouragement every time I poked her in the other hole.

"Sodomize me," she said sweetly, slipping her arms out of the housecoat and rolling onto her stomach. I was amazed she knew what the word "sodomize" meant. She thought that since I was bisexual, I was an expert at this form of sexual expression, when she was obviously the more experienced partner. I was a virgin at anal intercourse.

Kim was adamant about having me enter by the "back door" and responded angrily when I tried to surreptitiously penetrate her vagina because, as she explained, she was "saving herself for marriage." The back door was very wet and, after a minimal amount of pushing, I was inside her. Her face was pressed into the pillow, muttering muffled obscenities: "Ass hole!" "Harder!" "Fuck!" "God!" "Fuck me God!" My hand was under her, twiddling her clitoris, and I was moving in and out. I admit that I liked it, loved it. It felt terrific. The scene was incredibly erotic, naughty and irreverent; being associated with God was profoundly complimentary. Then the phone screamed as loudly as a fire alarm, interrupting our concentration. It was the loudest ring I had ever heard.

"Excuse me," she said, edging away.

"You're not going to answer it, are you?" I asked.

"I have to. It might be my mother. She'll be mad if she thinks I'm out partying this late."

"Does she mind you getting fucked up the ass?" I asked.

It wasn't her mother. It was who I was afraid it was, her boyfriend, "Honeybum." That was what they called each other, "Honeybum." How appropriate! Kim whispered on the phone, giggling, and playing with my limp penis. Apparently, Honeybum was drunk and frisky, making the most outrageously lewd comments imaginable. Kim reproached him sternly, threatened to hang up, giggled, and groaned with lust. Honeybum was uncontrollable. I stared at the puppy dogs and pussy cats. I pretended that I wasn't paying attention.

"Got to go, Honeybum. Classes tomorrow."

Giggle giggle. "I love you, too."

Giggle giggle.

Click!

Kim was dying to tell me everything about Honeybum. She discussed Honeybum with the same starry-eyed devotion that she discussed God. When Honeybum got an erection, Kim explained, he would hold it vertical under the blankets and transform the entire bed into an Egyptian pyramid. His penis was so huge that after making love she couldn't sit down for a week. But it was worth it! "It hurt good," she said. Honeybum had an indomitable sex drive, excellent technique, and uncanny staying power. He could make love three days straight without ejaculating.

Why do women love to talk about the outstanding sexual performance of their last boyfriend or, as in Kim's case, their present boyfriend? As if his sexuality was interesting by way of contrast to mine. Needless to say, I felt intimidated, feeble, inferior. The conversation seemed improper. I wished we were debating the existence of God.

She rolled onto her stomach, spread her buttocks with her hands, and invited me in the back door. I went at her a second time, hurriedly, worried that another phone call would shatter my passion. I couldn't figure out if it was impolite to come inside her. In fear of inducing an enema, I withdrew before orgasm, ejaculating all the way to her scalp. I collapsed on top of her, spent and drifting on the edge of sleep. She slipped out from under me. Bang! I looked up, startled. She was slamming things, drawers, the closet door, whacking the chair into the desk.

"Anything wrong?" I said, feeling guilty for almost falling asleep.

"Ten seconds," she said, banging another drawer shut.

"Ten seconds?" I asked.

"Why did you pull out?"

"I don't understand."

"Ten more seconds and I could have come," she said, kicking the tin garbage can into the corner, producing a loud clang. "Now I'm frustrated."

"Sorry," I said sheepishly. It interested me that she could get an orgasm from anal intercourse. "I was afraid the phone would ring. We can do it again if you want."

"Don't do me any favors," she said, thumping a couple of library books on the desk and sitting down to write her philosophy essay on the existence of God.

"Do you want to sleep together?" I asked.

"I can't sleep when I'm like this," she said. "Besides, I don't mind having sex with someone I don't love, but I won't sleep with him. I'm religious, you know. I feel you have to draw the line at a certain point."

"Oh," I said. I couldn't understand the way she thought; I assumed it was because she was logical. I could never follow a logical mind, the mind of an "A" student. For me, it would take a lot more love to let someone give it to me up the bum than to sleep with me.

She reluctantly let me kiss her good night on the cheek. I put my ear to the door and waited for the coast to clear before ducking out and tiptoeing downstairs to my room, holding the corkscrew in my hand like a mangled penis.

Now that I had experienced anal intercourse, I felt like a man of higher knowledge, full of dark wisdom, spiritually uplifted. I was calmly exuberant, like a reborn Christian at a Jesus freaks' meeting. I danced around the room happily, cleaning, dusting, hanging up clothing. I put a fresh snot-rag on my desk. I liked to pick my nose while I did homework and deposit it on a piece of toilet paper, which I called my snot-rag. I crawled into bed, stretched, and squirmed comfortably. I had the bed to myself and appreciated the luxury of farting under the covers without complaint from a female companion. Sleep came easily.

Sleep came, and with it a dream, an epic, a mythological kind of dream that leaped over great distances and great chunks of time. Phil and I were at my mother's place preparing for a Herculean journey to Hades and back. I stopped in the doorway of the bathroom and watched my mother having a pee, an artist in action. I noticed she had a tiny penis.

"Mom," I said, "You have a penis."

"Women have a tiny penis and a hole," my mother said, standing up and showing me that it was true.

I went out to the front porch and Phil directed my attention to a young boy shyly asking a little girl for a kiss. It was cute. We laughed. My cap was on the step, but someone had urinated on it which was irritating because it meant I couldn't bring it with me. We walked to the bus stop. It was a dry, clear summer day. As I climbed onto the bus, I realized I wasn't wearing any shoes.

The bus was a world unto itself, a traveling microcosm. There was a house on the bus, and an enemy was hunting us. We ran through the rooms, cleverly eluding them, laughing at our own cleverness. The enemy was growing in number. It was becoming more difficult to outsmart them and we were getting nervous. I stood on a chair pretending to fix a light bulb as a decoy for Phil to escape. It was our last laugh, because the game had become serious, at least for me. While Phil was getting away, I concentrated on survival. I fled down the back staircase, across a field, and up to the top of a mountain. The enemy came from every direction. Anticipating combat, I built a barricade around myself. They scrambled across the field like a vast army of ants, circled the mountain, and wasted no time commencing the attack. They threw things at me, rocks, toy boats, rubber tires, anything they could get their hands on. I threw the same missiles back at them.

I was on the mountain for five years, The Five Year War. Although there was no lull in the fighting, a peculiar relationship developed between the enemy and me, a feeling of respect, a warmth which escalated almost into love. As a tribute to my perseverance, someone threw a pair of shoes up to me. The shoes fit and enabled me to run down the mountain and get away. I ran through the suburbs of Chicago, the enemy still after me, wondering whatever happened to my friend Phil.

A bus stopped in the center of the town of Stockton. I got off wearing shoes and a suit jacket. Walking down the street, I felt safe and confident and then overheard an excerpt of the news from the radio of a passing car. It said that anti-Semitism was on the rise. There was a crowd of reporters jostling to get into an auditorium to see the Shah of Iran. I joined the gathering because I was doing an article on "The Shah and Prejudice," and was concerned by the fact that my friend Phil was one of the hostages. I flirted with a woman reporter in the lineup.

"I'm sure either you'll be calling me or I'll be calling you," she said, disappearing into the mob.

"Don't be too sure," I thought. "You're not all that attractive."

Inside, there was a stage set up for the Shah who hadn't arrived yet. Everyone was talking excitedly, but I concerned myself with finding a bathroom. I had to urinate. I had to urinate so badly I was afraid of peeing my pants. The phone shrieked obnoxiously from the other side of the room. I awoke on my feet in a karate pose, my heart pounding; 4:15 a.m., read the clock radio. I struggled to quell the panic that raced through my body. The phone screamed in steady, even intervals. I picked up the receiver. I heard Elizabeth's voice, barely distinguishable through a background of disco music and hysterical laughter. Her voice was unusually high-pitched, which meant she was drunk, very drunk, so drunk she could hardly talk. It was a party. I could hear nothing but men, men swearing, maybe one other woman.

"Elizabeth!" I shouted, running around in a circle. She had put the phone down or dropped it on something soft, a bed. I heard noises in the background, noises that made me nauseous, sexual noises.

"Elizabeth!" I shouted, sensing that someone had picked up the phone.

"Which one?" asked a male voice, as if Elizabeth was a pork chop. The phone dropped on the bed again.

"Ride her!" said a distant voice.

"Elizabeth," I shouted.

"Have you seen my car keys?" laughed a male voice into the phone. He had a European accent.

It felt like it was a dream, a nightmare, and yet it was real. "Get me Elizabeth, you Greek bastard," I yelled. "She has a name, Elizabeth! If I get a hold of you, I'll kill you. I swear I'll kill you, you fuckin' ugly wop."

"I didn't bother with names, if you know what I mean," said the European voice, unalarmed by my threat. "What does she look like?"

"She's got curly brown hair," I said.

"It's curly all right, and there's a hunk of meat hanging from it," he laughed and hung up the phone.

I was left with a picture in my mind. Elizabeth on a bed, one other girl, a lineup of greedy pigs with moustaches and hairy backs, who drive Trans-Ams and have fluffy dice dangling from their rear-view mirrors, cheering each other, competing, taking turns climbing between her legs, a gang bang. Vultures preying on a wounded deer, stabbing at an open gash. They saw bleeding flesh, a free meal, not a desperate little girl gasping for oxygen, clutching at anything that would save her from herself.

I continued to hold the receiver.

"Elizabeth!" I yelled.

11. Elizabeth Is on the Roof

The Barren Room was bolted shut, a closed casket. I knocked and kicked and whimpered at the door. I climbed onto the banana seat and rode my bike to Father's old apartment building where he no longer lived. From behind a battered '69 Strato-Chief in the parking lot, I watched dispassionate eyes enter and exit, as if today was like any other day. They stepped over dead bodies and confronted the apocalypse with busines-slike detachment. I sneaked up to the back door, abhorring the thought of having to meet someone, or talk, or even nod at a stranger. I tore my social security card into shreds in an unsuccessful attempt to slip open the lock. In the past, the door had no lock, but security was tightened because, recently, an attractive young woman–who didn't live there–had managed to get in, take the elevator to the roof, and jump off. Suicide, an unseemly and profitless distraction from daily apartment living, had to be discouraged.

The violent nature of the death appealed to newspaper people. They came in droves, shoving cameras in tearful faces, squeezing every painful detail out of the parents' mouths, converting the tragedy into a cheaply sensationalized back-page cover story. Look what happened to the high school beauty! When she hit the ground, every bone in her shapely body was shattered; yet she climbed back onto her broken legs, standing up briefly before dying. The neighbors only remembered an unnerving thump, as loud as the clang of a church bell, but deeper, chest-felt. It was a fourteen story drop, and the sound carried an alarming distance. No one guessed it was the sound of a human body.

I had no retreat. Meditation held no salvation for me. My life was inside the Barren Room. There would be people at the funeral, Mr. and Mrs. Baldwin, Phil, friends, acquaintances, cousins, and I wanted nothing to do with people. I had enough to contend with without having to contend with people. I could contend with dogs because they didn't talk, but not with people. I left my bike unlocked against a fence, expecting it to be stolen, and walked downtown. I needed more time alone.

"The Barren Room is no place to socialize," I said aloud.

Elizabeth preferred me in my gentle moods. It was Elizabeth's day, and I resolved to be gentle from beginning to end. I would be attentive. Talk softly, listen compassionately, refrain from barking at passing dogs. I wouldn't refer to Elizabeth's mother as Mrs. Ajax. My hands were in my pockets. I fondled myself distractedly and studied my feet.

I imagined Elizabeth on my arm, radiant, laughing, hopping up to kiss my cheek. Strangers of the world united in envy, stared in jealous fascination at Elizabeth and me, a model couple, perfection. It was not uncommon to see a beautiful woman with an ugly man, or vice versa, but to see such an ideally compatible physical combination was a rarity. We were tailor-made for each other, fitting together like spoons in a drawer. We had the same complexion and the same features, except mine were classically male and hers classically female. We had the kinds of faces found on billboards across North America selling cars, clothing, toothpaste. We teetered high above society on a narrow pedestal, arms flailing, struggling to maintain our balance.

"Is a funeral anything like a gang bang?" I asked Elizabeth.

"Yes indeed! Everyone stands around and waits his turn while one person is lowered into the hole."

"You slut. You pig fucker. You . . ." I stopped myself. I felt weak all over. My legs were heavy as lead. I reminded myself, "It's Elizabeth's day."

Leaves blared forth their individuality in technicolor. In the fall, leaves alight from trees, engineers drop from clock towers, pretty girls jump off the roofs of apartment buildings. It was the season to witness the toppling of a golden boy.

"Can I forgive you, Elizabeth, for what you've done to October?"

Like the leaves, the engineers, and the pretty girls, hair was falling out of my head. I massaged my scalp for a few yards and dropped my arms. I decided that going bald was the best thing that could happen to me. Let me go bald and get fat and ugly with pimples, a humped back, rotten teeth, and bunions on my feet. I wanted to cultivate bad breath and bad habits, fart profusely, refuse to wash my crotch, flick snot into people's food. I wanted the comfort of being the lowest thing on earth.

"You can't fall off the floor," I said, using another one of my father's lines.

"You can fall into a hole," said Elizabeth with profound ambiguity, alluding to death and sex. I thought about it and massaged my head a little longer.

In my mind's eye, I lived with Elizabeth across from a graveyard downtown in a small flat above a second-hand book store. After some dangerous early morning detective work for the police, risking my life in a vain attempt to save a young girl from killing herself, I returned home to the bed Elizabeth was keeping warm. I felt weary, depressed. The coroner found two quarts of alcohol and a quart of sperm in the girl's stomach. Elizabeth awoke slowly, opened the blankets, and invited me to crawl in beside her. She welcomed me softly, soothing as sleep. I tapped my hand against her chest between her breasts. I liked the hollow sound it made. She got on top of me and we made love slowly, creating powerful sensations from a minuscule amount of movement.

"I love you, Ken."

Elizabeth's face was tender and moist. She was crying, crying as we made love, crying because that lousy-piece-of-shit-fuckin'-lonely-goddam feeling in the pit of her stomach was no longer there, crying because she was struck by such an overwhelming sensation of love that it hurt. "It hurt good," as Kim aptly put it, referring to her boyfriend's massive penis. I let the tears flood out and roll down my face, just tears, no wailing or gagging or embarrassing hiccup noises. We cried and screwed and screwed and cried. It was silent, impetuous, and agonizingly beautiful. It was what some people call a religious experience. I call it crying and screwing.

"What the fuck happened, Elizabeth, between you and me? There was so much fuckin' love, so much fuckin' love it hurt. It hurt good!"

I stopped and used my shirt sleeve to dry my face. There was a little girl ahead of me on the sidewalk. She was about five years old with a long brown ponytail extending down her back and wearing a pair of green corduroy pants that needed a stronger elastic in the waistband. She absentmindedly hoisted up her pants and cocked back her head as she walked. I couldn't fathom how her tiny head could produce such a thick crop of hair. She had a coquettish gait, and her nose stuck up in the air in a very snobbish and feminine manner. It was Elizabeth as a child. I was spellbound and followed her for quite a distance through a maze of residential streets and across a school yard.

It was my first experience with one of the most basic human instincts: paternalism. It was as startling a discovery as masturbation, but since it was the type of thing that didn't get much attention in the media like sex did, it was less expected. Children had seemed to me the most obnoxious little bastards on the face of the earth, shit-disturbers that deserved to be locked in a soundproof vault and dropped into the deepest part of the Arctic Ocean. I was mystified by their widespread popularity, by why their existence was tolerated at all, by why the adult world didn't unanimously conspire to wipe them out. Suddenly, I could see the appeal of having a child. I felt the commonplace desire to nurture and protect, to participate in the continuity of life-death-life, which was a tediously recurring motif in English literature essays at the university. I had Elizabeth to thank or blame for prompting this change in attitude.

Before being mistaken as a pedophile, or arrested on suspicion of child molesting, I changed course and made a bee-line for the cemetery. The graveside was crowded with familiar faces, but I avoided eyes. I hoped to discourage pre-funeral conversationalists and didn't want to be nodding "hello" like a maniac throughout the whole service. My mother came up behind me and, without uttering a word, gave me a kiss and a hug, and stepped back again, leaving me to myself. It was such a perfect thing to do I almost cried.

The preacher gave a heart-warming sermon about what a slut the deceased was, and that all sluts eventually kill themselves and rot in hell and that if a woman doesn't want to die and go to hell, she'd better keep her legs and mouth shut. He didn't say it in so many words, of course, but that was what he meant. Because his religion prevented him from having sex, he didn't want anyone else to have fun. It was the most insensitive, dogmatic, cavalier monologue I had ever heard. He exploited the opportunity to parade his chauvinism and intolerance, pushing God with the brazenness of a used car salesman, offering nothing personal or insightful about the real topic of the day: Elizabeth. Not that I expected a great revelation on the source of Elizabeth's desperate unhappiness, but I did feel a touch of compassion was in order, at least for the parents' sakes. Thank God my sisters didn't show up. There was no telling what they would do. I had promised to be gentle, but I would have preferred to strangle the preacher with his starched collar and throw him into the hole with Elizabeth.

I gradually became conscious of the principal players around me. Paul and Ross huddled beside big Phil whose eyes were red, swollen, and guilty. Phil looked bigger and sadder than he had ever looked before. I realized that Phil was in love with Elizabeth. Elizabeth's parents looked about ninety years old, especially Mr. Baldwin who I don't think could have remained standing if his wife wasn't holding him up. Elizabeth had found a way to keep her parents together; no divorce marred the Baldwin reputation. Their only baby, the most beautiful baby on the street, or in the neighborhood, was gone, and they would stay together to keep the memory of her alive.

"So this is it," I whispered as the coffin was lowered into the hole. "This is what it's all about. This is the thing everyone makes such a fuss over since the very fuckin' beginning."

The preacher was butchering the air with words. My mother, who was not one for keeping her mouth or her legs shut, winged a dirt bomb over my shoulder and hit the man of the cloth in the chaste section between his legs. Mother never missed the bull's-eye, like Robin Hood splitting the arrow. The preacher doubled over and dropped to his knees. Most people were busy staring at the ground in front of their feet, which is the habit of someone who's being preached at, and completely missed the accident. There were one or two who thought they saw something thrown from our direction, but mother and I had absolutely solemn expressions, and suspicion died away. Phil and Mr. and Mrs. Baldwin noticed nothing, not even when the preacher was on all fours, taking deep, regulated breaths to regain his composure. The mourners forgot about him and filtered away from the graveside.

I stayed to listen to three blonde girls compete for the limelight. They didn't like Elizabeth when she was alive because Elizabeth was pretty and popular and because they were the types who disliked someone for being pretty and popular. However, they pretended that Elizabeth was their best friend and that they were hurt, hurt bad when she mysteriously stopped phoning them. But they loved Elizabeth now that she was dead. They screeched, retched, and hacked up phlegm, generally making a disgusting spectacle of themselves. I couldn't leave Elizabeth alone with three hysterical bitches and a preacher who was suffering from bruised testicles, not alone in the ground in a dark box, not when it was getting cold and winter was coming and she had nothing to keep her warm. The cold air made her nipples spring up like submarine periscopes. I could see Elizabeth's big brown nipples through her white blouse as she held onto my arm.

"I cried seven hours straight," bragged one blonde.

"That's nothing. I cried fourteen hours and didn't eat," said another proudly.

"I cried forty-eight hours and didn't eat or sleep," claimed the third blonde triumphantly.

"I cried for seven days standing on my head and made a puddle so big I almost drowned," I interrupted as they passed by. They stared at me compassionately.

I had shed more tears over the loss of Shultz than Elizabeth, which didn't necessarily mean anything.

Mother, who was not the type to go to wakes at the Baldwins' house, blew me a kiss and disappeared. Phil waited at his car and offered me a ride. I gladly acquiesced. Phil was relieved that I was no longer angry at him. What I felt for him was pity. Everything had changed between us, between everyone. Everything had turned upside down, and there was no way of slowing the pace or going back. The thought of going back, of basking in Elizabeth's love hit me over and over again, like a goddam sledgehammer, giving me a burning sensation in my chest. I was a glutton for the past and so was Phil. I gravitated to the past as naturally as the family drunk gravitates to the bottle of scotch hidden in the kitchen closet. But I realized, I realized over and over again, and this is the sledgehammer part, that I had no past to go back to. The walls were closing in on us all, and there was no time for petty grudges or feelings of enmity.

"I didn't sell enough hair driers," confessed Phil, his voice barely discernible over the hum of the engine. "I was fired."

"Maybe you threw too many hair driers out the window."

Phil had presented himself as a model of success, bounding up the corporate ladder with the agility of a mountain goat, as extravagant and as wasteful as anyone would ever want to be. I expected him to be king of the hair driers by the time I obtained my useless drama degree, taking me out for meals on his expense account, credit cards, double martinis, and conservative pinstripe suits. I was surprised to discover that it was untrue. Phil relied on this public image of success and youth. Failure was morally shameful, an indecency that should be kept from the light of day. He would make this confession to no one but me. To everyone else, he quit, told the boss to "Fuck himself," had a better offer from another firm. He was giving me a pound of his own flesh to equal the score. He didn't understand that I had come to believe in defeat, that I was fast becoming an enemy of billboards and public images, that his pound of flesh gave me no satisfaction.

"Brag about it," I said emphatically. "Be proud. Act like getting fired was the greatest accomplishment of your life. If nothing else, it'll confuse people."

Phil looked like he was wondering if I was going crazy. I knew he didn't care about the job itself. It was parting with the public image of success and youth that bothered him. When someone's parents or a girl at a party asked him, "What do you do?" he wanted to say, "I'm the image of success and youth!" I wanted the courage not to have to say that. I wanted the courage to say, "I'm scum. I'm a piece of shit. Spit on me." I wanted to say that with supreme confidence, and if I could say that with supreme confidence, I'd have won the battle against public images. If I could say that with genuine confidence, the women would fight for my love because it would be the most valuable love in the world, and men would emulate me. Religious fanatics would recognize me as Christ, come for the second time.

Phil broke the silence by turning on the car stereo. With music playing it was like there was more than two of us, which was comforting. It released me from the obligation to talk. I could fade into myself, stare out the window, and let my fantasies roam freely. I imagined myself running beside the car, keeping up easily and tirelessly, dodging people, and charging over the roofs of parked cars. Then I was cross-country skiing, even though it was the Fall and there was no snow on the ground. The parked cars were ski jumps, enabling me to do flips and somersaults in midair. I skied only on grass and had to jump over driveways and patches of cement. I soon became frustrated with skiing and switched to riding a horse bareback which was my favorite.

I played road hockey beside the car. I took slap shots from out of the car window, watched the puck sail into the sky like a golf ball at a driving range, and waited until the car caught up to the puck again before taking another shot. As we neared the Baldwin residence, I caught glimpses of Elizabeth and myself standing in doorways kissing, falling on top of each other in front vestibules. Elizabeth and I embraced with the force of a sledgehammer, and it hurt, hurt good. I shoved my face in her hair and held on determinedly. My chin twitched a few times, but I managed to hold back the tears.

When I walked through the Baldwin's front door, I was hit by an odor so pungent that it nearly knocked me off my feet. It was the smell of Ajax. Inhaling Ajax fumes was better for destroying brain cells than sniffing glue. Everyone was feeling dizzy and stoned even before the liquor was served. Pools of Ajax were eating holes through the plastic runners and linoleum in the kitchen. I had a rum and coke which tasted like a full ounce of Ajax had been added. There were sandwiches and squares of lasagna which I couldn't eat because they were soggy with Ajax. Mrs. Baldwin disappeared into the washroom with a bottle of Ajax and when she came out her eyes were glossy and bloodshot, piss-holes in the snow. I was saddened and sickened to realize that Mrs. Baldwin had become an Ajax junky.

Her personality quirks were bizarrely exaggerated. Even during tranquil and happy days in the past, she tended to overreact to minor problems. Today, however, she went berserk over the most trivial malfunctions, was crazed and panicked because she forgot the silverware, and shouted at anyone who got in her way. In an effort to calm her, I made the mistake of offering to get the knives and forks from the kitchen drawer.

"No! Not those," she screamed, as if I had threatened to use some kind of cruel instrument of torture on her. It had to be the special silverware for special occasions. She finally located the special silverware and put it proudly on the table, but it didn't look right to me. Every piece was blotched and stained from having been soaked in Ajax.

Mrs. Baldwin patrolled her guests in the living room. No sooner would someone take his last bite of the meal than Mrs. Baldwin would scurry up to him, yank the plate out of his hand, and disappear into the kitchen. One woman hadn't finished her meal, and they wrestled over the plate a few seconds before she gave it up. The dishes were thrown into a sink full of hot water and Ajax. A piece of something fell off my plate. She scowled and growled at me and got out the vacuum cleaner. In the middle of dinner, surrounded by guests, she started vacuuming the floor. She put the vacuum cleaner away, fiercely snatched up a few empty plates, and rushed to the kitchen, returning with a cloth that reeked of Ajax, and began washing the plastic runner. Like everyone else standing around talking, I pretended not to notice her. I could only pretend, however, until she had washed my shoes with the cloth and was working her way up my legs.

I ran to another part of the room. Mrs. Baldwin stood up and got herself a glass of wine, spiked heavily with Ajax. Standing behind me were the three blonde girls. One girl explained that she wanted to be fashion designer, but was studying computer programming at a community college. The other girl wanted to own a little store in a small town, sell interesting things like plants, puppy dogs, and wool sweaters she would knit herself, but she got accepted at a school for urban planning, and figured she shouldn't pass up the opportunity. The third girl was getting married to a man she didn't really love, just liked. In fact, he was a very nice guy, and a friend of her brother. Her mother was organizing the whole thing. Wasn't that nice of her? They were full of excitement and giggles about the wedding.

"How's school, Ken?" said Mr. Simmons, the friendly neighbor with the billboard smile. I hadn't seen him since Mr. and Mrs. Baldwin's twenty-fifth happy anniversary party.

"Best years of my life, Mr. Simmons."

Mr. Simmons was operating a makeshift bar in the dining room, mixing and spilling drinks with his big clumsy hands. He looked bigger than usual, like Phil, and clumsier. The room was too small for him. It looked like he couldn't move without bumping into furniture and knocking over the glass ornaments in the china cabinet. He reminded me of a cartoon character. I could never think of him as a real person.

"The holiday is almost over for you," said Mr. Simmons, predictably. "Time to find work, a good job, a wife, get into a firm that'll look after you."

"No, Mr. Simmons, my whole life is going to be a holiday. The world is a huge playground and I intend to have lots of fun. But I'm not staying in America when I want to be in Portugal, or be a computer programmer or an urban planner or a chartered accountant, when I want to be a goddam actor and nothing else, if you don't goddam mind. I'm not even getting married to someone unless I'm goddam crazy about her, and even then I'd rather not. I'd rather just live with her because I've always felt that the institution of marriage is stupid and useless."

At this point in my monologue, I turned toward the window and was struck by a sight that made me gasp with fright. Mr. Baldwin was on the roof of the house, still wearing the suit from the funeral, and a baseball cap with a Sears Automotive insignia on the front, digging the leaves out of the gutter with a hand spade. The task commanded his total concentration. I was afraid he would fall, afraid of the sound of the drop, of him hitting the ground. I knew the horror of that sound. I turned to Mr. Simmons, who had been joined by Elizabeth's cousin, alias Porky. Porky was ravenously stuffing his face with Ajax-flavored lasagna and listening to Mr. Simmons' lecture on the state of the economy. I rushed to the bathroom.

Locking the door, I pulled down my pants and opened my shirt. I stared at myself in fascination, studying my face, chest, hands, genitals. Everything was in working order; perfection, as a matter of fact. I had never looked better, sexier, more captivating.

"I know where you are, Elizabeth," I said loudly to my reflection. "I've found you. You're with me, inside me, seeing what I see. I need you here, your presence, your guidance."

I wrapped my fist around my penis and pumped. My penis was hard as iron, purply red, gorged with blood. I steadied myself with one hand on the counter and bent my knees. I squeezed and pounded until sperm flew in every direction, landing in puddles on the counter, splattering against the mirror. I was still as hard as ever. I wanted to do it a second time, but I heard shuffling noises outside the washroom door. I pulled my underwear over my erection and cleaned up with Kleenex, flushing the evidence down the toilet. I threw open the door to discover one of the blonde girls waiting to get in, the one getting married to the nice guy, her brother's friend.

"I heard you talking to yourself, making noises," she said. "What were you saying?"

"I was reciting a love poem," I said.

12. The Sex King

"Would you like to make love?"

"No thanks," I sighed, sinking comfortably into a billowing easy chair. "I'm a bit tired tonight."

Heather smiled at me slyly and swaggered up the stairs, wiggling her hips flirtatiously. I followed.

"I'll have to get a condom out of my knapsack," I yelled after her. I carried a supply of condoms on my person at all times, equipped for bizarre and unexpected liaisons with a wide variety of women.

"Get six!" rang Heather's voice lustily from the bedroom.

Heather pulled the sheet up to her chin, watching me as I undressed, and placed a towel over the lamp-shade to give the bedroom a more romantic combination of light and darkness. I enjoyed roaming around naked in front of a woman. My penis pointed straight out like a diving board. Her eyes were on me fixedly, sensually, which made me tingle inside with a graceful, erotic kind of energy. Heather giggled as I fluttered and pirouetted across the room like a ballerina, pointing my toes and leaping into the air. I was on stage which was where I belonged.

A long, cold, frostbitten winter had passed since the funeral. Although there were no permanent changes in my physiology, there were transitory changes in the way I presented myself. I now wore a thick, dark beard, which was thicker and darker than the hair on my head. My idol was D. H. Lawrence, The Priest of Love, and I emulated his hairy face and passionate glare. Now, summer was here. It was too hot for a beard; but I hadn't found a clean-shaven hero. My chest was wrapped in a bandage protecting three cracked ribs. I told Heather that I was attacked by a bear, but she countered with stubborn disbelieving logic. She asked when, where, how, and I was too slow with answers. I told her I had sex with a bear. She relented, respecting my privacy, worried that perhaps I was telling the truth.

"The most important thing in life is crawling into bed with someone you love and screwing your brains out," I said philosophically.

I stood by the window, permitting Heather a view of my profile, and stared at the moon. The moon was isolated and lonely, looking down upon a billion Ken Harrisons, watching a billion men make love to a billion women. I wondered how many men like me were making love to women like Heather. Too many. My life, family, friends, enemies, everyone I had ever talked to or touched, were as insignificant as a turd. Why did I feel so good, so free? Probably because I was about to get laid.

"The most important thing in life is the expression of love," I said.

"You don't love me," she said.

"I can love you for being a human being like me, for being lonely like me, for being horny like me."

"You like to love all different kinds of women. You've got a sweet tooth."

"I've got a horny tooth."

I lay gingerly beside her under the sheet, feeling my penis grow and harden. Because of my sore ribs, I remained on my back and waited for Heather to come to me. The anticipation of sex is a delectable preoccupation, worth prolonging to unbearable limits. My erection soared into the night like a pearly white spotlight, an enduring phosphorescent glow emanating from the center of my body, casting the town of Stockton in a spiritual illumination. I enjoyed being hard, the cool sheets on my bare bum, squirming like a baby. Heather approached me with suspenseful hesitancy. I waited for her touch, the sensation of her prickly fingers on my penis. She hovered above me, poised, slowly bobbing up and down, teasing us both, and finally easing down on me. My eyeballs spun in their sockets like the wheels of a slot machine.

"I'll be careful not to hurt your ribs," she promised.

"Don't worry about it," I said in a hushed panic.

Black hair poured down one side of her head reaching the pillow. She had a dark beauty which was uniquely her own and a glossy look in her eye when she made love. I needed physical contact with another person, to touch another human being, contact with something that had blood pumping through its veins. That was what sex meant to me. I told her that with my eyes. I didn't move a muscle. Heather did the moving. I concentrated on sustaining the state of elevated sensitivity, walking precariously along the edge without falling over. I stopped her and pulled out, had half an orgasm, and went back in again, more sure of my capacity to make it last. As the tension in her body mounted, I increased the harshness of my movement; we exploded together, grinding out the final sensations.

We kissed and hugged quietly, careful not to put too much pressure on my rib cage, until Heather was suddenly asleep in my arms. I had to urinate and managed to slip away without waking her up, but her roommate was using the bathroom. I was sleepy and returned to bed without emptying my bladder. Heather had complained bitterly about her roommate occupying the bathroom for unnaturally long periods of time, marathon showers, workouts with her long thick-handled electric toothbrush. There are only so many things you can do with one of those electric toothbrushes. I had marvelously sordid fantasies about her in the washroom with that toothbrush plugged in and humming.

Heather and I were at a tenuous stage in the dating cycle. After having slept together three times, it was almost time for a decision to be made, for the relationship to become more serious, or be abruptly extinguished. Or, an arrangement could be made to be friends, and only sleep together occasionally, which was what usually happened to such relationships until one or the other of us found someone else. We had to define things, the way we felt, predict the future, make forecasts. The pressure was there for both of us whether the question was raised or not. We had to know for ourselves. I loved her and wanted her forever. She was beautiful.

My mind, unclouded by sleep, dallied over events of the summer.

"I've got no money, but I'm incredibly virile," I said with a hint of a smile, leaning on the bar at Ring Stadium. I had an expression of self-assured humor on my bearded face which women found especially irresistible.

Smiling across from me was a redheaded girl with milky white skin and pretty features. I wasn't strictly and narrowly a brunette man, although I had a history of primarily brunette girlfriends. I was liberated, open minded, and interested in women of every shade and hair color. There was a softness about the redhead, a frailty that made my heart bloat up like a helium balloon and float into the clouds. I had a kingdom of love to give her. I wanted to give her the world, not to mention my heart, my soul, and my money. I wanted nothing in return, not love, not support, not sex. I was possessed by a vast, abstract kind of love burning inside me like indigestion. I needed to bleed my heart like a radiator. I needed to loosen the valve and release a little pressure.

"Did you know that most nymphomaniacs have red hair?" I said happily, trying to make her laugh again. She had an uncontrollable, high-pitched laugh which was spontaneous, awkward, and very attractive.

"Brag some more," she chided warmly, "I like hearing you brag. Tell me how great you are."

"I haven't exactly experienced greatness yet, but I fully intend to one day. I was never a great hockey player, not big-league calibre, although I don't hesitate to say I was good. I love music, rhythm and blues, rock, jazz, folk, but I'm no musician. I'm probably the most tone-deaf person who ever existed. I like art, and have good ideas, but I've got retarded fingers and could never paint or draw the images that flash through my mind. I'm certainly not a great student. I'm not even good, just average. I could be a great actor one day, but I recognize the risk in that. It's possible that I'll never be better than good, which will be something I'll have to live with. I do have something that's growing inside me, something that's definitely great, that's creative, powerful, and sane. It's a capacity to generate love. Love oozes out of every pore in my body. Does that sound hysterical?"

I continued with churlish conceit. "The woman who gets me will be one lucky girl to have all that passion to herself. She wouldn't know what to do with all of it. She would probably take advantage of it, squander it, not appreciate its greatness until she lost it. My love explodes through the boundary of womankind and embraces all humanity. I'll look across the bar and see some guy with a moustache and a hairy chest and enough gold chains around his neck to sink a battleship, and I'll be overcome by an incredible feeling of love for him. I'm not gay. It's got nothing to do with sex. I just see how hard he tries. I see something pure and human and vulnerable in him, even though I'd probably think he was a jerk if I knew him personally. I feel that my love is contagious. I feel I can fill up Ring Stadium, Stockton, the universe, with my love. I have enough love for everyone, and it's my duty to spread the wealth around."

"It's true," said Henry Kissing-Balls, verifying my speech with an absolutely solemn expression which produced a comic effect. I hadn't realized that Henry was standing behind me. "He loves everyone," emphasized Henry.

A lot of women wanted to be Henry's friend because it was fashionable and chic for a women to have a homosexual male friend, someone to escort her to bars, to run to if she's being bothered by a guy she doesn't like. Henry was confronting these women one by one and trying to seduce them. Henry and Chris had a lovers' spat, something to do with spending time with me, and Henry decided to take the heterosexual route. If he had to endure the petty quarrels of a monogamous relationship, he might as well do it with a woman. At least you don't feel inclined to sneak around when you're involved with a member of the opposite sex.

"I didn't have a single beer today, so I can get drunk tonight," Henry joked. He was concerned about becoming a first degree alcoholic.

"I didn't drink last Tuesday. It's Friday, so it's still all right for me to get drunk tonight too," I said. "I'm a firm believer that you should stay sober one night a week."

There was an awkward silence in which it was apparent that he wanted to ask me something. "Can I talk to you privately?" said Henry.

"She's one of us," I said. "She can keep a secret." I turned to the redhead. "Henry loves secrets."

Henry looked around shyly, nervous about being overheard.

"This girl and I are going to have wild sex. Do you have any of those things?"

"What things?" I asked.

"You know!"

"Condoms?"

"Right."

"How many?" I had a supply of condoms in my knapsack.

"Two," said Henry quickly. He knew exactly how many he needed.

"I may be needing some myself tonight," I said, glancing furtively at the redhead.

The redhead bought the next round of beer which was a good sign. It meant I wasn't boring her with my relentless and impassioned prattle. I had come out of a silent stage where I was breathing in and had moved into a talking stage where I was breathing out. I couldn't shut up. I enjoyed hearing my own voice. I fascinated myself. She found me amusing too, an off-beat artsie, an adventurous, irreverent, lecherous drama student. Drama students were known to be erratic, promiscuous, and sexually unconventional. The average drama student was in love with five women and three men at once and sleeping with most of them.

She was marriage-oriented. Her ambitions were humble; find a reliable income and a reliable husband. She wanted to be surrounded by a family which she could love and support. She had no desire to lead revolutions, climb mountains, to take the art world by storm. I was far too egotistical to be a reliable husband with a reliable income. I needed a woman as strong and egotistical as myself, like the women I was brought up with. My mother and sisters weren't exactly helpless cupcakes. I longed for a relationship with double power, two energy forces working together.

"The waitresses call you the Sex King," she said.

"Come with me to the enchanted Sex Palace," I answered.

We left Ring Stadium holding hands. Holding hands! What a luxury! I had forgotten how to hold hands. I knew how to have oral sex, anal sex, and sex missionary style. I even knew what to do with two women in my bed at once. But I hadn't held a woman's hand for a thousand years, and it was the most inspiring, sensual, emotionally rejuvenating thing I had ever experienced. It made me feel like barking, which I did. Chuck's dog responded enthusiastically as we passed his door.

"I'm so good-looking without a beard that I intimidate women," I explained to a curly-haired blonde sitting at an easel. I posed naked on a double bed. "A beard tones down my striking good looks and makes me more approachable."

"An interesting theory," said the curly-haired blonde. She was sketching me vigorously, ferociously, as if I was about to get up and run away before she finished. Male models were difficult to come by, especially ones that gave such a specialized service as myself. Her hands were covered with charcoal.

I got off the bed and walked behind her. She didn't stop sketching or break her concentration until I had studied the drawing a few minutes. She was shading, giving me depth, playing with my expression. It wasn't bad, but it lacked humanness. It looked like a caricature of a murderer or a rapist. She was more adept at drawing women. She drew women with a poetic compassion, probably because she was more familiar with the female body and had worked more with female models.

"You drew my penis too small." I reached down her top and lightly caressed her breast. My penis swelled. "Look! That's its real size."

"It's an imaginative interpretation of reality," she said.

"Next time, imagine it bigger, not smaller. I'm going to have to eat more bananas. They cause your penis to enlarge."

"Where do you get these theories?" she asked.

"I don't know if I read them somewhere or if I make them up. I think my mother told me that one."

"I prefer to draw a woman's body," she said. "Don't be offended. You've got an excellent build for a man, muscular and trim, but I find a woman's body flows easier. The lines are subtle and gentle. Artistically speaking, women have superior bodies."

"You just haven't got the feel of the male body yet," I said. "The physique of a man is easily as beautiful as a woman's. Think of Michelangelo's 'David,' the ripples of muscle on the stomach, the fullness of the chest, arms, and legs, but nothing that's crudely bulky. Your drawing has technical accuracy, but you don't capture the spirit of me because there's no imagination in it. I look stilted, oppressive, cruel. You have to learn to be me, a man, and love me, before you can project me onto a sketch pad or a canvas. It'll make you a better artist and a better lover."

"I'll try," she said suggestively, clutching my testicles with a charcoal-covered hand. She unbuttoned her top with her other hand.

"Leave your clothes on," I said, doing up her buttons again. "Stay dressed and I'll stay naked. Be conscious of my body only. Make your breast disappear, grow a penis and testicles. Become me."

"How?" she said.

"It's an imaginative interpretation of reality," I said. "Think penis. Meditate on the word. Repeat it in your mind, over and over again. Penis, penis, penis."

Sitting at her easel, she was at the perfect height to take me into her mouth. Her head bobbed up and down with an unbroken, fluid rhythm. Her concentration was focused on the mantra. She was trying to become a towering, quivering erection. Usually she sucked with such force it felt like she was going to bite off my knob, chew it, and spit it out. This time I didn't have to pull away in pain. Yet she wasn't afraid to make her presence felt. She knew what I wanted. How I wanted it. Where I wanted it. Why I wanted it. It was an invasion of my senses, my consciousness, and I surrendered to it with relish. I was drunk with sensitivity. I was her mouth, erect nipples, a swelling wet crotch. We were conscious of each other's body, of our own body, of a burning sensation inside, of everything burning and rising inside.

She swallowed my sperm, but there was that bit which spilled out the corner of her mouth and rolled down her chin. I pulled her up and kissed her. She was as supple as butter. I was still hard. Her clothes slid off and dropped to her ankles. We shuffled to the bed.

The second course of sex was consumed with the appetite of a connoisseur, not in the brutish rush of a starved glutton. I was on my back, on my side, on my front, on my knees. Afterwards, sleep hit me like a huge army of ants, picking me up, distributing my weight, and carrying me away. I awoke briefly to discover the naked, curly-haired blonde sketching at the easel. The movement of her hand was not agitated or convulsive, but smooth and graceful. She was an out-of-the-ordinary kind of person, with an out-of-the-ordinary kind of beauty. I was deeply in love with everything about her. The veil dropped, the haze returned, and I drifted back to sleep.

"It's been a drag the last fifteen years, all this anger and hatred between men and women," I said to my professor of Women in Literature who had wavy brown hair and stood at the front of the class. Despite her athletic figure and large shoulders, she had an attractive, feminine appearance. "You don't have to tell me it was necessary. I know that. But it's not necessary any more. It's time men and women started loving each other again. I'm ready."

I sat in a sea of women, blissfully contented, my heart pumping happily. I felt confident and generous and charming and witty. Women gave me energy, brought me to life. I glowed. There were five males in the class of thirty. They came and went in a small flock, like a clump of grapes, nervous and uncomfortable. I frolicked with the women like a puppy dog on a spring day.

(After class the girls and I liked to meet at the Artsie Fartsie to gossip and drink tea. There were usually about eight women, and I positioned myself as close to the center as possible, and we would have a merry gab. Gossip is a weakness of mine. I never tire of hearing about who is sleeping with whom, and who is breaking up with whom, and who is cheating on whom. I could discuss sex and relationships for hours. The conversation inevitably ascended to a higher, intellectual level and inevitably descended again to a superficial gossipy level. It was an ungodly mistake to interfere with the natural flow. It was best to enjoy the ride.)

"This whole Margaret Atwood thing is getting a bit boring," I said authoritatively, unable to resist an audience or an opportunity to open my mouth. "She hates men, hates women, hates fuckin' pig Americans. Hate! Hate! Hate! Let's sit around and have a good hate. She's supposed to be profound because she perceives that life is empty and meaningless, and if you want to be profound too, you have to perceive the same thing. Then we can sit around and hate some more and feel smug and superior and laugh at the rotten unintellectual slobs who can't see that life is a waste of time. If you say that life's meaningless in your first book, why write the second one? So you can say the same thing? Can anyone deny that a positive loving force exists in people? Life's only meaningless if you're incapable of love, and someone who's incapable of love can't grow as an artist. Love is the source of an artist. An artist must be able to project love onto the world. It was Dostoevski who said that hell is the suffering of being unable to love."

"I like Margaret Atwood," said my curly-haired professor. "She expresses a phase in the development of women. She says a lot of things that a lot of women have been dying to say for a long time. You do tend to get an empty feeling at the end of her books, but some of her stuff is more cynical than others. What books of hers have you read?"

"None, to tell you the truth," I said. The class laughed. "I read the first thirty pages of one of her books, but I forget which one. I have my most refreshing insights in a state of complete ignorance. I have lots of passionate theories on things I know absolutely nothing about. Information and facts cloud my intuition."

The class was familiar with my unfounded opinions and theories on literature. They didn't take them too seriously because it was obvious that I didn't mean them too seriously. I dropped opinions as fast as I picked them up and had no qualms about making glaring contradictions from one day to the next. I was an actor, not a politician or a fastidious academic. I had opinions for the sake of drama, to be amusing or to shock. The professor appreciated my presence. My wild, flamboyant generalizations were sure to provoke heated class discussion. I had been exposed as a literary charlatan once before. I was in the middle of a sophisticated tirade about Dostoevski, proclaiming him to be the greatest writer who ever existed. Eventually it came out that the only thing of his I had read was a novella, *The Double*, back in my freshman year.

"It's a vicarious release for me," said one tiny, soft-spoken girl. "I purge my frustrations through Margaret Atwood. I feel wonderful afterwards."

"Margaret Atwood is old already," I said. "And an artist isn't allowed to get old. It's not the seventies anymore. The seventies were a long time ago. I have a premonition that we're coming into the greatest decade of the century. Men and women are going to start getting together in the nineties, start understanding each other for the first time. It'll be more exciting and more mature than the sixties. John Lennon was really a nineties man, and he died on the cross for sanity between the sexes. *The World According to Garp*, a novel by John Irving, is another harbinger of the nineties. They represent a new, positive force which is getting stronger and about to burst into prominence. When that happens, Margaret Atwood will be an anachronism."

Although there were many Atwood supporters, everyone was enthusiastic about my optimistic prediction of the future. The majority of the class knew me from the Artsie Fartsie and had talked to me privately. They were willing to enjoy my ideas without casting themselves in the role of enemy or friend. They weren't threatened by the bombastic presentation of my opinions. The professor flung back her wavy brown hair and smiled at me. I smiled back.

"I've never had an orgasm," said my professor as she lay down on the rug of her office floor. Behind her head was a vast bookshelf, overstocked to the ceiling with cumbersome leather and hardbound books, shoved in at every angle. The curtains were closed, and the office had the perfect mixture of light and darkness.

"It doesn't matter," I reassured her. "You don't get a medal for having an orgasm."

There were two irate young men waiting impatiently outside the locked door of the office. They wanted to complain about bad marks they had received in Women in Literature, convinced that the professor had a prejudice against them because they were men. From my perspective, it was an unfounded accusation.

There was something exciting about making love in an office on the fourth floor, in the middle of the English department, with students waiting in the hall. She kept warning me to be quiet until I had penetrated her, and then I was warning her to be quiet. She coaxed me to go faster and harder. Her dress was pushed over her breasts and her panties circled one ankle. The frantic movement caused her head to thump against the bookshelf. I was worried that she would hurt her head and tried to get her to move away, but she wouldn't budge. She had a powerful grip. She squeezed her arms around me and insisted that I do it harder and faster.

The thumping of her head was causing the whole bookshelf to waver and books began to shower down like a monsoon rainstorm. They bounced off my bare ass, hit the back of my legs, slammed to the floor beside my head. I was locked in her iron clasp, an unyielding bearhug. Books sailed through the air like the debris of a tornado. She jerked suddenly with a mighty force. There was a crack. I screamed. Chaucer's *Canterbury Tales* lay broken and exposed beside me. The bookshelf crashed above us. Stopped by the desk which prevented us from getting squashed.

"I came!" whispered my professor to me in the back seat of the car as the two guys who were in the hallway drove us to the hospital. I had waited until we were both fully clothed before crawling through the wreckage and under the bookshelf and unlocking the office door.

"You sure love sex," I whispered.

"It's the greatest," she said. "Except maybe for food."

"Ya," I said, without taking offense. "Food's pretty good too."

She had a minor concussion.

I was treated for three cracked ribs.

"I've had a broken heart, a broken ego, and three cracked ribs, and I still think the world is a great place to hang out," I said to Barb who sat across from me at the Artsie Fartsie. "I provide a stud service for lonely women as my contribution to the human race."

"What about yourself? Don't you get lonely?" asked Barb.

"I'm a little in love with loneliness. Loneliness can be a real bitch, but she has a definite sexual appeal. She has wonderful breasts and long shapely legs that wrap around you."

"Where is she now?"

"She's inside me. She's the woman inside. She's not my enemy anymore. We work as a team. She helps me with women, guides me."

"What's her name, this woman inside you?"

"I don't know . . ."

"Bullshit!" said Barb. "You know her name. It's Elizabeth Baldwin."

I couldn't help smiling. "You remind me more of my mother every day." I learned forward. "Can you deny that Elizabeth is guiding me, teaching me? My life has gone straight up since the day she died. Things couldn't be better for me. It's not luck. It's Elizabeth helping me. Yes, she's the woman inside me."

"It's not love you feel for these women you run around with," said Barb. "At least it's not all love. It's love mixed with guilt. It's the guilt you feel about Elizabeth. You've projected that guilt on all women. You're exorcising your personal feelings of guilt on womankind. Nothing was your fault. Things just happened. You don't have to feel guilty."

"We have a debt to pay," I said. "Men, I mean. Do you want to know a horrible secret? I'm glad Elizabeth is dead. I'm glad because I know no one else can have her. I couldn't stand the thought of someone else having her. In a way, she's all mine. I never had her to myself when she was alive."

I awoke with a swollen bladder. I could have pissed out my ears like a lawn sprinkler. I could have submerged the town of Stockton in a polluted sea of urine. Pressure! I could explode. 8:00 a.m., said the digital clock, which was unusually early for me. I moved with painful slowness to the bathroom. There was the sound of an electric toothbrush. The door was locked. When I returned to the bedroom, I noticed the smell of smoke. A hole was burnt through the towel over the lampshade. The light had been left on. I turned it off, kissed Heather on the temple, between the eyes, on the end of her nose, and left. I peed against a tree on the way home.

"If I can't have eternal love," I decided aloud as I relieved myself with immense pleasure, "I'll settle for a few good years. If I can't have a few good years, I'll settle for a good night, a few good hours, a good ten minutes."

13. Inside a Jar of Peanut Butter

I studied my bowl of Alphabits Cereal and spelt obscene words on my spoon like "shit" and "fuck." "Cocksucker" was more challenging. It required three c's and two k's. I finally had to nibble a b into the second k. The Artsie Fartsie was where I ate breakfast, lunch, and dinner and had numerous coffee breaks in between. It was my surrogate womb, a place where I was well-known and well-liked, where I could be myself and feel secure. The old ladies who worked there had taken a motherly shine to me, old ladies often take a motherly shine to a golden boy, and regularly quizzed me on my diet, bullying me into eating something more healthy. My popularity with the opposite sex was a great source of delight for the old ladies and when I came in with a new girl they whispered and giggled among themselves, greeting her with huge smiles. They perpetually warned me not to get a girl pregnant because she would manipulate me into marrying her. My mother had given me the same advice since I was nine years old. I showed them my knapsack full of condoms and they roared with laughter. They looked after me, and if I was short of money, they gave me meals on credit.

Heather arranged to meet me for a coffee. I arrived early, feeling anxious and fidgety because I always felt anxious and fidgety about a woman I had slept with more than three times. I got this paranoid feeling that I was her boyfriend and she was my girlfriend. That was what I thought I wanted, but when things began to move in that direction, I felt an urgent need to hide in the nearest closet or submerge myself in a body of water with a snorkel, where no one could shatter my privacy. I considered wearing dark sunglasses so I could see her and she couldn't see me, but there was something immoral about that.

"You smell nice," she said to me once, after having sex, which was a sure sign she was falling in love. It's always the smell you fall in love with first, and that stays with you the longest.

I loved Heather, or at least something moved inside me periodically when we were together, especially when we were together in bed. But it certainly wasn't a monogamous kind of love. It wasn't the kind of love that could grow into something exclusive, unique, and romantically self-contained. It was the love I felt for many women. What was the magic ingredient that made me feel a psychic attraction to one woman over all others? Why could one woman cause me to be consumed by an eternal fire and another woman, equally attractive and suitable, only spur my emotions momentarily? What did that special woman have that I needed so passionately? What was it that touched my heart? Silly things! The way she brushed her teeth using a toothbrush with flattened bristles or how she looked when she was naked and blow-drying her hair after a shower or the way she pronounced my name. I could feel it if I overheard her use my name in a conversation with her friend or if someone said something nasty to me at a party and she defended me. I loved that kind of woman.

I looked down at my bowl of Alphabits. The word I had spelt on my spoon was "Elizabeth." I swallowed it.

Henry Kissing-Balls landed in the seat across from me with a tray-load of food. For breakfast he was having a hamburger, french fries with gravy, a coke and a chocolate donut for dessert. He looked disheveled and worn, a couple of pimples breaking out around his mouth.

"That's disgusting!" I said, referring to his meal.

"What?" asked Henry innocently.

"How can you eat that crap for breakfast?" I said with paternal indignation. "You have the unhealthiest diet of anyone I've ever seen. It's amazing you're still alive."

"This stuff is good for you," claimed Henry firmly. He stuck his fork into a few french fries and dipped them into a puddle of grease, gravy, and ketchup.

Henry caused my motherly instincts to surface. I nagged him to eat properly and to get enough sleep. He was a helpless child without me. Philosophy majors lack a practical understanding of survival and of pleasurable living. You have to tell them everything. While their minds busily attempt to comprehend the universe, you have to remind them to wear a sweater when it's cold, eat when they're hungry, sleep when they're tired. Otherwise the philosopher gets mixed up. He'll wear a sweater when he's hungry and eat when he's tired. I lectured Henry to get sun on his face. The sun would inject vitamin D into his system and clear up the pimples forming near his mouth. Henry was trying to stop overworking his brain and let the other parts of his character catch up. He needed to return to earth and be with people again after drifting alone in the cosmos for so many years. He needed to develop an awareness of his senses, a sensitivity to the physical world.

"Two condoms weren't enough," said Henry boastfully. He couldn't wait to tell me.

"Congratulations, you big hunk of bisexual, you," I said. "At least you know you can still do it with a woman. Have you told Chris? He'll probably blame me. I actually do deserve some of the credit. I've given you moral support."

"When we got into that bed, it was just me and her. No one else was around to help me. I rose to the occasion, and not once, not twice, but three times although I couldn't do it the third time because I had no condoms left."

"Don't let it go to your head and start acting tough. You haven't set any world records yet."

"Are you still assembling the largest harem in North America?" asked Henry.

"I'm trying to cut down. . .but Rome wasn't built in a day."

The cereal didn't curb my appetite. Henry was fishing through the gravy for the last few french fries. He dunked his hamburger in the gravy. There was enough grease on his plate to make Stockton the lube job capital of the world. My skin felt slimy just looking at it. I envisioned Henry's face sprouting pimples like dandelions.

"Mmmm! Delicious!" exclaimed Henry, sipping his coke and moving on to the donut for dessert.

"You're making me sick," I muttered, unable to suppress my motherly instincts. I couldn't leave the subject alone. "That meal's as fattening as hell."

"That feels much better," said Henry, ignoring me and holding his stomach. "It finally came to me last night, after sex, that first line of poetry. Only it wasn't a poem. It came as the first line of a novel, a poetic novel."

"What's the line?"

"You won't understand it yet."

"Tell me anyway."

"The first line is, 'I like to be a little person, unable to affect people.' "

"What's the novel going to be about?" I asked. He was right. I didn't understand.

"It's about being young, virile, and sexually frustrated."

"Sounds good," I said. I could understand that!

"That first line," said Henry with a strange confidence which I had never seen in him before, "is a kernel of wisdom that will flower into great social change. My brain is teeming with thoughts. I have this character inside my head. That first line captures his spirit. Everything about him, what he will go through, how he will change, is consistent with that first line, that first line of poetry."

Henry stared at me forcefully, burped forcefully, farted forcefully, and left the table laughing forcefully.

"You're a pig," I said forcefully, pushing his greasy tray to the next table. The truth was that I liked it when Henry farted. When other people farted, I found it offensive and juvenile. When Henry farted it was funny. He wasn't the kind of guy you expected to fart.

"I'm going to put some good farting scenes in my book," said Henry gleefully, waving good-bye and bobbing brilliantly. "I like a book with good farting scenes."

The Artsie Fartsie was an informal atmosphere, to say the least, and when the old ladies were busy, I was allowed to wander behind the counter and make myself something to eat. It was a privilege granted solely to the regulars. I preferred to make my own peanut butter sandwiches because no one else spread on quite enough peanut butter. I liked a generous serving of peanut butter.

When I lifted the top and peered into the jar, however, I was stung by such a scary sensation that my breathing stopped, and I wasn't capable of moving a single part of my body. It was a flash of déjà vu, and I was frozen to the spot. My life was condensed into one moment, past and present fused, and I fell into a pit of timelessness. Inside the jar of peanut butter, shaped unwittingly by past peanut butter users, was an exact replica of the Barren Room.

My head whirled, I swayed dizzily and had to cling to the counter. I felt like I was toppling over and over again like a barrel rolling down a hill, bouncing unevenly at first and gradually gaining momentum. I caught glimpses of things above and below me, a tottering ceiling tile, a dirty piece of paper stuck to the linoleum floor, a stain on the counter.

In my mind, I rolled head over heels off the counter and onto the floor. I was rolling and rolling and rolling, rolling in the Barren Room. I struggled to remember if I had been drinking, if I was drunk, if it was night and I was at a bar, my head spinning from beer. I couldn't remember drinking. I remembered nothing. It came to me, suddenly, in a frightening wave, that I had to stop rolling or I would die. The forward roll perpetuated itself like a metronome on top of a piano. If I allowed it, it would take me to a place from which I could never return. I concentrated on arresting the movement, pulling out of the spin. My early attempts were ineffectual. My head slowed down and finally stopped. I returned the lid to the peanut butter jar without making my sandwich.

I sat in my seat with cup of tea, trembling, immensely relieved, appreciative of my sanity and my self-control. My time of privacy and solace was brief. Heather took the seat in front of me.

She looked exceptionally sexy with dark hair and dark eyes and clearly erect dark nipples pressed against a white blouse. She wasn't wearing a bra. I wanted to touch her little breasts with the big dark nipples. My mind clouded and my eyes fogged. Inside my pants, I was thick and hard. I wanted to drag her into the bushes behind the Artsie Fartsie and make love against a tree. I struggled not to think of her crotch. If I let myself think of her crotch, it would be all over. Heather sat up and kissed me and sat back in her chair.

"Heather, we're finished," I said softly, almost crying myself. I couldn't think of a more tactful way of putting it. Our relationship is on the roof, I thought of saying. It would have been an inappropriate time for a joke.

It took a few seconds for the statement to sink in. I read her face. Her eyes looked hurt and moist, but she didn't cry or get hysterical. We hadn't known each other long enough to justify a tearful scene. I could have hung around a few years, played the role of boyfriend, benefited from that juice a man gets from a woman, but I couldn't give her the kind of love she wanted, the kind she deserved. Staying with her would have been an act of cynicism. It would have been cowardly and corrupt.

"Why?" she asked. The question was as inevitable as death.

"Because I'm in love with someone else."

"Who?" her voice cracked. I wished I could make her happy and feeling good about herself. I wished I could make everyone happy and feeling good about themselves. I was having a hard enough time making me happy and feeling good about myself."

"Elizabeth," I said.

"She's dead," exclaimed Heather tactlessly.

"Not in my mind. In my mind she's alive and with me every day. Whenever I sleep alone, I sleep with her. Whenever I beat off—I still beat off an awful lot, by the way, especially during exams for some reason or after a day in the library—in my mind, I'm making love to Elizabeth. Sometimes I bump into a girl in an elevator or sit beside a girl in class and she smells like Elizabeth. The smell burns into me. The smell hurts. I'll see a girl with a long mane of wavy hair like Elizabeth's hair, and it takes all my will power not to stick my face in it, or at least play with it with my hand. Once I actually did it. This girl was sitting in front of me on the bus. I grabbed a handful of her hair and stuck my face into it. She got angry and threatened to get the bus driver and call the police. I pretended I was retarded; retarded people do that type of thing. It was a great acting job. I told her that if she called the bus driver, I'd shit in the aisle. She felt sorry for me and only made me promise not to do it any more. I met her later at Ring Stadium and we ended up getting along very. . ."

"I thought you were over Elizabeth," interrupted Heather, her anger visibly rising. "You acted so cheerful and optimistic. What was I to you? You've been living out a fantasy about your old girlfriend through me. I've been used as a watered-down substitute for Elizabeth."

"Not at all," I said. I hoped my voice sounded comforting. "You were a very good substitute."

That was the wrong thing to say. She got even angrier. She said, "The only *good* thing about our relationship was fucking." She was trying to sting me back.

"At least that was good," I said.

"Elizabeth's been dead for almost a year."

"That's not a very long time," I said. "I do feel something for you. I'm not fantasizing about Elizabeth while I'm making love to you. When I'm with you, I'm with you, mostly. It's when I'm alone that I'm with Elizabeth, that I feel her presence."

"You don't look miserable and heartbroken to me."

"I'm happy," I said."Elizabeth doesn't interfere with that. She's not on my mind so much as she's in my mind. I'm not usually conscious of her, but she's there, inside me, dominating my dreams at night. We occupy the same body."

"I feel sorry for you," she said, at a time when I was busy feeling sorry for her. "Why is it I meet nothing but fucked up men? Maybe all men are fucked up."

"It could be," I said. I didn't really believe that, but I was doing my best to make her feel better. I believed that men and women were equally fucked up.

"I read in the paper," continued Heather, "that a man in Stockton is grabbing five-year-old girls off the street in broad daylight and raping them. That makes me want to throw up."

"I didn't do it," I said.

"I know," laughed Heather scornfully. "You're a necrophiliac."

"I dwell a bit on the past. That doesn't make me a necrophiliac."

Heather was the first bridge I burned. I had a lot of burning left to do. I had to be there one hundred percent, one hundred percent aware, one hundred percent tuned into a woman, or I didn't want to be there at all, at least not for more than two or three nights. I couldn't be half or three-quarters or nine-tenths in love. It was everything or nothing, or almost nothing, maybe a little sex now and then. It wasn't that I expected serenity from a relationship. I was open for disputes, but I had to be there, right with her, all of me, one hundred percent. It's that limbo area where you're with someone and yet somehow far away that creates dead people.

There's a lot of dead people walking around the street, numb to life, and that's the reason they're dead. They can't get close to anything.

Eventually, Heather's tone of voice softened. At last we made that resolve which everyone makes and almost no one keeps for any length of time when they break up. We promised to be friends. The only thing I wanted to do was get out of the Artsie Fartsie and be alone. I would have promised to be anything, friend, enemy, father, mother. I would have allowed her to give me a swift kick in the balls as penance if I was guaranteed she'd leave me alone afterwards.

It was a short walk from the Artsie Fartsie to the athletic center. The campus was crawling with rapists and child molesters, hiding in the shade of the trees, glaring malevolently out of shifty eyes. Every male I passed was a filthy pervert. I tried to imagine myself raping a five-year-old girl, her hairless little body, pigtails, tears streaming down her face, uncomprehending fear. It was a monstrous act. I could never perform such a heinous desecration. What if I was locked away in a library for a year, deprived of the God-given privilege of every free man to masturbate, forced to ferment in my lust by a cruel and sadistic torturer? What then? Could I be driven to it? Sanity has its limits.

The summer heat made my beard itchy. After dumping my knapsack in my locker in the athletic center, I took my leather kit bag and placed it on the sink. Timing was of the utmost importance. I glanced obsessively at the clock on the wall of the change room, disrobed, and stood naked in front of the mirror. The occasional naked stranger passed by dripping from the shower, too preoccupied with his own body to notice me. I removed the instruments of my symbolic rebirth from the kit bag, shaving cream and a razor blade.

"Off with the mask," I exclaimed to myself theatrically.

It was the unveiling of a masterpiece, a classical sculpture. My face was slowly exposed; shaving off a beard is a tedious process. I felt a slight prickle of enthusiasm, then a growing excitement, and finally an incredulity; surely I wasn't that good-looking. I had forgotten about the sensual dimple on the chin, the perfectly formed jaw, the finely chiseled features. Covering my face had been a criminal offense.

"I forgot how good-looking I am, but only briefly," I said to myself.

Time was running out. I dried myself and swung the towel around my neck. My face was bleeding in a couple of spots, and I dabbed on tiny squares of toilet paper. The toilet paper gave me character. White shorts, white socks, both freshly washed, and running shoes were added. The clock ticked. Classes ended in thirty seconds and I intended to be caught in the rush. I applied the baby oil, just the right amount to darken the skin. It made me glow without being obvious that I was wearing oil at all. I tied on my dirty red bandanna. The effect was sublime. I felt a surge of love for myself and my body exuded high-voltage energy.

I romped and frolicked happily through a crowd of students pouring out of the Landscape Architecture building. There was something sexually alluring about women who majored in Landscape Architecture. A pretty girl stepped in front of me. I bumped into her in a miraculously gentle manner, like a slow motion embrace, both of us tumbling painlessly to the sidewalk. I lifted her up and apologized profusely; she profusely reassured me it was all right. I made a great fuss as to whether I had hurt her, inspecting her knees and questioning her on the workableness of each body part. She promised that everything was in working order. I said that I believed her. She smiled. I smiled.

I continued my run, unable to shake the idiot grin off my face. It felt good to be a full-fledged golden boy again. I sprinted down a road that cut through the heart of the university. The sidewalks were flowing rivers of students. The wind filled my sails. There were jealous, adoring, and lustful eyes on me. It was impossible not to look at me, sailing down the middle of the street practically naked, surrounded by the mass movement of students. I loved being watched. Someone whistled at me. There was sprinkled giggling. I ran even faster and fought to suppress my grin.

I passed the University Center, turned onto a walkway, and headed in the direction of the Arts Building. I reached into my shorts, pulled on my knob, and adjusted my penis to face left. I hate the way a penis tends to shrivel during intense physical exertion. There was a stairway which was densely populated by leering and lascivious females, and I bounded up three steps at a time. My leg muscles strained and burned as I arched over the final steps. Beautiful women eyed me seductively, beautiful women with unattractive, dull-looking men.

This was one of my pet peeves. Why did so many enticing young women choose such uninteresting boyfriends when many of them could have someone like myself? It didn't make sense. I figured they had known each other since early childhood at a time when they had equal sex appeal, and the woman blossomed and the man didn't. The relationship was a bad habit, like thumb sucking. They stayed together because it was easy and safe.

I drifted off the campus and onto neighboring residential streets. It was boardinghouse land. Stockton families often rented a room to a student. I was sweating heavily. I stopped and hunched over to catch my breath, dizzy and exhausted. I always overdid it when I had an audience. A little girl skipped past me. I looked up. She was about five years old. I decided to walk for a short distance to regain my breath.

The little girl walked ten yards ahead of me. I kept pace with her. She marched along in her imaginary world, brown ringlets bouncing down her back, her feet slapping the pavement noisily. She was a miniature adult. It was difficult to believe someone that tiny was a real person. What was going on in her little brain? What would she grow up to be? Who would she grow up to love? I hoped she'd grow up to love someone like me.

That paternal urge rose inside me again, like a falcon spreading its wings and taking flight. I wanted to protect her from the roving bands of perverts and child molesters who stalked the streets. I wanted to prevent her from falling down, from falling off the roofs of apartment buildings. She turned randomly, left, left, right, right. It was getting dark. I followed her, afraid to leave her alone. She must have been lost.

I barked loudly, two or three times.

She stopped, turned around, barked back. I barked. She barked. We barked indiscriminately and emphatically; we barked at each other, at fate, at the absurdity of life.

"Hi," I called. "Where are you going?"

"Nowhere," she said. As I drew closer, I noticed dirty streaks down her face from crying. She had a pretty face, with a button nose. One of her running-shoe laces was undone, wrapping around her other foot occasionally and tripping her. She wore a tank top which was cute. She knew she was supposed to cover her tits, but her tits were non-existent.

"Just walkin'?"

"Ya."

"Me too," I said. I wondered why she didn't admit to being lost. I repeated, "Where are you going?"

"You already asked me that," she said. She was a smart little kid.

"Where do you live?"I said.

"Twenty-nine Elora Street." She was miles away from home and walking in the wrong direction.

"If I had a car I'd drive you home," I said.

"Why don't you drive me home anyway?"

"Because I don't have a car."

"Oh," she said and started to cry. She thought all big people had a car. I reached down and did up her shoelace, and she immediately calmed down.

"You're walking in the wrong direction," I said, taking her by the hand and turning her around. "I'll walk you home. You shouldn't be walking the streets when it's dark. And you shouldn't be talking to strangers."

She nodded. She could bark, cry, and feel bored within a span of five minutes.

As I walked down the street holding the little girl's hand, I started thinking about the soap Elizabeth gave me to use when I slept over at her house. It was called Pears soap, and it was almost clear enough to see through and had a different kind of smell. Pears soap became popular later, but no one had ever heard of it at the time. Elizabeth discovered it before anyone else. That was the type of woman Elizabeth was. She would be the first one to discover an interesting bar of soap. That was one of the reasons I fell in love with her. I needed to find another woman who could do that.

A few months later I had returned to Elizabeth's place for a night. I couldn't believe it, she gave me a different kind of soap to use in the shower. It was blue with dark blue stripes through it and a distinct smell of its own. She had done it again. I loved that smell. God, I loved her for that! I loved that soap because I had never seen or smelt it before. Elizabeth came up with these things out of nowhere. Anyone else would have had to spend half their life sniffing bars of soap in a drug store, but not Elizabeth. She wouldn't even say anything about it. She'd just give me this great bar of soap I had never seen before and not say a word.

"Shit," I exclaimed. Ahead of me, walking towards me, was Penny. I didn't want to face her, chat like old friends, pretend I liked her. I quickly pulled the little girl across someone's front yard and hid in a clump of bushes. I waited for Penny to pass.

"Come out of those bushes," shouted a deep male voice.

"Keep your filthy fuckin' hands off the kid," said another deep male voice from the opposite direction.

I looked out and saw two plain-clothes policemen, one on each side of the bushes, guns drawn and pointing at me. A fat woman was standing on the sidewalk. Three police cars squealed to a stop in front of the house. I was thrown against a tree and frisked, which didn't take long since I was only wearing a pair of shorts. Penny arrived on the scene. I didn't look at her. The little girl was scared by the police and crying.

"You idiots," I shouted at the police in exasperation. I finally looked at Penny. "You're a jerk and an asshole and you don't deserve to be alive," I said. I felt the whole problem was her fault.

They gave me the spiel that you hear on television, about having the right to remain silent, and pushed me into the police car.

"Is this when you take me to the station, put a paper bag over my head, and torture me?" I asked.

"You watch too many movies," said the police officer.

"I saw that weirdo barking at the girl," said the fat lady.

"You'd be attractive if you lost about two hundred and eighty pounds." I said to her sarcastically.

The interrogation lasted hours. They asked me a thousand questions and made me sign a thousand pieces of paper. They asked the same question four and five and six times. A doctor made me pull down my shorts and put a powder on my genitals. The powder proved I hadn't raped a little girl. In another room, they asked the little girl questions and investigated her genitals.

Heather was phoned. She told them I had no abnormal sexual quirks. Evidence mounted in my favor.

"You idiots," I said to the police, exasperated.

14. The Fringe

My home is a single room in the downtown core of a big city. The kitchen and bathroom are shared, but my little room is all mine. It's my kingdom, my creation, shaped to fit the curves of my personality like a finely tailored suit. Spanning one wall, in contrasting primary colors, is the word "arts." I stole the idea from the "Happy Anniversary" streamer Elizabeth made for her parents. The other three walls are hidden under a matted array of posters, paintings, and looming shelves of second-hand novels. Opening a new book is like breaking into a virgin. I prefer to read things that are sleazy, tattered, second-hand. I have collections of plays piled in a corner and propped along the windowsill.

I sleep on a futon because I like to be close to the ground. The futon is large, firm, and encourages deeper penetration during sexual intercourse. There are two framed self-portraits of Vincent Van Gogh and a life-sized poster of Marlon Brando in his prime. There's a desk and a comfortable chair for reading. There's a mountain of wax on a small table, different colored veins of wax solidified in abstract designs pouring over the edge of the table and down the legs. A half-melted candle is stuck into the top burning brightly, casting monstrous shadows across the room. There's one other item centrally located against the longest wall. It is a full-length mirror.

"I like to be a little person, unable to affect people," I say to the shadowy reflection of my naked body.

Although my hair is thin and getting thinner, my fear of going bald was slightly premature. No obvious signs of baldness are visible in the obscure lighting of my room. No evidence of physical deterioration mars my person. I have sexual magnetism and the talent to be a great actor. Modeling pays the rent. When I can't find work modeling, I pile boxes. A box moves down a conveyor belt, G-34 stamped on the side, and I put it in the G-34 pile. I work in a basement warehouse with artificial lighting and no windows. The ceiling is low and my head almost touches the long tubular lights. It makes me feel like a marijuana plant. I don't know what's in the boxes. I don't care. I meet interesting women in strange bars. I try to seduce them and often succeed. I look for acting jobs.

I've heard that clinging to a single dream for too long is a crime, and I believe it. The price tag is too high. There is room enough inside a person for many dreams. But Elizabeth holds onto something inside me, stubbornly, like a mule refusing to move. I've heard that you're supposed to face and define and resolve things that bother you, and I believe that too. I'm a great facer and definer and resolver, perhaps the best in the world, but the past still plagues me like the withdrawal symptoms of a drug addict. There is one thing that cheerful, smiling, middle-class couples refuse to admit. A dream doesn't just disappear, no matter how much facing and defining and resolving you do. One dream extinguishes another. One love extinguishes another. These couples don't want to believe that the hold they have on each other is so tenuous.

"Elizabeth is asleep in the closet!" I say to my reflection. "Don't disturb Elizabeth; she's sleeping in the closet."

When will my time of joy and liberation arrive? I'm capable of moments of soaring happiness and jubilation. Freedom will come to me. Freedom will come on a sunny day, on a boat in a vast body of water with a full wind in the sails and Tchaikovsky blaring from hidden speakers, echoing off the clouds. Freedom will come in a field of long grass as high as my shoulders. Freedom will come in the middle of the big city at a bar surrounded by warm people and loving music. Freedom will come in the form of a woman. It'll always involve other people. Independence is a myth created by little people who want to be big people. I don't believe in independence or God. I believe in little people. I enjoy my little moments. I don't intend to jump off the roof of an apartment building.

During my bouts of nostalgia, I often think of Phuc Wildfong. Phuc quit hockey the same time as me and teamed up with two of my sisters, Candy and June, in operating a home for rape victims and battered women. Phuc has a sincere sympathy for people who've been fucked and gang-banged by society. He's one of the few men in the business. I see my sister Ruth regularly, the tall one, closest to me in age who is sexually attracted to midgets. She tells me that Phuc mentions my name every time she sees him. Ruth lives with Angel Pie in the same neighborhood as Wendy, Mary, and May. Angel Pie is as short as ever. Phuc is as Oriental as ever. Ruth has taken to walking on stilts for a hobby. It was suggested to her as a joke by me. She takes the things I say too seriously.

"Orientals never lie," I say to myself. "And they have no fear of dying." I'm going to give Phuc Wildfong a phone call one of these days.

Bruno is the only player from the Dixie Queens who still plays hockey. He's a second-rate goon in the American League known only for his ability to butcher the opposition with his stick. Since I don't play hockey anymore, Bruno feels sorry for me. I feel sorry for him. If you're not a superstar, hockey is a lousy way of life. Bruno had one moment of greatness. He played one game in the NHL and got one shift. He was hired to break heads. He charged around the ice cross-checking players on the back of the neck. That's Bruno's specialty. He was called for a five-minute misconduct penalty and never got on the ice again. I watched the game at Ruth's place because I don't own a television. The camera flashed through the crowd looking for pretty girls, but for some reason stopped at pathetic old Winfield. They did a close-up of Winfield's fat head and bloated face.

"Winfield! You're as ugly as ever," I exclaimed, getting up and turning off the set.

Steve Lawson didn't graduate from the University of Stockton. He was lured away by big money and high times to play hockey in Germany. Hockey in Germany is gaining popularity. By going to Germany, Lawson has thrown away any possibility of playing in the NHL. Lawson is smart. He knows he's good, but not quite good enough, and intends to make the most of his hockey career. He is a hero in a foreign land. At home he would be another frustrated nobody in the American League clutching aimlessly at the fruits of fame and fortune.

"I want the courage to be an absolute nobody," I say to myself. "Courage! Where can you buy that stuff?"

Phil and I fell out of touch after Elizabeth's funeral, but now I visit him occasionally. He is married and has a baby boy. He lives in a different world than me, a world of hairspray commercials, subdivisions, getting together for a beer with the boys, Saturday afternoon sports events on TV, sex two nights a week after the eleven o'clock news, a respectable position in the sales department, and lineups at Sears. He thinks reading is for women and gets pissed off at the machine when he loses at Pac Man. There's nothing wrong with the way he lives. It's narrow, uninteresting, and depressingly self-satisfied, but there's nothing wrong with it. Phil and his wife call me "Uncle Ken" around their baby. I must admit that I like being called "Uncle Ken."

In a certain way, I'm envious of Phil. He seems content with his life. He's as stable as a tree. I'm a bundle of need and desire, sexually, financially, emotionally. Phil and I like to reminisce, but we never mention Elizabeth. I think Phil is in love with Elizabeth. Sometimes I'm convinced of it. When that thought gets lodged in my mind, I feel I understand Phil. I feel fraternal and protective. I want to kiss his baby. I feel we have never lost that high school bond which was once powerful and uplifting.

Phil keeps me informed on tidbits of gossip concerning Paul and Ross. Paul has gastritis and drinks a solution of honey and vinegar every morning to reduce his farting. Ross impregnated a fifteen-year-old girl. She had a miscarriage in his bed. He put the fetus in a jar of ethyl alcohol and keeps it on his shelf. He acts like a proud parent, uses the fetus as a center piece when people are over for dinner, and brags that his child never cries in the night or wets the bed. He has the perfect child. He asks the guests if they want him to heat up the fetus for dessert. It'd be tasty with ice cream on top. When Phil is in the same room as the fetus, Ross calls him "Uncle Phil." Paul hasn't changed, but Ross has developed a perverse sense of humor.

Blind Chuck graduated the same time as me. Chuck was walking to school on the final day of classes. Suddenly, his seeing-eye dog got a little pink erection and jumped on a cocker spaniel. The cocker spaniel was blind and being walked by a beautiful seeing-eye woman. Chuck was deeply moved and thought it was wonderful that a seeing woman was walking a blind dog. As their dogs humped, Chuck got to know the woman and turned on the charm. Two weeks later, I was invited to their wedding which I gratefully declined. Everyone from the Institute for the Blind was invited, and I knew that if I attended I would be convinced of my own blindness by the end of the evening. I mailed them two flea collars for a wedding present.

My fanatical passion for dogs has resurfaced. It's not a sexual attraction. It's spiritual, a spiritual kinship. Dogs love to love, love to be loved, love to make a room vibrate with love. They're loyal and protective. I want a dog more than anything else in the world, except perhaps the right kind of girlfriend. If I had a girlfriend and a dog, I'd have the courage to tackle any project that confronted me. I couldn't keep a dog in my little room. Some callow fools suggest I get a cat. How insensitive! Cats are nothing compared to dogs. One dog is worth a thousand cats. I'm abusive to cats. Whenever I see a cat, I bark and stomp my foot on the ground. Some cats run away, and some just stare at me. The only surviving dog in my family is Tanka. Whiskey was hit by a car. Tanka will probably outlive the whole Harrison family.

Henry Kissing-Balls and I have remained close friends. Henry's novel has recently been published. I give readings of his first chapter on the poetry reading circuit and other events to promote his book. It's the only regular work I get as a real actor. I give a dramatic reading. I shout and whisper and cry and pull down my pants. The crowd loves it. There are always a few pseudo-intellectual-frustrated-poet types who complain that the reading is too much fun and entertainment. Their argument is tediously predictable. Great literature can't be fun and entertaining. Great literature must be verbose and humorless.

"It's good for what it is. I just don't like that kind of stuff," said this stranger to me after a reading. He thought he was liberal-minded because he wore a beard. He probably graduated from English Literature at some university and was programmed into thinking that serious literature must be about misty moors. "I guess different people like different things," he said, trying to impress me with his generous spirit and open-mindedness.

"Right! And some people have good taste and some people's taste is up their ass," I said. You don't tangle with an artist's ego.

Everything has come together for Henry. When he finished college he knew exactly what he wanted, and he took the most direct route possible to get it. Henry surprised a lot of people, especially me. The most surprised person of all is Henry himself. Henry has more than writing ability, more than talent. There's a magic in what he puts down on paper. He is often chastised for being offensive and obscene, yet no one can deny there is something strikingly honest about what he writes. He can write, but he can't read. He tried to give his own reading once and it was a disaster. He stumbled over every word and bobbed with mounting severity, repeatedly cracking his head against the wall behind him. He was semi-conscious by the time he staggered off the platform. Reading and writing involve two different muscles.

"Your book is sick and perverted," said one zealous defender of God. Henry was flattered by the comment. It was the type of comment that had been made about Shakespeare, D.H. Lawrence, and Salinger. Henry was in good company. He said, "Don't blame me. I'm not responsible for what I write."

"If you're not, who is?" asked the attacker.

"It writes itself. It takes on a life of its own. I open a door and whatever comes out, comes out. I try not to interfere with the flow. When you go to sleep at night, you can't be responsible for what you dream. It comes out of you, but you don't necessarily understand it. It may even be sick and perverted. For me, it's the same thing with writing. It's not my fault what comes out of me. You say my book is sick and perverted. What you really mean is the world is sick and perverted. Which is not what I put in the book. You have to be sick and perverted to think my book is sick and perverted."

Henry Kissing-Balls wasn't a philosophy major for nothing.

"What's the most frustrating aspect of your life as a writer?" asked a young woman during one of the many question periods after a reading.

"Spelling," said Henry. "I keep forgetting how to spell. I'll be able to spell everything for a few months. Then, for no reason, I can't spell a thing. I have to look up every word. I don't even get close enough to find the word in the dictionary. I have to phone someone to get the first three letters. I've spent hours combing through the 'f' section of the dictionary, only to remember that the word starts with "ph."

Someone in the crowd yelled scornfully, "You think you're great."

Henry piped up for himself, "I'm a turd, but my writing is great."

There is another person who plays on my mind, perhaps more than anyone else, and that is Mrs. Baldwin. I've gradually developed an irrational hatred for Elizabeth's mother. I haven't seen the Baldwin family since the funeral. I haven't heard a word of gossip about them, yet I find myself constantly lecturing Mrs. Baldwin. I work myself into a rage. I fantasize about meeting her on the street and stopping to talk. The conversation is friendly at first. She asks me what I'm doing. I know what she wants to hear. She's status-conscious and wants to feel superior. She wants to hear that I'm lazy, and stupid, and unsuccessful. No matter what I tell her, that's what she'll hear. She's always felt that way about me.

"What are you doing these days, Ken?" asks the imaginary Mrs. Baldwin.

"I'm an actor!"

"An actor? Ha. Ha. But how do you make a living; how do you eat?"

"I give blow jobs to fags on Rush Street for twenty bucks a shot."

Elizabeth had some nice qualities, but a mind of her own wasn't one of them. Mrs. Baldwin manipulated Elizabeth against me. She tried to push Elizabeth to be political, bargain with her sexuality to win a man with money and high social standing. She told Elizabeth to use her head, not her heart. Elizabeth's head was spinning. When I think objectively about Mrs. Baldwin, I realize I should pity her. She lost her only daughter, whom she loved. But I imagine myself meeting Mrs. Baldwin on the street again and the same kind of conversation happens.

"You're a petty, frustrated old bitch, Mrs. Ajax," I say out loud. "You wouldn't know greatness if you fell over it."

It's easier for me to feel sorry for the old man, Mr. Baldwin. He wasn't much good for anything but loving his daughter. Although it's more difficult for me to have a conversation with Mr. Baldwin than with anyone else in the world, in retrospect I like the man. He's oblivious to almost everything. He had no idea what was going on with his wife and daughter. There's something endearing about his boyish naivete. I'm sure the only thing he wants in life is to have his little baby back. I'm sure he gets drunk with his best friend Mr. Simmons and cries and admits that life means nothing without his baby girl. I wish I could help him. I wish I could resurrect Elizabeth. He's a nice man and didn't deserve to lose his baby.

"You're not the only one who misses her, Mr. Baldwin," I say to myself. "I miss her too, you know."

A month after I graduated, Mother came to me in a panic. She began to stammer about the economy, unemployment, high interest rates, and the dismal future of America. It had finally occurred to her that I intended to be an actor. She emphasized job security. Computers are where the money is. The walls are closing in. Everyone is being laid off. Mother was worried for my survival. Unemployed workers are becoming violent. The news is full of protesters, protesting the government, protesting private industry, protesting the price of licorice cigars, protesting protesters. Newscasters use paranoia to sell the news. Face facts! A great depression hangs over the country. Join the protesters. Join the paranoid.

"Fuck the economy," I said. "Don't bore me with that shit."

"You had fun at college. Now you have to work!" said Mother.

"Work!" I exclaimed indignantly. "I haven't got time for work. I've got too many more important things to do."

"You used to be such an ambitious young man," she said. "What have they done to you at that university?"

"I still am ambitious, but I'll never be a nine-to-fiver. I want nothing to do with rush hour. I live on the fringe, Mom. I'm part of the fringe."

"But the economy," she repeated. "The economy!"

"If the economy is so bad, why are there so many fat people?"

Mother pulled me into her car, squealed out of the parking lot, and raced to Stockton. While on the highway, the speedometer never dipped below eighty-five miles per hour. It was a miracle we didn't get stopped by the police. Mother stormed into the Drama department. I was trailing behind her, jogging to keep up, asking her what she intended to do, and pleading with her to turn around. She marched past the secretaries, not giving them an opportunity to budge, and kicked open the door of the department head. We stood in his office. He recognized me, but he was shocked by the intrusion and unable to speak.

"What the fuck have you done to my son?" she demanded.

"Pardon?" he said.

"You've ruined him with your goddamn ideas."

He looked at me, hoping I could shed some light on the situation.

"Excuse me, sir," I said. "I'd like you to meet my mother."

Mother may be a nuisance when she doesn't understand something, but when she does understand and agrees, there is no stronger support system. She's like a team of bulldozers. She's the source of everything inside me, everything that's confident, positive, and courageous. She's what spinach is to Popeye, the raw material of a conqueror. She has come to believe in me as an actor, nothing else is good enough for Ken Harrison. Mother is always there, always behind me no matter how many miles away she is. She's there to inspire my enthusiasm, destroy my enemies, celebrate my accomplishments. Her love never wavers. On top of that she's pretty. She feeds me energy like a hydro-generating plant, and she's pretty too.

I told her what I wanted life to be. She thought about it and said, "Fuck the economy!"

"Fuck the economy!" I shouted joyfully and kissed her on the cheek.

Mother got so excited she drove back to the city and quit her job. She sold the house, gave Tanka to my sister May, and bought a sailboat with her boyfriend. I haven't seen her since, but she mails me a letter from somewhere in the Caribbean every other week. They live off the sea and give rides to tourists for extra cash. Mother wrote a successful cookbook for sailors. Her boyfriend plays the piano, has a custom-built, portable piano which he bolts to the front deck when they're in port. He takes an occasional job playing piano in nightclubs. I'm thrilled when I get news from Mother. When I open up her letters, a twenty dollar bill falls out of the envelope.

If it was possible to harness my mother's sexual energy, by sticking a tube in her vagina and playing with her nipples, you could keep the lights on in Los Angeles for years. I know what she's doing with that poor man of hers down south. She's putting impossible sexual demands on him. She did the same thing to my father.

There's no use holding this against Mother. She can't help it. Nymphomania runs in her family. Who am I to criticize her? I'm not exactly celibate. I look at her from the perspective of a son. She's given more to me than any other person in the world. It's foolish to think I could ever repay her. You can't even say something as trite as "Thank you." You can only take the bounty and walk away.

"You're a slut, Mom, but I love you anyway," I say to my reflection.

When Mother sailed south, Father flew north. Father quit his job when Sara forced him out of the condominium. The change in Sara was a mystery to Father. She started out madly in love with him, became silently disapproving, then openly hostile, and finally hysterical and violent. The cycle was all too familiar. Sara threw a fork at him once. Another time she attacked him with a huge lead candlestick, which was heavy enough to club an elephant to death. It got to the point where he couldn't feel safe in his own home. He slept with one eye open. Father claims to understand nothing about relationships. He's not lying. He really doesn't. Father's friendly, easygoing nature frustrates and enrages women.

Although elevators will remain a central part of his life, Father has taken an interest in a new career. He wants to go back to school and train to be a brain surgeon. I don't know how he got the idea in his head, but I'm sure he'll make a good brain surgeon. He's good at everything; that's his problem. I'm glad I'm retarded at most things. It forces me to channel my energy into specific interests. I agree with Father that doctors perform a wonderful function in society, healing people. My father wants to heal people. He doesn't want to preach, moralize, or crush the opposition party in a political debate. He wants to heal people, and he's spending a bundle to do it. He lost a fortune in Florida. He's broke, but has noble intentions, my father.

"I can only afford the necessities, like booze and drugs and prostitutes," joked my father.

"That's an original line, Dad. I like that one."

Father and I belong to the legion of lost and lonely men scouring the city for true love, or not-so-true love, or any kind of love at all. Father goes to bars, drinks, meets women, fat ones, skinny ones, stupid ones, witty ones, sad ones, bitter ones. Sometimes he goes home alone. Sometimes he has company. Sometimes, when he has company, he wishes he was alone. He goes back and looks some more. It's not so bad. Every night is different. He thinks of going out and feels tired. He goes out anyway. Once he's at a bar, he's glad he didn't stay home. He decides that the next night, he'll try a new drinking establishment, new faces.

Father shares my loneliness.

Barb lives with her boyfriend. They are on the fringe of society like myself, going through part-time jobs like a sprinter jumping hurdles: mopping floors, secretarial work, stacking empties in a beer store. It's demeaning, but it's no more than twenty hours a week of being demeaned, instead of the usual forty. It's a creative lifestyle, bohemian. There's no billboard image of youth and success to lean on and not much to boast about in coffee shops. Part-timers have no rights. Only full-timers have rights. Fringe people spend their time thinking, talking, screwing, pursuing an interest in the arts. They plan excursions. Fringe people are world travelers.

It's the private realm that matters to the fringe people, not public images. They want a rich inner life and are willing to make sacrifices. There are many ways to attain subsistence, and a creative approach can make a little go a long way. It's an alternative to selling your body and mind for job security and a gold watch after twenty-five years' service. It's an attempt to make your life your own. It may or may not work. It's just an alternative. Like everyone else, Barb wants more, but she's young and willing to wait for the right direction, the right opportunity. Penny, Barb's friend, is full of surprises. She's not the same woman. She lives with us on the fringe.

"I can be a miserable bitch," said Penny.

"I can be a miserable prick," I said.

We ate grapes and made love. Life on the fringe agrees with Penny. There's not the kind of pressure that makes a person old. She's even become more physically attractive. The sexual aspect of our relationship stopped when Penny moved in with a man, but the friendship has remained.

Sex is here to stay. My life revolves around sex like the planets revolve around the sun. Sex is the nucleus of my being, forever on the forefront of my mind. Sex is immortal and omnipresent. I can't look at a woman, on the subway, walking down the street, in a hamburger place, at a bar, without wondering what it would be like to make love to her. I can't help glaring at women, often with my mouth open and my tongue thick and salivating. I identify body parts, nipples through a blouse, curves of a buttock, lips, the dimple of a crotch, legs, fingers. These are the things that obsess by mind. I wake up with an erection and go to sleep with an erection. Throughout the day, I get an erection every fifteen minutes with clockwork regularity. I get an erection as often as some people smoke cigarettes. I'm a chain smoker when it comes to erections. The genital area of my jeans is worn white from adjusting my hard-ons.

This physiological condition is not exploitive or sexist. You can respect women as equals and still have a healthy sex appetite. The liberation of women has nothing to do with abstinence or impotence. I wish everyone enjoyed sex as much as me. I meet the odd woman who actually seems to enjoy sex more than me. New Age women, for example, can never get enough sex. I dated a New Ager for a short time. She scratched me so badly during sex that after a week my back was covered with scabs. I like to be scratched a little, but I don't want permanent scars. It got to the point that I made her put on oven mitts before we got into bed. The sex was fun, but I felt like the loneliest man on earth when she talked about politics. I didn't want to take a stand and debate. I wanted to exchange secrets. She called me apathetic. I pulled my erection out of my pants. There's nothing apathetic about my penis.

"I look good tonight," I muse to myself. "It's a shame no one is around to see me."

When will I find a woman I can love? When will I find the woman I long for? I want her more than anything else in the world. My heart is crying for her, screaming for her. There are beautiful, creative things inside me I can share with her. She's out there somewhere looking for me. She's more important than the economy. I smell her, taste her, hear her voice, but I haven't found her yet. I look for clues and pursue possibilities. She doesn't have to be flawless. She doesn't need a magnificently contracting vagina. I consider a good lay to be someone I enjoy having breakfast with the next morning. She just has to have that pervasive quality, that aura of love. I'll recognize the glow inside me and around me. Everyone seems to have a girlfriend but me. I hate to see couples holding hands. I figure they're in love and going home to screw. It's not fair that I have to go home alone.

"Fuck! Elizabeth," I say to my reflection, "what did you have to go and die for? That was a dumb move!"

I want the courage to be absolutely nobody. There's power in anonymity. There's power in little people. There's power in the Barren Room. There is something in the center of everyone that's as frightening as death. It's where nightmares come from. I live in reverence of this power. It lifts me up and throws me down. It's bigger than me. Simple-minded people call it God, as if it's a person. I think of it as a landscape.

"The Barren Room is a nice place to visit," I say to myself, "but I wouldn't want to live there."

I study my naked reflection in the mirror. I yawn. I prepare myself to sleep alone. I walk around the room collecting items: a squash racket, flowers out of a vase, my favorite album, three paperback novels, a suitcase full of Christmas decorations from the closet. My arms are bulging. I drop one of the novels and have to bend over and pick it up. I get into bed and push the pillow between my legs. I carefully place everything around me and in my arms. I sneeze. I let the candle burn.

I masturbate twice before falling asleep.